Cat-astrophic

by

Sue C. Dugan

The Cat with Nine Lives, Book 1

Cat-astrophic

Cover Art by *Lisa Dawn MacDonald*

The Wild Rose Press, Inc.
PO Box 708
Adams Basin, NY 14410-0708
Visit us at www.thewildrosepress.com

Publishing History
First Edition, 2023
Trade Paperback ISBN 978-1-5092-4754-7
Digital ISBN 978-1-5092-4755-4

The Cat with Nine Lives, Book 1
Published in the United States of America

"Hi, I'm Nick." He sat in the vacant desk next to her.

"I know."

He crossed his arms. "How?" Two could play that game.

She sat looking at him, not responding to his question.

Finally he broke the silence, hoping this chick wasn't a drama queen bent on causing problems. "You're Catherine?"

"I only answer to Cat—or Chaton," she said with a wink.

He studied her features then. She looked a bit like a cat with her black hair, topaz-brown eyes, and long fingernails. He tried not to stare, but she was so different from the other girls in school.

"So which is it? Cat or Chaton?"

"They mean the same. *Chaton* is 'kitten' in French."

"I don't know French."

She quirked a brow at him. "Are you sure?"

"Yes, I'm sure." *Whatever. Oui. Je suis sûr.* Oh, damn, where had that come from? He clamped his gaping mouth shut.

"I was once a cat," she said.

Nick remained quiet. His thoughts skittering around like a mouse being pursued by a...Whoa! First he was thinking in French, and then she tells him something like that? How was he supposed to respond? He frowned, studied the top of his desk, and said nothing.

"I have eight more lives to go," she added.

Praise for Sue C. Dugan

"I like your novel. You have chosen my favorite backdrop for a story: Teens in high school. High school teens are in another dimension with a life style kept exclusively unto themselves, high energy, raging hormones, and impulsive behavior. All of this gives a writer exciting characters without any restrictions in genre."

~ Don

"Very enjoyable reading. Ideas that come from left field? I love it. Makes me think. Keep on doing!"

~ Reno Reader

Dedication

As always, this book is dedicated to my family, but also to friends and fellow writers (the Tuesday afternoon critique group). I must especially thank Marti, Amy, the staff at Wild Rose Press (especially Dianne Rich), Terry, Don, and Meghan. Of course, I've probably missed someone, but I dedicate CAT-ASTROPHIC to the 'village' that helped me create Nick and Cat's story.

Chapter 1

All talking stopped when an unusual girl came into the high school cafeteria. Unusual, according to Nick, an all-American jock.

This was a typical small-town high school with all sorts of kids—the jocks, the cheerleaders, the student leaders (like his girlfriend, Emily, who was president of their Junior class), the band nerds, the computer geeks, and the cowboys, with a few oddballs thrown in. The girl dressed in a black leotard and neon-bright leggings would be in the oddball category. Laketon was a small rural town in western Michigan where they grew blueberries, apples, and cherries. A lot of the kids participated in the rodeo and 4-H. Kids wore blue jeans, flannel shirts, and cowboy boots here. But this girl, dressed in a black leotard, rushed into the middle of the cafeteria and twirled around on her toes, hair flying, pirouetting with the grace of a ballerina. It almost seemed as if she was auditioning for them. For what, he didn't know.

Nick grimaced. Unfortunately he knew what pirouetting was because his mother dragged him to the Nutcracker ballet each Christmas until he was twelve—when he flat-out refused to go even with bribery. Nick may have known what a pirouette was, but he also knew a touchdown, a tackle, a sack, a punt, and other important things about football—no self-respecting male said "pirouetting" without getting laughed at or, worse, jumped and beaten up.

Still, the girl kept them spellbound as she continued to twirl. He looked over at his girlfriend, Emily. She had her chin in her palm and didn't take her eyes off the girl's performance. The girl's stance changed as she bent at the waist while still moving in a circle. Her hair was in tiny braids, and as she twirled, they flew around her head like the blades of a helicopter. You could have heard a pin drop in the usually noisy cafeteria.

When the girl slowed and stopped, several people clapped, including Emily. Emily whispered, "She's good."

Nick looked over at Emily. That was one of the things he loved about her and made her a good class president: she was nice to everyone.

Nick also heard someone mutter, "What a freak." The comment jarred him from thinking about Emily's goodness.

Freak or not, the girl had held their attention with her grace and fluid movements.

The girl bowed ever so slightly, and then her eyes rested on his. Nick couldn't look away. Her brown-eyed gaze held his, and an unspoken language passed between them. She whirled away and out the door. Her performance was only about five minutes but seemed longer.

Emily nudged him. "Did you see the way she looked at you?"

"No," he lied.

"Yes! She looked like she knew you."

He mumbled, "I don't know her," and he shrugged.

Time to change the subject.

"Do you think she's a new student?" he asked, not because he was interested, but he didn't want Emily commenting on the look that passed between them.

"Wait!" Emily slapped her hands lightly on the table. "I might know of her! She moved into our neighborhood! She didn't look like that when I saw her by the mailbox. She wore jeans and an Oregon sweatshirt, but I think it's her!"

Gary, Nick's best friend, walked by wearing a Lions sweatshirt, and Nick's attention turned to football and the Lions. Nick gave him a thumbs-up, and Gary gave him a low "tweet" whistle—his signature greeting.

The Lions' first game of the season was tonight. Nick would be sitting side-by-side with his father— both of them wearing their Lion jerseys, pumping their fists and urging the team to win.

"I'll ask Veronica about her," Emily said.

"Whatever," Nick said, forgetting all about the new girl. His eyes strayed to the clock. "Gotta go." He took the last swallow of his protein drink, kissed Emily before tossing the carton in the trash, and headed for his first class.

Chapter 2

"We need to talk." The girl from the cafeteria stepped from around a recessed door in the hallway. She had changed into jeans, but he still recognized her, and she was every bit as exotic when he studied her up close—large, brown, almond-shaped eyes and a longish nose that gave her the look of someone from Egypt or the Middle East.

Nick tried to ease by her, but she stepped closer. "Do I even know you?" he asked.

"Look in my eyes. What do you see?"

He wanted to tell her she had the eyes of a crazy person, but something sparked a memory—a girl with a long skirt, dancing by a fire.

He inhaled sharply. Phlegm caught in his throat, causing him to sputter and choke. The vision was gone, and the bell conveniently sounded.

"We'll talk later," she said.

He didn't want to talk to her, now or later. She made the hairs on his arms stand up.

He went to the drinking fountain and drank until the lump in his throat was gone and so was the new girl with the strange request.

Nick wiped his mouth on his sleeve and went to World History—his favorite class—and to his horror, that girl was seated in the back, watching him enter. He hesitated, seeing her reaction—a small smile—before taking his seat.

The girl's long legs were stretched out. She must be a junior, but holy moly, she didn't have the same body as most of the girls he knew. Nick took a closer look—her black jeans were tucked into tall boots with tiny heels, crossed at the ankle—certainly they weren't the boots a cowgirl would wear to ride horses or work around the barn. Ridiculous boots for show. Nick smirked.

The usually noisy room was quiet today, everyone breathing in unison, waiting, wondering about the new student. Everyone knew each other at Laketon. A new person stood out. And a new person dressed in a black leotard and jeans in a sea of blue denim and flannel? Well, that was an anomaly.

After taking roll and welcoming Catherine—Nick learned that was her name—Coach Sullivan said, "We're going to be doing a research project about World War II, and I'll be assigning work partners. You'll have about five weeks to work together. After I call all the names, please sit together."

Everyone waited expectantly as the coach called names. Who would have to work with the new girl— Catherine?

With growing dread, Nick waited for his name to be called. As people paired off, odds were Nick would get stuck with Catherine.

Bryan Cranden poked Nick's back. "I bet you get the strange chick, Reverend," he whispered.

"Shut up, Bryan. Don't call me that," Nick replied.

Cranden had been a continual thorn in Nick's side since the water incident when Nick teased Bryan about peeing his pants when the drinking fountain sprayed his crotch. And then there was Emily. Another bone of contention—Bryan wanted Emily but, lucky for Nick, she only wanted him.

"Bryan, do you have a question?" Coach asked, not looking up from his tablet.

"No, Coach."

"Okay, then." He nodded. "Nick and Catherine."

Bryan snorted, and Nick heard several giggles.

"People!" Coach raised his voice.

Catherine remained motionless, and when Nick turned to look at her, she nodded to him. Did she know his name? Since she hadn't moved, he stood and walked to her desk.

"Hi, I'm Nick." He sat in the vacant desk next to her.

"I know."

He crossed his arms. "How?" Two could play that game.

She sat looking at him, not responding to his question.

Finally he broke the silence, hoping this chick wasn't a drama queen bent on causing problems. "You're Catherine?"

"I only answer to Cat—or Chaton," she said with a wink.

He studied her features then. She looked a bit like a cat with her black hair, topaz-brown eyes, and long fingernails. He tried not to stare, but she was so different from the other girls in school.

"So which is it? Cat or Chaton?"

"They mean the same. *Chaton* is 'kitten' in French."

"I don't know French."

She quirked a brow at him. "Are you sure?"

"Yes, I'm sure." *Whatever. Oui. Je suis sûr.* Oh, damn, where had that come from? He clamped his gaping mouth shut.

"I was once a cat," she said.

Nick remained quiet. His thoughts skittering around like a mouse being pursued by a...Whoa! First he was thinking in French, and then she tells him something like that? How was he supposed to respond? He frowned, studied the top of his desk, and said nothing.

"I have eight more lives to go," she added.

He moved his gaze to hers, assessing her statement. Was she teasing? She stared boldly back at him, blinking slowly. Her eyes in this light glowed yellow; just a minute ago they were greener. No, she wasn't teasing. She was serious.

Neither of them spoke. Nick looked away and down at his notebook. What high school student, in her right mind, said she was a cat once and had eight more lives? *The crazy ones?*

Coach Sullivan continued after everyone had moved into their working pairs. "I'm going to give you fifteen minutes more to discuss what you might want to research." The noise level steadily rose as the discussions and negotiations began.

"So..." Nick said, tapping his pencil on his World History notebook. "What do we want to do for our project? Do you want to read over my notes on what we've covered, you know, before you came?"

"Saumur. Let's start there."

He frowned. "We haven't discussed Saumur."

"No? Don't you remember it?"

He flipped through his notes. "No, I don't remember anything about Saumur." He looked up and frowned before going back to perusing his notes. "It wasn't one of the major battles."

"Think, Nick." She moved a finger with a long red nail up to her temple. "You were there."

He drew away from her slightly. "I've never been to a place called Saumur."

Nick's mind scrambled around, searching for that town.

"You know, Saumur," Cat said. "You said you would come for me."

"What the heck are you talking about?" The queasy feeling in his stomach intensified.

"The last time I saw you." She raised her brows over her heavily made-up eyes, studying him. "In Saumur."

"N-n-no," Nick stammered. "I don't know you at all."

"Not like this," she said.

Nick's brows furrowed. "Not like what?"

"Not in this life. Not in this body."

"What?" Nick's breath seemed to stick in his throat, a cotton ball strangling him, making him cough and pound on his chest. "How?"

"I recognize your eyes." Cat's pupils seemed to dilate as she talked. "The eyes are the mirrors to the soul, Nick. I know your soul."

He blinked rapidly. Sure, her eyes looked familiar, but nothing else. Another stirring in his gut. "Are you trying to say…" *What was the word?* "I've been re-in-car-nated?"

"That's one name for it," she said. "And yes, that's

what I'm saying."

"I don't believe in that stuff."

"Nick?" Coach asked. "Are you and Catherine okay over there?"

"Still deciding," Nick answered. He lowered his voice and continued, "Look, Cat, I don't remember meeting you. Sorry." Nick searched his mind where he might have known her. The homeless shelter? His church group volunteered there.

Again, the blink and stare from Cat.

Nick eased out of his chair. "Coach." He raised a finger. "Can I speak to you?"

"Certainly, Nick."

He leaned on Coach's desk and lowered his voice. "That girl." Nick's voice shook. "Do I have to work with her?"

"She's new, Nick," Coach Sullivan said, expectation in his voice as if he anticipated this question. "I paired you two together because you take good notes and really enjoy history. I thought you could help her get caught up."

His heart did a little tap dance in response. "She's weird," he mumbled.

"Nick…" Coach gave him the *are you joking* frown.

"She's really freaking me out."

Coach leaned forward as he studied Nick. "Why?"

"She told me some weird stuff." His voice rose an octave as he talked. "I've never heard of Saumur." Nick noticed several heads turned in their direction. "What the heck is Saumur?"

"Where have I heard that?" Coach Sullivan frowned and drummed his fingers. "Oh, I know, it's a battle site."

"So it's a real place?" Nick asked, his stomach sinking. "Where?"

"France, I believe." Coach switched on his tablet and typed the name in Search, scratched his head, and typed in something else. After several tries, he said, "Yes. Here it is."

Nick leaned over and read: *Saumur was the site of the famous Battle of the Loire where the students of Cadre Noir held off the elite Nazi soldiers at the end of WWII.*

Then in small letters: *Montreuil-Bellay. French internment camp. A forgotten camp.* Only two short sentences. A memory of barbed wire flashed through Nick's mind.

"It's not one of the major battles or internment camps," Coach said, "and you'll have to do some digging for sources, but it might be an interesting project."

Nick's stomach sank farther. "You really think that would be good for our research?"

"Sure." Coach flipped off his tablet. "It would be something different. She's obviously done her research."

Nick started to turn away, dejected. "Okay." He sighed.

"Oh and, Nick"—Coach looked up—"the scout from Michigan is coming to one of our home games. We'll need to work on your A game."

"Wha...?"

Coach Sullivan nodded. He knew Nick's father had played for Michigan, and Nick wanted to go there too.

"Uh, sure thing, Coach!" Nick turned and trudged

back to his desk, imagining a poor grade because they were researching something obscure like Saumur. Cat watched him sit.

"Okay, we can start researching Saumur, and the battle, and the people who were imprisoned there," Nick said.

"The Romas." Cat yawned.

"Romans?" Had he heard her right? "No, this is WWII."

"Romas," she repeated slowly, emphasizing each syllable. "You call them Gypsies," she said with a sneer. "I don't need to do research. I know."

"Well, I don't know anything about Gypsies." Nick leaned back and slapped his palms on the desktop.

She blinked at him. "Oh, but you do."

He shook his head. "No, I don't."

"You do," she insisted, staring at him with her tigerlike eyes, lazy but alert at the same time, unsettling. "You were at Saumur too. On the other side. I've been searching for you. Wondering when we would get together again." She smiled. "Even though you left me to die."

"Don't talk so loud," Nick whispered. "Someone might hear you." Their conversation was beyond the bizarre and a bit frightening.

"So?" she said.

"This is crazy," he whispered.

"I can't believe we're together again!" She sat up a little straighter and tapped her fingernails on the desk. *Click. Click. Click.* Then she gave him another Mona Lisa smile.

What the heck? He had never seen her until she whirled into the cafeteria this morning. He would have remembered a tall, mysterious girl, wouldn't he?

Chapter 3

Nick would be lying if he said he didn't think about Cat for the rest of the day.

"Nick? Are you with us?" his calculus teacher asked.

"Huh?" He was there physically, but his mind was a chaos of images and visions, mainly of a boy carrying a large rifle looking too big for him to tote.

The calculus problems on the board looked foreign too. He blinked. "Sorry." He dragged his mind back to the present, leaving the picture of the boy with the rifle behind. Was he imagining these things from the World History discussions and what he knew of WWII? After all, his grandfather had shared stories and books about the war, feeding Nick's imagination.

And later still, Emily noticed his distraction. They sat on the bleachers before Nick went to football practice.

"Calling Nick. Earth to Nick," she said, giving him a little punch on his arm. "I don't have a lot of time today. We've got the homecoming planning committee meeting in"—she looked at her phone—"five minutes." She rested her daisy-patterned sneakers on the seat in front of them and moved her knees slightly as they talked.

"Sorry," he said. "Thinking about our World History project and working with Cat."

"Who?"

"That new chick."

"She couldn't keep her eyes off you!" Emily said with a giggle.

"I got paired with her in World History this morning," he said, running his fingertips over the ridges on the bleachers.

Emily frowned.

"She's kind of weird." Nick hoped that would alleviate his feeling of dread. "She said we used to know each other."

"I told you!" She punched his arm lightly. "A girl knows that look. She had *that* look."

He hadn't seen "the look," but obviously Emily had.

"How does she know you?" Emily demanded. A frown creased her normally smooth forehead.

"I have no idea why she said that, but it kind of bugs me." An image raced through his head, a girl with a multicolored skirt, not Cat or Emily but someone else. He shook it away.

"Maybe just mistaken identity?" Emily asked, sneaking another peek at her phone.

He didn't think so.

"She looked at you like she knew you. Is she an ex-girlfriend come back to haunt you?" Emily joked.

"Hell no! I don't know that girl!" But those topaz eyes kept him spellbound.

She smiled. "I know!" She smacked his arm. "I was just teasing!"

He let out a long sigh.

Emily touched his sleeve and gave him a smile. "I'm sorry."

"I've never seen her until this morning," Nick said.

"She moved into my subdivision," Emily said. "You know, that big house where Dr. Kawalski used to live?"

Nick knew the house.

"Do you think she's pretty?"

"With all that black makeup?" he said, grimacing. "Hardly!"

Emily shrugged. "I saw Bryan trying to talk to her by the lockers."

Bryan liked to hustle the new girls.

Emily continued, "There are all kinds of rumors floating around about her."

"Like what? She escaped from the loony bin?" He gave a half-hearted chuckle to ease the tension he was feeling.

"Veronica lives next door to her and said she was some big-deal dancer, here to heal after an injury."

Nick rubbed the back of his neck and moved his shoulders around. "Why would anyone move to Laketon to recover from a sports injury?" Laketon was a small farming community by Lake Michigan. The nearest big hospital was in Grand Rapids.

"I have no idea." Emily sneaked another look at her phone. "Like I said, that's what Veronica told me." Emily took a final sip of her apple juice, making the straw gurgle in the box. "What are you going to do?"

"I don't have a choice." He did a little one-shoulder shrug. "I have to work with her."

She squeezed his arm. "I know." She smiled and nudged him. "Hey! If anyone can handle it, you can."

"Ha! That's what Coach said."

Emily squeezed the empty juice box. "I've got to

run. Call me later?" They parted with a kiss and assurances of a call before Nick headed toward the locker room and Emily to her meeting.

The rest of the football team was already in the process of changing, banging lockers open and closed while shedding clothes for practice jerseys and shorts.

"Hey, Rev, how's Goth girl?" Word got around fast in such a small school.

"Name's Nick, not Rev." He hated being called a minister because of his father. He saw Bryan putting a hand to his mouth, trying not to snicker. "Shut up, Bryan. You heard Coach assign partners." Nick stripped off his shirt, reaching for his practice uniform.

"Hey, when did you get that?" Gary asked with a low whistle, pointing to Nick's chest. Most of Nick's scars were from his exploits with Gary.

Bryan turned back to his locker and began putting on his shoes.

"What?" Nick looked down to see where Gary was pointing.

"That scar." Gary motioned toward his chest.

His scar was red and hurt for some reason. "Had it for as long as I can remember." He touched the tender spot. "My folks said I fell out of a tree." He must have done something to irritate it, but he couldn't remember what.

"I don't remember it," Gary said.

"Before we moved to Laketon."

Gary was Nick's oldest friend. They had swimming lessons together and played make-believe war with tiny plastic army men.

"Does it hurt?" Gary asked.

"Not usually."

"What's your project on, Rev?" Bryan asked, stretching out "Rev." "Figure it out with that weirdo?" Snickers from others behind open locker doors. "Weirdo or not, she's a snack, right?" Bryan said, elbowing Nick's ribs, and Nick shoved him away. "Right?" Bryan kept laughing.

"Quit," Nick snapped irritably. "French internment camps," he said and slammed his locker shut. "End of discussion." More snickers came.

Coach Sullivan walked through the locker room, carrying his clipboard and looking pointedly at his watch.

They jogged outside to the football field. Nick forgot about the locker room conversation as he took to the running track; he needed to be in top physical shape for the Michigan scout. As he ran, finally hitting his stride, he thought about why Cat thought she knew him. He considered every scenario and came up with nothing. Finally, with shaking knees and sweat pouring into his eyes, he stopped and hunched over, catching his breath.

"Moderation, Nick! Moderation," Coach called.

He nodded as he straightened, his breath coming in gasps. Usually, running the track didn't have this effect on him.

"Save it for the scout," Coach said with a smile.

"Yes, sir, Coach." Once they started on the football plays for Friday's game, he needed to concentrate and keep his eyes on the ball, but his vision became cloudy and unfocused, only coming out of the fog when the ball slammed into his chest and he dropped it. Damn. And again, his breath came in gasps.

"Concentrate on the plays!" Coach yelled. "Nick! I

need you to be *in* the game." He definitely wasn't on his A game this afternoon.

"Yes, sir!" Most times Nick had the ability to focus only on the task at hand, which was beating the opposition. Today, it was all he could do to track the ball.

When practice finished, he showered, changed, and drove home expecting the Lions game to be on the TV. He pulled into their circular drive and studied their two-story farmhouse that was in need of paint. The upstairs windows looked half-lidded and sleepy at him. They had lived here since Nick was in elementary school.

He was starving. Good thing his parents always had something delicious to eat.

The aroma of pizza coming from the kitchen made him drop his backpack on the chair and head in that direction. He frowned. The television was strangely quiet. Only Minnie, their cat, meowed loudly for her nightly scratch. What was going on?

He stopped and rubbed Minnie between her ears. Minnie's eyes reminded him of Cat's. Maybe Cat had a pet cat at home? It was uncanny how some people started to resemble their pets.

He gave Minnie one more scratch before pushing through the swinging door that separated the living room and old-fashioned farm kitchen. He found his parents huddled together, talking at the scarred butcher-block table.

"What's going on?" Nick asked, reaching for the breadsticks. "Are we going to watch the game?"

His father looked up at him and gave him a pained smile. "Your grandmother's in the hospital again. We've been in Grand Rapids most of the afternoon."

"Why didn't you text me?" Nick asked, dropping the bread back into the box. "Is Grandma okay?"

"Grandma's getting good care," his mother said, placing the pizza and a bottle of Chianti on the table before taking a seat herself.

Nick's father said grace. Nick waited a beat before piling four slices on his plate.

He frowned at his mother's cell phone on the table. "In case the hospital calls?"

She nodded wearily.

"It's serious?" Nick mumbled between bites.

"Heart palpitations," his father said. "Possibly a stroke."

Nick frowned and wiped the grease from his mouth. "That doesn't sound good, Dad."

"It isn't. Grandma's heart is out of whack, not beating normally," his father explained. "They're running tests. Maybe a pacemaker."

"But she's safe and being watched in the hospital," his mother said, not really eating, just picking at the mushrooms and drinking her wine.

As a way of distracting his parents, Nick said, "You want to hear about the thing that happened at school?"

"Sure, tell us about your day," his father said.

Nick frowned at his father's detached blank stare but decided to tell them about Cat anyway. "We're writing research papers in World History and were assigned partners."

"That doesn't sound all that unusual," his father said, frowning at the pizza left in the box and his empty plate.

"My partner's different." An understatement. Cat

was different and spooky.

"Gary?" his father asked, taking another slice of pizza.

Nick wished he was partnered with Gary. "No." Nick shook his head. "Someone new. Catherine. She calls herself Cat."

"That's not so unusual," his mother said.

"She said she was a cat once."

"All children fantasize," his mother said, moving smoothly into her social worker mode.

"We're sixteen, not children anymore, Mom."

The phone vibrated on the table; his mother looked at the number. "The hospital," she whispered.

"Go on." Nick's father motioned.

She answered and was silent for a while, then finally eked out a "Thank you," before adding, "We'll be right there."

"What's wrong?" Nick asked.

"Grandma's had another stroke." She grabbed her purse. "We need to be there for her."

His father pushed back his chair. "I'll get the car. Nick? Do you want to come?"

Before he could respond, his mother said, "I think it's better you stay here. Finish your homework. We might be quite late."

"Your mom's right. Watch the game without me," his father said, taking his keys from the hook by the door.

"I'll clean up," Nick said. He'd tell his father about the Michigan scout and Cat when Grandma was better.

His mother gave him a tight smile. Cleanliness wasn't one of his strong suits.

"Thank you, Nick." She hugged him. "Tell Grandma I love her."

Chapter 4

When his parents left for the hospital, Nick continued looking at the plates of half-eaten pizza. He had promised to wash the dinner dishes. Instead, he picked up his mother's glass of wine and took several swallows.

Minnie came into the kitchen and wound her way around his ankles.

"Minnie, I met a friend of yours today. Cat." That statement made him grimace. He rubbed his temples; already they were throbbing.

Minnie was unimpressed and continued to meow and rub against him.

He brought the wineglass to the sink and put a scoop of kibble into her bowl, which she circled sinuously before crouching down to eat her food. Nick began stacking the plates, when an image of a boy with a gun appeared. He tried shaking away the vision, but the boy—about his age, wearing a uniform, looking ill at ease while holding the gun—refused to budge. Nick wasn't an expert on rifles, but that one looked like a picture his grandfather had shown him.

The image left, and he began scraping the food into the garbage disposal and rinsed the dishes before putting them in the dishwasher.

When the dishwasher could hold no more, he started it and surveyed the remaining dishes. As much as he hated washing dishes, he didn't want to leave a mess for his mother; she had enough on her mind with Grandma. He'd wash the rest in the sink. With a sigh, he filled the basin with hot water and soap.

As he stood at the sink, looking out the window at their now-dark backyard, Nick's reflection showed faintly on the panes. He looked down at the sink and selected a plate to be washed, and when he looked up, a stranger stared back at him. It was his reflection, but he was the boy with the gun with a look of fear and desperation. The boy's hair was darker, and he was leaner and had a look a soldier might have—grim determination. The eyes—they had the same eyes, and the realization jarred Nick, and he stepped back onto Minnie's tail. He jerked when she hissed, dropping and breaking the plate.

Then another image appeared. A boy swathed in a white apron, elbow-deep in soapy water, surrounded by mounds of dishes. A boy washing endlessly, hands red from hot water and harsh soap. A boy who hated washing dishes as much as Nick did.

Nick looked away, shook off the images and the fuzziness in his brain, before kneeling down and picking up the plate pieces. Who was that person? His mother said the eyes were the windows to the soul. Cat had said the same thing. Was he looking into his soul?

He put the broken china in the garbage. When he glanced up, the strange reflection was gone, and only Nick remained.

Nick turned away from the window, preparing to leave and turn on the game, when his phone vibrated. He held his breath as he looked at the caller ID and then let it out noisily when he realized it was Emily and not a call about Grandma.

"Hey!" he answered.

"What are you doing?"

"I just finished cleaning the kitchen for my parents."

A pause. "Really?" She sounded skeptical.

"I know." He chuckled. "I'm a slob." He paused. "They're at the hospital with my grandma."

"Oh no!" Emily gasped.

"Yeah, she had a stroke."

"I'm so sorry, Nick! Do you need company?"

It was tempting to have Em come over, but it was almost eight thirty, and he had homework and wanted to watch some of the game. "No. It's okay. I need to do some calculus." And too, Emily would want to talk and ask questions during the game.

"Okay." She sighed. "Let me know if you need me."

That was just another of the reasons he loved her. *So supportive.* "I will."

Nick turned on the game and placed his calculus book on the coffee table. He chewed his pencil and tried to do his homework, but his focus kept shifting to the images on the window and the Lions on TV. Lions were down 7–3.

He sighed, flipped his book closed, and went upstairs to finish calculus, but instead opened his laptop and switched it on. He was curious about reincarnation. The Methodist church believed there was one soul per body. They didn't entertain the notion of souls floating freestyle in the atmosphere, waiting to be snagged by a body.

He typed in *reincarnation.* He couldn't believe the

amount of information about the topic. But as he scanned the text, his belief was confirmed. Reincarnation was a religious concept of Buddhism and Hinduism—Eastern religions, not Christian or Jewish faiths.

He sat back, satisfied. Cat must be a Buddhist and Nick, a Christian—as simple as that.

With a sigh, he began to work on calculus in earnest, only sneaking a peek at his phone for the football score between problems.

Chapter 5

Nick slept poorly. His frantic dreams clawed at his subconscious. *Hands reaching out from a black hole in the ground. Also, there was that boy again—wearing a ragged uniform, holding a rifle, and some random man running toward him.*

"You are a thief, Jean Claude Rousseau."

Jean Claude Rousseau, a name. The boy's name?

When his alarm sounded at 6:15 a.m., Nick wearily swung his legs over the side of the bed, picked up his phone, and saw a message from his mother saying they had stayed at the hospital with Grandma. Although groggy and unfocused, the name Jean Claude Rousseau stayed with him.

Before showering and getting ready for school, he turned on his computer and typed in "Jean Claude Rousseau": he was a movie director, a real person. Could Nick have watched one of his movies? He scanned the list, but nothing looked familiar.

He turned off his computer, took a shower, and checked Minnie's water bowl before heading out. The closer he got to school, the more hesitant he became and eased up on the accelerator and coasted into the school parking lot. He dreaded seeing Cat again. She had irritated something deep within himself, like a sore on the back of his heel that nagged him when he walked.

Nick parked next to Gary. "Hey, man!" They bumped shoulders. "You get calculus finished last night?"

Gary nodded and gave a low whistle. "I had trouble concentrating. My sister was practicing her trumpet. And then I was trying to watch the game."

Nick grimaced. He could imagine the noise Gary's little sister, learning the trumpet, could make.

Gary whistled and waved to his girlfriend, Tiffany. "Later," he said to Nick as he jogged over to her.

Emily waited by Nick's locker, swaying from side to side on the balls of her feet, always energetic and busy. Today she wore red-white-and-blue sneakers and pink-and-white polka-dotted socks. "How's your grandmother? I've been waiting for you to get here to find out!"

"About the same. Mom sent a message they stayed at the hospital last night."

"How did you sleep?"

He yawned in response, his fatigue visible.

"You look exhausted," she said.

"That obvious?"

The bell sounded, they kissed, and he opened his locker and shoved his calculus book onto the pile of papers, notebooks, a forgotten sweatshirt, and several pairs of smelly socks that made him wrinkle his nose. Wearily he closed the door. When it was time for World History, he dragged his feet, knowing he had to sit next to Cat.

"Hello," he said softly, glancing quickly at her, watching the others file in for class. Cat was studying her phone and obviously didn't hear his greeting. It appeared she was dressed for gymnastics or dancing in a low-cut leotard and multicolored tights with a flimsy skirt. He looked away from the swell of her breasts. The only time Emily showed off her breasts was in the summer when they went to the beach.

He shifted in his seat, trying to get comfortable, but the chairback, rigid and unyielding, pressed into his spine. "Good morning," he said. "Are you a gymnast?"

"Dancer." She glanced at him and smiled. "Morning." She slipped the phone into her bag and handed him a piece of paper. "My contact info."

Nick looked at the paper blankly for a moment.

"So we can talk about our paper if needed," she said.

"Ah!" Nick put her contact info into his phone and gave Cat his number.

She smiled at him again. She had a nice smile even with bright-red lipstick.

Coach Sullivan tapped on his desk to get the students' attention. "We're going to continue talking about what happened in the European countries after the start of the war." Looking down at his wristwatch, he added, "And halfway through class, you can all work on your projects."

As Nick listened, he doodled on his notepad, writing a fact here and there. Hitler, Goering, Patton, Churchill, Colonel Michon. He lifted his pen. Had Coach said "Colonel Michon"? No, Nick had added the name on his own. Who was he? He circled the name and looked at Cat and then down at his notepad. Her eyes narrowed at seeing the name.

Nick pointed to the Colonel's name and raised his brow, questioning.

Cat wrote back: *Superintendent at your school.*

Nick wrote back: *Which school?*

Cat: *Cadre Noir*

Huh?

Coach continued his lecture, but Nick only heard a buzzing in his ears. When Coach finished, the room erupted in a hum of voices. Hands raised and students asked, "Can we change our topic?" and "What if we can't find any research?" and "Why do we have to do this?" The questions went on and on.

"I don't understand," Nick said to Cat, pointing again to Colonel Michon's name. "I've never heard of him."

She studied him. "He was the head of your school in Saumur."

Her comment still didn't explain why Nick wrote his name. *A thin face with a goatee flashed in his head.*

"People!" Coach rapped on the board for quiet. "Stop talking over each other! Raise your hand if you have a question."

Nick turned to Cat, whispering, "Do we still want to write our paper about Gypsies?" Or what had she called them? Romas? A boring topic, in his estimation.

She crossed her arms over her chest. "Yes, and I prefer we call them 'Romas.' 'Gypsy' is a trash term."

"Oh." Nick swallowed. "What if I want to do something else?"

"Then you'll be working alone," she said, raising an eyebrow at him.

Nick paused and thought about her comment. Part of him wanted to work alone and research Patton, but he was drawn to Cat and the Gy—er, Romas. And the battle Coach had told him about.

"Okay," he said. "We'll do it your way. But I need

to narrow down the topic." Truth was, he didn't know anything about Gypsies. Images of a woman wearing a turban looking into a crystal ball was pushed away by a girl wearing a multicolored skirt with a red flounce at the bottom. The vision of the girl was vivid, and she seemed familiar, but he didn't know who she was. Maybe she just resembled someone he had once seen?

Cat began speaking and jerked him away from the flirty skirt that flared out when twirling.

"The treatment of French Romas during World War II. The Romas interned at Saumur. Narrow enough for you?" she asked.

He laughed. "I guess."

They were silent for a moment. "Coach mentioned a battle there. I'll cover that."

"Yes, the students against the Nazis."

He quirked a brow at her. So she knew about that too?

"And you can tell me why you left me," she added.

Wait. "What?"

"I think we have unfinished business between us, and that's why we found each other," Cat said. "That's the usual reason 'souls' find each other."

He shushed her and used his hand to indicate she lower her voice.

"Is that why you looked mad when you saw me in the cafeteria the first day?" he whispered.

"Probably."

"I think there needs to be another explanation. I've never been to France."

"I slowly starved to death in my prison hole," Cat said.

"Huh?"

"Starved. Do you know how painful and slow that is?"

His stomach twinged. He had forgotten to eat breakfast. Could he imagine starving? His stomach grumblings multiplied by a hundred? He frowned and scrubbed at his chin.

"No, I've never been starving." He smiled. "I thought I was, but I wasn't."

She cocked her head at him, her fingers tapping on the desk as she regarded him, deciding if he was serious.

He added, "No, I can't imagine how horrible that would be."

She gave him a quick smile in response.

They had gotten off to a rocky start. Maybe they could start over and get their paper written. Maybe he would learn something new.

Chapter 6

Nick sat with Emily before football practice started. "Want to go to the library later?" he asked.

Emily raised her brows into a V. "After football practice? Um..." She looked at her phone. "I don't think so." She shrugged apologetically. "I've got homework, and it's my night to cook dinner."

In Search on his phone, he typed in "Cadre Noir" and frowned at the picture of a gigantic building on the screen.

She frowned at his phone. "What are you looking at?"

"A school in France."

"Oh?" She leaned closer. "Is that part of your research?"

"Umm." Nick rubbed his chin as he read the descriptions: Black Cadre, French Military Riding Academy, and Equestrian Display team. He wasn't sure how the three-sided building with at least four stories played into their research, yet Coach had indicated it was. Nick thought the school looked like a fancy apartment complex. "I think so. A battle."

"What exactly are you researching?" She moved her animal print sneakers with purple and white striped socks impatiently.

"Gypsies and this battle." This school was important. Then he read, "The school's cadets held off the German's elite Panzer division for three days."

"Wow! That's impressive," Emily said.

"Where'd you find that topic?" She frowned. She also had Coach Sullivan and the same research project. "I don't remember Coach telling us about that."

"Cat."

"Oh?" She rolled her eyes. "Gotta run. Talk to you later!" They kissed briefly, she hopped off the bleachers, and he went to the locker room to change.

Later when football practice finished, Nick walked the short distance from the high school to the Laketon Library. It was still light out, although just barely, and yellow leaves swirled on the sidewalks. Even in mid-September, the trees were preparing for winter. Nick gave an involuntary shiver.

He sent a text telling his mother he had stopped at the library, before pulling out his wallet, checking to see if he had his school ID in case he wanted books or Internet access. Even though he guessed Cat was crazy in some ways, he wanted to know more about this Saumur place and the colonel.

Once there, he asked the librarian, "Do you have books on World War II?"

"Do we ever!" she said with a shake of her head. "We have a whole section on that subject." The librarian motioned. "Would you like me to show you?"

"Yes, how about France and World War II?"

"Let's take a look," the librarian said and showed Nick to the history section. There were several books written by and about the French in the war. Nick selected two that looked interesting.

"Anything else?" the librarian asked.

Nick indicated he was good before flipping to the

back of the books and running his finger down S listings, looking for Saumur. As he perused the books, he fumbled in his backpack for his emergency stash of jerky and chewed thoughtfully as he read.

He next read about Colonel Michon, the school superintendent responsible for leading students in a revolt against the Germans.

The colonel was legendary in the area because he took a stand against Hitler's Panzer tanks when they invaded the Saumur region. But the article said nothing about camps or Romas. Were the internees and the battle linked in some way?

He finished his jerky and searched for another in his pack, his appetite never fully satisfied.

A sign over the computers said they had access to the Michigan State and University of Michigan research banks. Something Nick wouldn't be able to access at home. He hoped to attend the University of Michigan when he graduated. He needed to keep his high grades and football form.

Nick sat at an assigned computer and searched for Saumur. Before the computer had finished the search, images of grapevines in neat rows flashed across his mind. France was known for their wine, he reasoned. He lifted his nose and smelled the perfume of overripe grapes, overly sweet and ready to burst. His imagination had taken over, adding sensory details, or maybe it was the air freshener the library used.

There were many pages about Saumur, a wine-growing region, but nothing about an internment camp.

He next searched for "Saumur World War II" and "Saumur internment camp" and the epic battle led by Colonel Michon.

He continued scrolling down, looking for anything that would help him, until he came to a site about France's interned Gypsies. He rubbed his chin. The internet referred to them as Gypsies, so why was Cat so touchy about it?

He shrugged and began to read. The information started with a black-white-and-gray picture of a group of prisoners. Nick squinted at the image. One of the men looked familiar. Was the man someone famous? Maybe he just reminded Nick of someone he knew? His knuckles smarted, and he had the urge to suck at them to ease the discomfort. He must have done something during practice.

More images in his head of barbed wire with prisoners pressed so close against the fence, it etched their skin. Sunken faces and eyes begging, begging for release, begging for food. Where were all these images coming from?

Nick sat back when his stomach gurgled, not a hungry sound but an upset feeling. He looked at the clock. It was well past dinner time. Was this the feeling the body had to starvation? A hollowness that echoed with hunger pangs? A headache started behind his eyes, and he rubbed at his forehead before deciding to go home.

He stood, switched off the computer, and gathered up his backpack.

"I hope you found what you were looking for," the librarian said as Nick walked past her desk.

"I did, thanks." But he was left with more questions and images of places and things that were unfamiliar, yet they weren't. He unlocked his car and drove home.

Once at home, he went into the kitchen and pulled leftover pizza from the refrigerator. He unwrapped the foil and wrinkled his nose. Was he hungry? Marginally, so he took a small slice and put the rest back. While he waited for the microwave to reheat his food, he checked his phone for messages. His parents were on their way home from the hospital. Emily had sent him a smiley face, and he grinned and sent a heart back to her.

He paused as the image of a large kitchen used for preparing huge quantities of food flashed across his mind. He mentally compared their kitchen and the one in his head. No, they were nothing alike. One had a large wooden box for holding food and blocks of ice. Their kitchen had a regular refrigerator with an ice maker.

He heard his parents enter the front door. "Nick?"

"In the kitchen."

He finished his pizza.

"What are you doing, son?" his father asked, coming into the kitchen, taking note of Nick's empty plate. "Going back for seconds?"

"Nah!"

His father nodded. "Leave anything for me?" he joked.

"Maybe." He smirked, then sobered when he remembered where his parents had been. "How's Grandma?"

"Stable but still at Spectrum."

"Can she have visitors?" Nick could swing by after school and have a quick visit.

"I think so."

"Good. I'll go see her," Nick said, watching his father take most of the remaining pizza and reheat it for dinner.

The next night after football practice, Nick drove to the hospital to see his grandmother. Nick knocked on the door before opening it. "It's me, Grandma."

"Nick!"

He stepped cautiously in and looked around at the sterile room with machines that beeped and blinked. They seemed to be connected to Grandma in some fashion.

He pulled up a chair and sat. "How're you doing?"

"About as expected for my age."

"You look the same."

She smiled and reached up to pat her hair. "I must be a fright."

"No."

"Let's talk about you," she said. "I'm tired of doctors talking about me!"

Nick leaned forward and rested his elbows on his knees. "We're writing about WWII in World History." Nick moved his head. "I just wish Grandpa was around to tell me more."

Grandma pursed her lips as if thinking about what he said. "You might be old enough to read his journal."

"A journal?" Nick sat up straighter. "Can I see it?"

Grandma smoothed the blanket over her lap. "Of course!" She laughed. "He'd be pleased someone wanted to read it."

"Did Grandpa fight in France?" What a silly question to ask. "Grandpa told me about D-Day."

She chuckled. "Oh, yes. D-Day," she said and, after a pause, added, "Part of the liberation of France."

"Where's grandpa's journal?" He wanted to read it. That might earn them extra points on their paper.

Again Grandma paused, and a look of confusion crossed her face—probably because of her stroke, Nick reasoned. "There's a box of stuff in the storage closet, I think."

"Do you mind if I look for it?" he asked, pushing himself out of the chair. He couldn't wait to read about his grandfather's adventures during the war. He had heard the stories from Grandpa, but the journal might shed some light on what was happening in France during that time.

"Be my guest. I don't know why I need all that old stuff anyway. It's yours, Nick."

"Thanks!" He took a step toward the door, stopped, and went back to kiss her cheek, promising to come back soon.

Once in the parking lot, he looked at his phone. It was after eight. Should he go to Grandma's apartment or go home? He texted his parents.

—*Going to Grandma's for Grandpa's journal.*—
His mother replied.
—*It's after 8.*—
—*For my project.*—
—*K.*—

Chapter 7

Nick drove to his grandmother's apartment, found the key on his key chain, and let himself in. He switched on some lights and looked around the plant-filled living room with the multicolored quilt neatly folded on the back of the couch. He breathed in the familiar smell of Grandma's surroundings: potpourri, talcum powder, greenery, and coffee.

Nick knew there was a storage closet on the balcony. He turned on the outside lights and opened the sliding door. The closet was crammed with stuff: Christmas decorations, folding chairs, various pots, some tools, and boxes stacked on the back of shelves. Which one held the journal? Nick began taking each one out and opening it, squinting at the contents under the weak overhead light. He used the flashlight on his phone to get a better look. Box number one held family photos, mostly black and white. He groped around for something that resembled a journal—but found only pictures. He opened box number two which held greeting cards. Nick recognized a birthday card he had made for her in grade school, but no journal. In box number three, he found the battered journal along with his grandfather's medals and newspaper clippings about D-Day. Grandma had said it was his. He put away the photos and cards, turned off the lights, and cradled the box under his arm as he locked the door and got into his car. He couldn't wait to study what was in the box when he got home.

Once there, after greeting his parents, he shook the box at them. "Grandma said I could have it."

His mother raised her brows. "You're the only one who likes history."

Nick's father cleared his throat. "I like history too."

"True," his mother said before returning her attention to scrolling through messages on her phone.

"I'm starving," Nick said, but "starving" had a new meaning after meeting Cat.

Nick reheated his dinner and began laying out everything from the box that was held together with tape that was curling and peeling around the edges. The journal was first, then the medals, some letters, and yellowed newspapers announcing the D-Day invasion.

He began by opening the journal. The cover was torn and stained in several places. Nick wondered if Grandpa had carried it into battle. *Earl William Chesterfield, June 1944.*

The ink had smeared on the pages, making it difficult to read. But he was able to make out: *We're not to keep journals, but I want to remember everything. We're preparing for a top secret invasion. We can only guess at what it will be. There are rumors, but we haven't been briefed on what exactly we'll be doing.* Nick yawned and rubbed his eyes. He guessed his grandfather was referring to D-Day—a top secret invasion they had learned about in class. As much as he wanted to read the rest of the journal, his eyes began to close. He crawled into bed, vowing to get up early to read more. His dreams were filled with war too. Jean Claude Rousseau visited him again. This time he was running toward a large gate guarded by men with guns.

Then the shooting started, and he was jarred awake. It took a moment for him to realize he wasn't in the dream anymore, but in bed and he had slept through the alarm. He was late to school.

"Nick?" his mother called. "You're going to be late. Are you up?"

"Coming."

He'd take the journal to school to show Coach Sullivan. It would be far better to write about D-Day and share some of his grandfather's writings than the Gypsies—Romas. Who even cared about them?

When Nick arrived at World History, he carefully eased the journal out of his pack to show Coach.

"What do you have there, Nick?" Coach said, frowning at the worn and partially tattered journal.

"This was my grandfather's journal when he was part of D-Day."

Coach gingerly opened the cover to study the handwritten pages. "Have you read it?"

"No, I just got it last night. I thought I might look at it during lunch or something."

"I'd like to look at it again." He clasped Nick on the shoulder. "We're getting ready to cover D-Day, so maybe you can read some of it in class."

"Sure! That would be great!" He envisioned extra-credit points coming his way.

Nick scooped up the journal and took his seat near Cat. "Can I show you something?"

"Sure," she said.

He slid the journal across the desk for her to see. "This is my grandpa's journal he kept during WWII."

She raised her brows and flipped open the book.

She grimaced. "This is from 1944. Saumur happened in 1940."

"Maybe we want to switch to this instead?" he asked.

"No, I want to know what happened to us."

"Cat…" He was silenced when Coach began to take roll. He didn't believe in that reincarnation stuff. But just when he thought that, disjointed images flooded Nick's mind. A castle. The boy in a uniform watching a bonfire through the shelter of trees. Nick couldn't make out what he was looking at; the images flashed and were gone. Who was that boy he kept seeing?

"Does anyone have any questions?" Coach asked.

Nick jerked his head up, so engrossed in the images, familiar yet not. The lecture was over. The time had slipped away. What had he missed? Apparently everything.

"What did I miss?" he asked Cat.

She shrugged. "It'll cost you."

His shoulders shook as he suppressed a laugh. "I've got five bucks in my wallet."

She kept her lips together, chuckling silently.

"Okay," Coach said, waiting, eyes scanning. "If no one has any questions, I'll give you the rest of the class period to work on your project. Who is still having problems narrowing their topic?"

Several hands raised and Coach went to them. Nick turned to Cat. She watched him with laughing eyes rimmed in shimmering black.

"So you don't want to switch to D-Day?" He tried again.

"No." She folded her arms across her chest.

He let out a long sigh and closed the journal cover. "How do you know about the camp and Gypsies? I mean Romas." Suddenly remembering the face of the prisoner and the barbed wire. "Are you related to someone in the camp?" Nick asked after a considerable silence. There had to be a logical answer.

"I *was* in the camp," she said.

"Did...did it have barbed wire?" Nick asked.

Cat's eyes narrowed.

Of course it did. Most prisons had that deterrent.

"And deep holes?" he whispered.

To this, her eyes widened in surprise, and tears welled up.

Her reaction troubled him and made his chest hurt.

"I died in one such hole."

"Oh." *Yes, she had mentioned that.*

She lowered her head and looked away.

The images kept coming. A vision of buildings, converted barracks constructed for one reason but used for another stuck in his head. The internment camp, holding hundreds of Romas, smelling of excrement, perspiration-soaked clothing, and unwashed bodies with crippled and ill prisoners sitting or lying in the corners.

He needed to get those thoughts from his head. He stood, swaying slightly on his feet.

"Nick?" Coach Sullivan asked.

"I think I'm going to be sick." He rushed into the hallway and vomited into the nearest trash can.

Chapter 8

Nick skipped football practice and went directly home after school. No need to explain his absence to Coach Sullivan after getting sick in the hallway. His stomach was a hollow void and grumbling at being empty.

He unlocked the door and went in, checked his messages for any updates from his parents. They were at the hospital, but Grandma was better. Dinner. He needed dinner. Nick went into the kitchen, where Minnie wrapped herself around his legs and looked up with her effervescent eyes, reminding him of Cat, but only for a moment. He was starving and remembered there was one piece of pizza left.

He plugged in his phone, grabbed an apple, and heated the pizza and pulled out the journal to read more. While he ate, he read Grandpa's words: *We've finally been briefed on Operation Overlord. We are part of the allies landing on the beaches of Normandy to cut off the Germans. We never dreamed this was our mission. We're quite excited but also worried. When our landing craft got closer, we were faced with sheer cliffs. The Germans are entrenched and began picking us off like sitting ducks. We'll have our work cut out for us. Those of us who made it to the beach were trapped. Behind us were cliffs and in front of us was the ocean. Some of our tanks were sunk.* Nick finished eating and closed the journal, wondering how D-Day and Saumur were connected. Maybe they weren't. But from what he remembered of Coach's lectures and what Grandpa had shared, it was all pretty terrible. Were the Romas another piece of the puzzle?

Deep in the night, Nick heard his parents come home. He took a cautious peek at his alarm. Two o'clock. He turned over and went back to sleep only to be visited by images of a Gypsy girl, her familiar topaz eyes rimmed with more smokiness, wearing a white blouse embroidered with flowers on the sleeves, her multilayered skirts raised to reveal a bare leg. The wind swirled her hair, making it dance on the breeze until a sharp noise startled him.

Nick sat up in bed, turned off his alarm, and rubbed his sleep-encrusted eyes. His dream was so vivid. What was her name? The name eluded him, on the tip of his tongue as she floated away. He stretched and pulled the quilt tighter; he didn't want the dream to end. Even though he was groggy and unfocused, the girl was real to him. Outside, the sky had lightened for the new day. Reluctantly he got up and showered.

While he dried off, he read the text from his mother saying they left early for the hospital and dinner was in the refrigerator. Nick finished dressing, grabbed an apple, took his backpack, and went to school.

In World History, he took his seat next to Cat, yawning widely, making his jaw crack.

"You look terrible," she said.

Nick rubbed his face and hunched his shoulders. "Weird dream."

She leaned back and studied him, giving him the once-over. "And what did you dream about?"

Should he tell her he was haunted by a Gypsy? Would she believe him?

"Nothing important." He wasn't sure if his dreams were fueled by Cat or reading the journal. Although Grandpa didn't say anything about Gypsies or even the Jews.

Her face registered disappointment.

"Maybe there is something…" He stopped when class began and Coach started talking.

To tell Cat or not to tell Cat? Would he be validating her belief they were once other people in a past lifetime?

When Coach finished his lecture, Cat turned toward him expectantly.

He let his breath out noisily. "I've been having dreams."

"And?" She moved her head for him to continue.

"About a prison and a boy with a rifle, and a girl."

"What kind of girl?" Cat asked.

There was only one way to describe her. "A Gypsy girl."

"I was once a Roma girl," Cat corrected. "Among other people." She gave Nick a shoulder shrug like it was no big deal.

"Do you suppose…"

"So you do remember me?"

"I'm not saying that, maybe just the power of suggestion. You know." He moved his hands. "We've been talking about Gypsies, Romas, so they keep popping up in my dreams."

"Don't you think that's a weird coincidence?"

Probably. He shrugged. "Maybe. I've been reading my Grandpa's journal about D-Day."

"Nick." She drew out his name.

"I need more to convince me."

"More than remembering?"

"Yeah." Nick put up his hand. "My family doesn't believe in reincarnation."

"Can't they be wrong?" She let her shoulders rise and then fall.

"My father's a minister and is pretty sure on the subject."

"Is that the end of it?"

"I guess."

She sat back and folded her arms, looking perplexed and doubtful.

****

After school, before football, Nick met Emily on the bleachers. This had been their ritual since they started dating. Today the soft breeze fueled by Lake Michigan ruffled her hair, making strands dance around her face. He bent over and kissed her nose, red from the chill. She pushed up her glasses and smiled at him.

"How's your grandmother?" she asked.

"About the same." He moved his shoulders. "I miss having my parents around. I never thought I'd get tired of leftover pizza, but I am!"

Emily laughed and rocked back on the bench. "And here I thought you could eat anything!"

Nick watched the team file into the locker room. "I better go."

"You can come over tonight for dinner?" Emily asked.

"I'm always late because of football."

"I'll save you a plate," she said.

"Thanks, but let me check and see if they'll be

home. Love you!" He gave her a final kiss and jogged toward the entrance to change for practice.

Football took on a familiar pattern. Warm-ups, running, push-ups and sit-ups, throwing the ball, catching, kicking, and sprinting. After warm-ups, they played mock games practicing different formations. As much as he tried, Nick's head was fuzzy and unfocused. He rubbed his face. The lack of sleep was getting to him.

He missed catching the ball that was thrown to him. It sailed past Nick's head, and Bryan caught it easily and gave him a shit-eating grin.

"Nick!" Coach called. "Concentrate! Anticipate!"

"Concentrate," Bryan mimicked. "Anticipate!" Bryan's voice was low, so no one but Nick heard his heckling. "Rev…er…end."

Nick glared at Bryan. *Would the guy never leave him alone*? "Shut up!" he snapped, which only fueled the ghoulish glee on Bryan's face.

When football practice mercifully finished, Nick headed home, hoping his parents had returned from the hospital. He needed to eat and get a good night's sleep. There were lights on at the house, meaning his parents were home. He parked and went inside.

"Nick?" came his mother's welcoming voice from the kitchen.

"It's me," he said, dropping his backpack next to the front door. A weight seemed to lift, knowing they were home.

"How's Grandma?" he asked, going into the kitchen and lifting his nose. No dinner smells, only a bag of Chinese takeout.

His father was sitting at the table reading the

newspaper. "Better." He massaged his temples. "She's better but will need rehab."

Nick remembered the lag time between Grandma's thoughts and her words. "She seemed okay when I saw her."

"It'll just take time," his mother said, yawning.

"I really missed having you guys home." He noticed, too, the dark circles under his mother's eyes. The lack of sleep was getting to them as well.

"We missed you too," his mother said, turning away from her computer and stowing it away.

"Let's just enjoy our dinner knowing Grandma's in good hands," his father said.

Nick went to the sink and washed his hands. "Will you be able to go to the game on Friday?"

"Hopefully," his father said.

"Let's eat," his mother said, putting spoons by each carton.

"Dad—" Nick took a deep breath. "—can I talk to you after dinner?"

"Sure." His father nodded.

Nick's mother raised her brows and frowned. "Sounds serious?"

"Not really." But was that a lie?

When they finished eating, Nick and his father went into the office.

"What do you need to talk to me about?" His father sat and waved his hand for Nick to do the same. "Certainly not the birds and bees conversation we had when you were in fifth grade."

"Nothing like that." Nick sat on the edge of the chair and clasped and unclasped his hands. "It's kind of silly, but people have been talking about reincarnation at school." *Lie! Only Cat was talking about it.* "What does the Bible say about that?"

"To begin with, the Bible doesn't mention reincarnation. In fact, it says men only die once." His father flipped open the Bible on the desk. "You can read it in Hebrews for yourself."

Nick nodded. "I will."

"Let me ask you something." He cupped his chin. "What good would it do to keep living the same sinful life over and over?"

Nick shrugged. "What about finishing stuff left undone?"

"Nope," his father said. "If that was the case, your mother would be hounding me over and over to clean the garage." His father chuckled. "The Bible says nothing about coming back to our earthly bodies. It says one soul, not a reconstituted soul—no, just one per body."

Nick considered his father's words. "Isn't reincarnation something the Buddhists believe in?"

"I think so." His father tilted his head, studying Nick. "Interesting school conversation, don't you think?"

Nick smiled ruefully. "You know how it is, Dad."

"It's been a long time since I've been in high school, but I don't ever remember discussing that."

"Whatever." Nick's phone vibrated in his pocket. "I need to get my homework done." *And see who called him.*

He took the steps two at a time and went into his bedroom and closed the door and looked at his phone. Emily.

He called her back. "Hey!"

"What're you doing?"

He let out a sigh. "Homework."

"Just homework?"

"Not just homework. Everything."

"I hope you're not too busy for me?" Emily's playful tone held a bit of sarcasm. "How's your project coming?"

"I don't even want to think of that right now."

"What's she like to work with?"

What was Cat? Stubborn, relentless in her pursuit of discovering what happened to the Romas, antisocial. But he had seen a crack in her façade, a smile and a playful comeback.

"Nick? Is she that bad?" Emily asked.

"She's just stubborn and wants to research Gypsies."

"That's an odd topic," Emily said.

"That's what I thought."

"Do you think she's pretty?"

He wouldn't describe her as pretty. Emily was pretty. Cat was more exotic. "No!"

Nick ran his fingers through his hair. He didn't want to distract himself by thinking of Cat. "I've got to go. Homework."

"Sure, Nick. See you tomorrow." She sounded disappointed.

He took out his calculus book and flipped it open to start on his homework. He hadn't done his homework last night and now had two days' worth to do. Other things crowded in, and he couldn't focus: Cat, the scout, Grandma's illness, Grandpa's journal, and Emily all vied for his attention, and he began to feel a tightness in his chest, like he had too much to do and not enough time.

****

The next morning in World History, Coach Sullivan asked, "Nick, can you stay after class for a second?"

"Sure thing." Maybe it was about the scout. Sure, he wasn't playing his best, but he'd pull out all the stops for the scout if he had to.

"Mrs. Klaich is worried about your grade in Calculus."

Not about the scout.

"It's a hard class," he explained.

"I know that, but you've been getting A's, so when she said you've dropped to a low C, I was concerned."

"I know." Nick rubbed his temples with his palms. "My grandmother's in the hospital, and things are kind of upside down at our house right now."

"Understood. But your academics come before football." Coach clasped him on the shoulder.

Football had been Nick's life.

"I know. I'll get caught up. I will."

"See you at practice," Coach called after him.

Nick waved his hand as he left the class and then pounded his fist against his forehead once in the hallway. *Get in the game! Forget all the past-life BS until after the scout visits.*

Chapter 9

Western Michigan had an early frost on the night of Laketon High's first home football game, against Century High. The excitement for the game swirled around the stadium like leaves in the wind. Nick rubbed his hands together, warming them. He liked the cooler nights the best. He saw the ball location clearly when unhampered by sweat dripping down his face. Before changing into his uniform, he took a couple of swigs from his water bottle fortified with some vodka.

As the team took the field and his eyes adjusted to the glare of the overhead lights, he wondered if his parents were able to leave Grandma and attend. They hadn't missed any of his home games. Emily would be here, of course, but it wasn't quite the same as having his father in attendance. And what of the Michigan scout? Coach hadn't said anything about him being there.

The game buzzer sounded, and all Nick's concentration went to the game, but strangely his legs slogged through icy water, slushy and hard to keep his balance.

"Nick!" Coach Sullivan called. "What's wrong?"

He shook his head, trying to clear the ice from his brain. "Nothing."

"You're playing sloppy and unfocused." Coach frowned. "You should have easily caught that ball. It was coming right to you."

Nick nodded and tried again, only to be rushed and tackled. All the air knocked out of him, and he lay on the turf, looking skyward, the stars dimming in sympathy or winking conspiratorially.

"Take a rest," Coach said with a flap of his clipboard. "Bryan! Need you now!"

Gary gave him a hand up and helped him over to the bench. He watched as Bryan took his place on the field. He locked eyes with his best friend, Gary, to judge his reaction. Gary, in turn, gave him his signature whistle-tweet and moved his hand to tell him it was okay.

When they headed to the locker room at halftime for hydration, a pep talk, and to catch their breath, he saw his parents and Emily with her gaggle of friends. She gave him a lopsided, sympathetic smile. They were behind by two touchdowns.

Nick's father nodded. "You'll do better next time," he yelled.

"Sure," Nick called back. He followed morosely behind his teammates. Why was he doing so badly? His heart wasn't in the game. His concentration was taken by those visions running in his head.

****

When the game finished, Coach gave them his usual speech about losing.

"Losing is tough, but it's part of the game. What we need to do, each of us, is to analyze what went well and what didn't. We'll do that as a team, but each man must decide for himself what it was he did or didn't do." Coach stared into Nick's eyes while he shifted uncomfortably, before looking away and down at the floor.

"This wasn't our best effort. You know it. I know it. What do we need to do to get back our winning attitude and drive?"

Bryan said, "Not everyone is concentrating." Bryan turned to Nick.

Nick's scalp bristled as eyes bore into the back of his head. *Was it that obvious?*

Gary muttered, "Suck-up!" Very few students challenged Gary because of his size, including Bryan.

"We all have outside influences that can't be helped sometimes. It takes determination to concentrate on what we need to do, and that's different for each man. See you all on Monday," Coach said as his way of ending.

Nick and Gary changed from their uniforms into jeans and sweatshirts.

"I know what'll make you feel better," Gary said, whistle-tweeting and then crossing his eyes. Gary was good at cheering him up by making a funny face or imitating a cartoon duck. They bumped fists.

Nick didn't think anything could cheer him up.

"Party at the beach," Gary said.

A public access area on Lake Michigan.

Did Nick feel like partying? The decision swung between yes, no, hanging in the middle. Emily would probably like to. "Maybe," he said.

"I know, man, tough loss"—Gary nudged him in the ribs—"but I got beer." He winked at Nick, and Nick cracked a smile.

Partying at the beach was much better than brooding over the loss. "I'm sure Em will want to go."

After showering and dressing, he found Emily

waiting by the locker room, tapping her green-and-white sneakers adorned with sequins.

"Do you want to go to the party at the beach?" she asked, taking a moment to pull up her matching green-and-white polka-dotted sock.

"Sure." Nick nodded. "We can swing by." He took a couple of swallows from his water/vodka bottle, feeling the warmth start to make its way through his body.

****

Nick and Emily heard the voices and laughter and the crackle of a driftwood fire as they parked at Fishermen's Beach. He lifted his nose to the odors of fish, sand, and smoke. Then another scent hit his nose—a smell from memory although he wasn't personally acquainted with it. Rabbit stew with vegetables and broth accompanied a vision of another fire and a circle of multicolored wagons. Nick stopped in his tracks. Emily flashed him a smile, and he shook away the thought.

He was pretty sure Cat wouldn't be at the lake, and he was glad.

The beach was a favorite spot for building fires, cooking hot dogs and s'mores, and making out or having sex.

They walked toward the sounds on the beach. The water stretched out, silvery and endless. A bonfire on the beach with friends, beer, and hot dogs might be what he needed.

"You don't seem very happy tonight." Emily grabbed his hand and hurried him toward the voices and the flames dancing off the water.

"I guess I'm not good company." He paused,

stopped, and kicked some sand. "That was a tough loss."

"It was only the first home game." Emily squeezed his hand.

"True." His head hadn't been in the game tonight.

It had been football, football, football for as long as he could remember. His father regaled him with tales of his playing days with the Lions. The passion for the game seemed to be deflating in him like a shriveled balloon, and he didn't know why exactly.

"You're right, only the first home game. Let's go." Nick squeezed Emily's hand back. He swung their entwined arms up toward the water as they walked down the path, the moon and the anemic bulb from an overhead light illuminating the way.

When they got to the beach, their friends had already piled driftwood high, and the fire crackled, greedily clawing at the night sky. Someone was setting off fireworks, and the spiders of light glittered over the water before falling away to be swallowed in the darkness. He flinched at the pop of the fireworks—so much like the shot from a rifle. Again he pushed the image away.

"Emily! Nick!"

Nick heard Gary's tweet-whistle as they joined their friends by the fire.

Nick raised a hand. "Hey!" He let out a loud sigh of relief to have left the game behind.

Gary was holding a can of beer and Tiffany a paper cup with something that smelled fruity.

"You need a drink?" Gary asked.

"Do I ever!" Nick said as he fished in his wallet for some money to help pay for the beer.

Gary pocketed the money and handed him a cold can from the cooler, and Nick took a long swallow before wiping his mouth on the back of his hand.

"That game was the shits," Gary said.

"You got that right." Nick tipped the can to his lips just as he heard a collective gasp from those clustered around the bonfire. He turned to see what was happening. Veronica was leading Cat toward the circle.

"Does everyone know Cat?" Veronica asked.

A few nods and affirmations.

Oh crap. He didn't want her here talking about reincarnation and Romas.

"Look who's here." Emily sidled up closer to Nick. She gave him a teasing grin.

"Yeah." Nick was hoping to avoid Cat and tossed back the rest of his beer.

"Another?" Gary asked.

"Yeah." He opened the blue can and took a long swallow. "Em?"

"No, thanks." She gave her cup a slight shake. "I'll stick to soda."

"Hello, Nick," Cat said, walking through the sand with some trouble on her heels. "Emily. Gary." Cat nodded to each of them as she said their names.

A chorus of mumbled hellos returned.

Cat rubbed her arms and gave Nick a sweet smile. "Nice night for a fire."

He hadn't seen her smile like that before, and the parting of her lips softened her dark features and lit her topaz eyes. She was beautiful and a bit exotic in the glow of the fire. "Sure," he agreed.

"Tough loss," she added.

"You were there?" Emily asked.

Cat nodded.

Nick studied the contrast between the girls, Emily golden and light, and Cat dark and mysterious. He finished his beer.

Gary motioned toward Cat. "Want a beer?"

"Sure," Cat said, taking the can and downing it in one gulp and wiping her mouth on the back of her hand.

Damn, she drank that quick.

"Another?" Gary asked, whistle-tweeting his approval.

"Sure!" Cat matched them beer for beer, laughing when it took Nick two swallows to finish his.

"What?" Nick asked innocently. "I'm slow, so what!"

"You have to do it in one long swallow."

Nick started to chug, when Emily tugged at his arm. "Nick! Slow down," she urged.

Cat quirked her brow at Emily. "You want one?"

"No, thanks." Emily looked down at her soda. "I don't like beer."

The girls stared at each other. Nick shifted uneasily until Emily grabbed his hand and led him away. "Can I talk to you for a minute?"

"What's wrong?" he asked.

"What is she doing here, Nick?" Emily whispered as she tugged at his arm.

"Hanging out like the rest of us." He pulled his arm out of her grasp, annoyed. He had no idea why she was here.

"She's here for you, isn't she?"

"No! She came with Veronica."

"She arrived with Veronica, but she's here for you!" Emily whispered, her eyes glaring. "I saw how she smiled at you."

"She's a friend. My research partner."

"Bullshit!" Emily said.

"You're wrong!" Nick called as Emily stomped away and joined a circle of her friends.

Nick stood looking after her until Cat came over and patted his arm. "Everything okay?"

"I guess." He let out a sigh.

"Maybe I shouldn't have come."

At that moment, Veronica took Cat by the arm, saying, "I want you to meet someone."

Cat teetered sideways on her pointed heels and tripped toward the fire. Nick lunged and caught her, keeping her from tumbling into the flames.

She straightened and smiled up at him. "You saved me! My hero!" Cat patted his cheek. "I guess heels aren't the best thing to wear to the beach." Cat laughed before Veronica tugged at her arm.

Nick watched Cat's swaying hips as she and Veronica struggled through the sand. Nick lowered his eyes and rejoined Gary, reaching for another can. "Em doing okay?" Gary asked.

"She's upset Cat's here."

"Women!"

Gary didn't know the half of it.

"Nick?" Emily asked, returning to his side. "What's going on?"

"What?" He took a drink. "Nothing."

"Four beers and we've only been here, like, ten minutes?"

Much longer than ten minutes. "Just want to relax after the game." He gave a slight shrug. He glanced over to where Cat stood with Veronica and several others. Cat's head was tipped back, her mouth open, laughing. Nick frowned, irritated his partner was laughing with another guy. Nick didn't want Cat laughing with Reg.

Emily followed his gaze and folded her arms, then mockingly said, "My hero!"

"Come on, Em. She was just playing."

"She's not playing!"

"Just work partner. Besides, she's talking to Reginald."

"Really?" Emily said, giving him a pout. "Reg? Who cares."

Gary sidled over. "Another?"

Nick moved the empty can. "Yeah."

"Designated driver," Gary said, poking Emily.

"No way," she protested. "I'm not cleaning puke from my upholstery again."

"Only one time," Gary said, trying to put an arm around her, but she pushed him away.

"Once is too much!" She looked at Nick. "Don't get any ideas."

"A couple won't hurt." He took another beer. And besides, he drove.

"That better be it!" Emily said, stomping off to see her friends who were clustered together, whispering and gesturing in Cat's direction.

Nick stood with Gary, who seemed oblivious to the stir Cat had caused at the party. "Damn, they grow those boys from Century big."

"Yeah, their quarterback Benson ran like his butt was on fire." Nick finished his beer, and the darkness brightened a bit.

"Another?" Gary asked again.

"Sure. Who got the beer?" Nick eyed the cooler set away from the fire. "I owe you."

"My brother bought me a case. I don't know about the rest."

Nick opened the can and sucked at the foam bubbling over the edge. "I couldn't seem to get my head in the game tonight."

"First home game jitters," Gary said.

Yeah, that was probably it. No, something else was bothering him, but he couldn't name it.

Fitting four hot dogs on one stick, Gary eyed him. "What else is bugging you? That girl?" He motioned with his chin toward where Cat was standing next to Veronica, her eyes mesmerized by the flames.

"Nah! She's just a little wacko!" Nick drank most of the beer in two long gulps. His head was clearer and more focused than before.

"Another?"

Nick glanced at Emily huddled together and laughing with her girlfriends. "I shouldn't but…" Nick watched as she tipped her head back, laughing at something Tiffany said. "Sure."

The beers went down easily, and after the fifth—or was it the sixth—he lost count.

"Hey! You okay?" Gary asked when Nick accidentally bumped him, swaying in place. "You should have something to eat. A dog?" Gary turned the stick roasting the hot dogs over the flames, making the skins bubble and turn black. He pulled the dogs off and slid them into buns.

"You might be right." Nick accepted the hot dog and ate it quickly, burning his tongue in the process.

Kenny sidled over. "You guys want some of this?"

He shook a silver flask toward them. Nick took a swallow, and the whiskey burned down his throat. He winced. "Gary?"

Gary gulped down a long swallow. "Whoo! That's some shit!" he said, laughing and then tweet-whistling.

"You guys want to play some flag football?" Kenny asked.

Ugh, football was the last thing Nick wanted to do tonight. "Go to hell." Nick fell over laughing, holding his stomach. But with the hot dog and beer sloshing around, the laughter turned to agony as they both burned their way up his throat and spilled onto the sand. He vomited until dry heaves contorted his body.

"Hey, man, what's wrong?" Gary kept repeating.

Nick nodded his head but remained on the sand, holding his stomach. Damn, that hurt.

"Well, well, well. If it isn't the honorable do-gooder, Reverend Dupont!" Bryan mocked.

Another person he didn't want to see tonight.

"Em!" Bryan's voice changed, dripping honey. "Do you need a ride home, sweetheart? Looks like the reverend is out of commission."

Nick saw Emily's sequined shoes, her legs wide in a defensive, fighting stance.

"I'm taking you home, Nick Dupont!" Emily was clearly mad, but he was deliriously drunk. "Give me your car keys!"

He struggled to follow her to where the car was parked. "Em! Who am I?" Nick tried to imitate Cat struggling through the sand in her heels.

Emily cracked a small grin. "Do you like that black lipstick?"

"A turn-on," Nick said, jokingly.

"Really, Nick?" She laughed and swatted at his arm.

"Yeah, I think you need some pointy boots and black lipstick!" He imitated Cat's lurching gait in the sand.

"You're so bad, Nick!" She tried to keep a stern face but broke into a wide smile.

He kept imitating Cat until Emily was laughing so much she was crying. Things were right between them for the moment.

Chapter 10

Nick awoke the next morning with everything hurting, even the pores on his face. His head throbbed, his neck and ribs were tender, even his pupils had pins sticking in them. The light coming from the lines in the blinds was painfully bright, making his eyes water. He lay as still as he could, trying not to move. Even breathing was painful. Shards of glass stabbed at the back of his eyeballs, jabbing with each beat of his heart. He needed some aspirin and something to settle his stomach, but that would mean moving, so he stayed as still as possible, willing his headache to go away. He awoke to the sound of something vibrating and footsteps on the stairs leading to his bedroom.

"Nick? You up yet?"

His father's words drilled into his ears. No, he was dead. He was sure of it. He was in hell for drinking and throwing up out the window of the car, leaving splatters on the side of the door. That he remembered clearly.

"No."

His father opened the shades, and Nick pulled the blanket over his eyes. "I think I'm sick."

"Yeah, I saw the evidence on the side of your car door." Nick heard the accusation in his dad's voice before he said anything. "Emily drove you home last night?" he asked, glaring. "Are you hungover?" He paused. "The car reeks of alcohol."

"Sorry." Nick sighed behind the covers. "I guess I got carried away."

"You need to shower and get up. Even if you're going to act like an idiot, you still need to be part of the family and do your chores."

"Just give me a minute." He started to sit up. "Can you get me water and some aspirin?" Or three or four? A whole bottle?

His father huffed but he left, and Nick heard him in the bathroom for the water and pain reliever.

"Here." Nick heard his father set the glass on the table and the ping of several tablets.

"Thanks. Give me a minute."

His father left, closing the door behind him, leaving Nick alone. Nick shifted his body cautiously, each movement excruciating. Nick sat at the side of the bed, breathing shallowly, willing his stomach to stop churning so he could take the tablets. The water in the glass swirled with waves of nausea. He swallowed the pills and washed them down and waited for his stomach to erupt, and when it didn't, he was able to shower. The pinpricks of water bore into him, easing the throbbing in his head, settling his stomach.

After dressing and texting an apology to Emily, Nick crept down the stairs, where he found his parents in the study drinking coffee.

"Do you want to tell us what happened last night?" His father set his coffee cup down with deliberate slowness, his fingers tense on the handle. His mother glanced up from her magazine.

"I guess I screwed up."

"Why?" his mother asked.

"That miserable loss."

"Everyone has off nights," his father said.

"But I played terrible."

"I remember many losses," his father said. "Don't be so hard on yourself."

Nick leaned against the chair and moved his head and neck around. "I guess I didn't handle it very well last night. I got carried away."

"We've all had a lot on our minds," his mother pointed out. "Your grandmother's stroke," she said.

"Just take it easy with that stuff," his father said.

"I know. I know." But he relied on his liquid fortification to get him through some days.

"We'll talk later. First you need to clean the mess off the car, and you should visit your grandmother."

Nick pocketed the keys and went out to the driveway, studying the vomit across the side of the Subaru.

Nick drove to the car wash, hosed off the Subaru, and wiped out the inside. Better, he reasoned, but he still smelled a whiff of vomit, so he purchased a car freshener before heading to the hospital. In his head, he rehearsed what he would say to Grandma, the sanitized version of the game and the party afterward. He wondered if his mother had ever gotten in trouble in high school. She was levelheaded like Emily, and he couldn't imagine his mother vomiting out the window. Emily either. Emily kept him sane when school was hard, football practice was intense, and the demands of life made him crazy. Punctual, organized Emily, leading their junior class and the designated driver of his life.

He drove to the small rehab hospital between Laketon and Grand Rapids, a twenty-minute ride, and went to her room on the second floor, 7B.

Grandma was sitting up in bed, the white blanket accentuating the paleness of her skin.

"Hi, Grandma."

She turned from the television to him. The left side of her face sagged from her stroke, but otherwise she appeared normal.

"Nick, my boy, so good to see you! Sorry I missed the game last night." Grandma turned down the sound of TCM—her favorite channel. A black-and-white film was playing, where everyone wore suits, smoked, and were drinking at a bar.

Nick grimaced.

"Are you sick?" Stroke or not, his grandmother didn't miss much.

Nick shifted uncomfortably, staring at the floor. "I guess I'm sick," he mumbled.

Her eyes bored into him. "I see."

"We went to a party after the game."

"Ahh," she said. "That kind of sick."

He looked up and gave her a pained smile. "I started reading Grandpa's journal."

"What did you think?"

"It's kind of hard to read."

Grandma nodded. "Yes, water damage from when we had a leak in the roof." Grandma shifted. "Can you use it in your research?"

"That's the thing, Grandma, my partner wants to research Gypsies."

Grandma pursed her lips as if deep in thought. "I don't remember anything about Gypsies." She turned her head as if looking to see something written on the whiteboard. "Only said he felt sick for the people they found when they liberated the camps." She licked her lips.

Nick shifted his feet as images of starving and sick people flashed through his mind—a terrible scene. "No, the thing with the Gypsies happened before D-Day. I wish we could use it, but my partner is set on Gypsies."

"Hmm. Not the Jews?" Grandma asked.

"No, I guess everyone always thinks about the Jews in that war. There were others who were persecuted." He cracked his knuckles as he talked.

"True," she said.

"Do you want the journal back?"

"No, you keep it. He'd want you to have it," Grandma said as she smoothed down the blankets.

Nick brightened, feeling better than he had all morning. "I'd like that."

The curtains parted next to the bed, and an orderly came in. "Time for physical therapy."

"Oh, I was enjoying my grandson! Do we have to?"

"I'll come tomorrow if I get all my homework done," Nick promised, standing and leaning over Grandma's bed.

"All right," Grandma said. "Will you go water my plants?"

"Sure." He squeezed her hand lightly and gave a lopsided grin before returning to his car, where he rolled down the windows, hoping the fresh air might somehow blow away the lingering smells. He drove to the retirement community where Grandma had moved after Grandpa died.

Her front door had several notes stuck to it. *Get well soon! Dinner when you return. Missed you at*

Bunco! The seniors here seemed to look out for each other. Mom was right; Grandma had lots of friends here.

He unlocked her front door and let himself into her small but neat apartment. There were several pots of green plants in her living area. Nick got a pitcher and began watering. On the table was an unfinished puzzle. Nick paused and fingered several pieces and studied where to place them. After fitting them into the picture, he went down the short hallway to Grandma's bedroom where she had a giant Christmas cactus that she tended faithfully.

As he went down the hallway, lined with family photos, he stopped to study the picture of his grandfather in his uniform. In some ways, Nick resembled him—hair color, the set of their jaws. There was also a picture of Grandpa with his unit. These men looked like boys, like they could be part of the Laketon High football team, not grown men fighting a world war.

Almost all the faces reflected apprehension and stoicism; only one man gave the camera a rueful half smile. Most of these men were dead like his grandfather.

He left the pictures and began watering the cactus as a long dark hallway with cold stone floors flashed through his head. *A fleeting glimpse of boys milling around as the boom of canons echoed in the background. Were they preparing for war too?* It was the same boy Nick kept seeing—Jean Claude Rousseau.

Chapter 11

Nick drove home from his grandmother's apartment and thought about what a boring Saturday it would be if Emily was mad at him for last night. It was dumb getting drunk at the bonfire. He needed to be more careful; Emily was lukewarm on drinking and didn't usually imbibe.

"Hey, babe, I'm sorry you had to drive me home," Nick said when he called Emily, and there was a long pause on her end. "I need to see you. Can I come over after dinner? Take you for ice cream or something?"

"I'm not mad, Nick."

"You're not?"

"No, your imitation of Cat made me realize you don't have feelings for her."

He wasn't sure how she had come to that conclusion, but he'd accept it.

After his parents left for the hospital, Nick went to Emily's house. As he drove into her development, he went by Cat's house, the one where Dr. Kawalski used to live—it was a large house with lots of windows and a three-car garage. The windows were dark, and he didn't see anyone moving around, which was just as good.

He parked in front of Emily's and knocked. When she answered, she beckoned him in.

"How are you feeling today?" she asked, folding her arms, studying him.

"So-so." He moved his flat hand, indicating he wasn't sure. "Just the loss." He smiled at her and stepped forward and saw her relax. He put his hands around her waist and kissed her. Things were always better with Emily.

****

After church the next day, Nick and Emily decided to meet at the library to research their topics for Coach Sullivan's class. They both had Coach Sullivan for World History, but at different times. Emily was lucky. She and her partner were researching Patton—Nick had wanted to do the same. When they arrived, the librarian assigned them computers in the back.

Nick began with some academic sites the library subscribed to. The first was in French. He stared at it blankly before realizing he comprehended what he saw. No, that couldn't be right. He didn't know French. He massaged his temples.

"You okay?" Emily whispered.

He turned his computer to face her. "Can you read this?"

Saumur—Saumur est un camp d'internement niché au cœur des champs de raisin d'Montreuil-Bellamy.

"No, why?"

"I can."

"What does it say?"

"Saumur was an internment camp nestled deep in the grape fields of Montreuil-Bellamy."

"That makes sense." She pointed to the words. "You're using the context clues. Camp. *D'internement.* Internment. *Raisin* means 'grape,' right?"

"Maybe." Nick was aware of his shallow breathing and a light-headedness as he continued reading with the growing realization he could actually understand the French text even without clues.

He selected another site and tried to concentrate on the English words and not French. How had he learned French? He had taken two years of Spanish. He didn't think the two languages were similar. Were they?

****

At home after the library, his parents were working together in the study, his mother doing casework notes and his father writing a sermon.

He cleared his throat in the doorway. "Can...I talk to you for a sec?"

"What is it?" His mother closed her computer and folded her arms on the desk to listen.

"I know we don't believe in reincarnation, but I've been having weird dreams since meeting Cat in class."

Nick's father put aside the yellow notepad he was making notes on and leaned closer.

"Wait a minute. Who's Cat?" his father asked.

"My research partner."

"Dreams about reincarnation?" his mother asked, her eyes narrow and intense.

"Cat said we knew each other in another lifetime, and now I'm dreaming about a boy named Jean Claude."

His mother inhaled noisily and tried to cover with a cough. "That sounds French," she said.

"Cat seems to think we knew each other during World War II. A place called Saumur."

"Saumur?" his mother's voice was hoarse with a strangled cough.

"You'd be older than Grandma," his father added with a false laugh.

"That's not physically possible," his mother said, her brows knit together in a frown.

"I know that, so why the dreams?"

"I…" She shrugged. "I don't know."

"She believes we were reincarnated," Nick said, pushing home the point.

"Is that why you asked me about the Bible and reincarnation?" his father asked.

Nick hung his head. "Yes."

His mother leaned forward, her mouth gaping open. "Why do you think she said those things?" his mother asked, her voice low and gravelly sounding.

"I don't know, but I keep having visions and dreams about a foreign place."

"Could just be the power of suggestion," his mother said.

Somehow though, Nick didn't think that was the case. The first time he had seen Cat, in the cafeteria before they even talked, he started remembering a town, totally unlike Laketon. His face must have betrayed his thoughts.

"I believe the power of prayer holds the answers to our troubles." His father held up a Bible.

Nick grimaced. "I know. Thanks."

As he went upstairs, feet dragging, his mind conjured up all kinds of scenarios and none of them good.

He didn't open his Bible. No, he flipped open Grandpa's journal to a page that was less water stained and read: *The weather was terrible for the crossing. We were to take Omaha Beach. But we got blown off course, and the Germans were entrenched. I saw some of my buddies drown in the waters or shot, held down by their packs and equipment. So many lost. It makes me sad to think I could have been one of those men. We fought our way ashore. The fighting was endless and brutal.*

As he read more, Nick's mind flipped to more images: an endless line of Nazi soldiers; a bridge being blown up; and the smell of gun smoke and the tang of death. He didn't think they were images from reading the journal. No, he had a more intimate knowledge of the bridge. Did these result from the power of suggestion? If he had done his research on Patton, would he be thinking of blowing up bridges? Perhaps. It was all so confusing.

Chapter 12

Nick dreamed about Jean Claude again, but he wasn't alone. He was with a girl. All the images were about her.

The glimpse of a girl, a girl my age with the body of a fully developed woman. Her image ran through my brain, hair flying, lips parted in laughter. And I was the boy. Yes, I was Jean Claude watching the dancer.

"I am Chaton, the Gypsy princess!" she said through laughter as she spun around the campfire, twirling her body as a ballerina.

"Chaton, my sweet kitten. Come eat. Stop your dancing!" a man with a pointed goatee called to her.

"Non! I want to fly!"

"Beware," the man said, giving me a hard look. "The cat has claws."

To which she only twirled faster around the fire's glow.

Chaton. A Gypsy kitten.

****

After a restless sleep, evidenced by his sheet and quilt in a tangle, Nick tried to recall his dream and the name of the girl. Her name was always just out of reach. Shannon? No, Chaton—a kitten.

He showered and went downstairs for his usual breakfast of cereal, yogurt, and a banana. His parents were huddled around the table, sipping their coffee, heads bent together, talking softly. Had Grandma taken a turn for the worse?

He heard his name and stepped back quickly—making sure he was unseen, and listened.

"Do you think we should tell him?" his mother asked in a near whisper.

Nick barely breathed waiting for the sad news.

"I'm not sure it would help," his father said.

"What if he needs to know?"

"I don't think he does."

Nick noted a bit of hesitation in his father's words. Their conversation wasn't about Grandma. He took a step toward the door but stopped when he heard more.

"What if it's just coincidence?" his mother asked.

"Have you ever heard of Saumur?" his father asked.

The whispered conversation was definitely about him. He stepped closer, his eye to the space between the door and the wall.

"Well, no...but it's easy enough to find," his mother said. "The Internet and all." As she talked, she moved her finger around the handle of her mug.

"It's not an Auschwitz or Birkenau." His father snorted.

"I know," his mother said. "Well..." She hesitated. "Some people believe..."

"We're not some people, Grace. I'm a minister and need to set an example."

Minnie bumped into Nick's leg. He picked her up before she started meowing loudly, and stroked her while he listened. She purred against his arms, rubbing her head against the scar on his chest.

With Minnie in his arms, Nick stepped into the

kitchen. "What do you need to tell me?" His parents looked up.

Nick's father looked down at his plate and cleared his throat, before saying, "Nick! Son! Sit down. We need to talk."

Nick put Minnie down and sat opposite his parents, waiting while his father cleared his throat again.

His mother swallowed. "When you told us about the girl at school...that she knew you from before..." She searched for words, her speech hesitant and halting.

Nick narrowed his eyes. Where was this leading? "Yes?"

"When you were about three or four, I think, you kept telling us you had been in a war."

His father shifted in his chair. "We thought you were playing make-believe after Grandpa told you about his experiences during D-Day," his father explained.

"Or you had seen something on television and were fantasizing about it." His mother spoke deliberately, but she kept her head down. "You told us your name was Jean..." His mother narrowed her eyes in concentration. "I called you for lunch, and you didn't respond. You were playing in the backyard..."

Nick remembered.

"Nick, lunch," his mother called.

Who's Nick? I was Jean Claude. *"I'm Jean Claude!"*

"You are not Jean Claude! Your name is Nick, and lunch is ready," his mother said, annoyed.

"No, I'm not. I'm a soldier, and I ride horses!" he chanted in a singsong voice. "Jean Claude. Jean Claude. Giddyup!"

"No, you're not Jean Claude!" she insisted.

Nick had the hysterical urge to laugh, but instead, black spots danced before his eyes, and his head felt woozy.

Nick stared at his parents, speechless, until he found his voice. "Why—why didn't you tell me this when I told you what Cat said?" he stammered.

"We weren't sure what to do," his mother said.

"We've been distracted about your grandmother's health. We probably should have told you earlier," his father said. "Your mother and I talked it over and prayed about this." His father clasped his hands together. "We decided you should know."

Nick needed to wrap his mind around this. "So what Cat said was true?"

"We don't know," his mother replied ruefully. "We believe there has to be some sort of explanation."

"How come I don't remember this?" But he remembered hazy visions. Pictures flashed across his mind.

"You were very young," his mother said.

"We were anxious and concerned," his father said after a long pause. "It was all so strange." His father shook his head sadly like he wished this conversation wasn't taking place.

His mother continued, "You knew some details about where you lived in France. About a memorial near Paris with your name on it."

"Could I have seen that on TV?" Nick asked, not wanting to believe even with this new revelation from his parents.

"You said some French words."

"It could have been on the TV," Nick said again.

"We considered that," his father said.

"There has to be an explanation. People don't just wake up and know a foreign language, do they?" Nick asked, pushing back the mounting hysteria.

"No." His father brushed something from his robe.

"How long did I talk about being soldier?"

"For a couple of years as soon as you could talk." His mother leaned forward as if her back pained her.

"And why did I stop talking about it?"

"We stopped it."

"How?" Nick asked, shifting from foot to foot.

Silence passed between his parents.

"What did you do?" he asked again.

His parents looked at one another in some sort of telepathic communication. His mom shrugged and his father sighed.

"A priest performed an exorcism," his father said. He kept his eyes down and didn't look directly at Nick.

Nick gave a bitter snort. "Like that old movie *The Exorcist*? Did my head spin?"

"Nothing like that!" His mother rushed to say, "A priest prayed for the evil spirits to leave your body."

"A priest? A Catholic priest?" Nick's voice rose. "But we're Methodist!"

"True," his father spoke. "I was still in seminary, and we lived in Ohio. I wasn't ordained yet, so I guess technically…"

"Methodists don't believe in exorcisms, do they?" Nick asked.

"No."

"But you did it anyway?"

"We were grasping at straws," his mother said, reaching out and squeezing Nick's fingers. Fingers freezing and numb.

"We were concerned." His father smiled tightly. "I read something about the power of the brain and exorcisms—"

Nick yanked his hand away from his mom.

"I met this priest at a conference I attended, so I called him," his father said.

"Did the exorcism work?" Nick asked. It must have; he had no memory of it. Wouldn't something like that be traumatic and stay with him? But just as he thought that, an image of a man, a priest, popped into his head.

"We thought so. You didn't talk about the war until now, until you met Cat."

"How can this be? I'm plain old Nick Dupont in Laketon, Michigan. I was born in Laketon Hospital!"

"I know!" His mom bit a fingernail. "It just doesn't make any sense."

"But when you said Saumur..." his father said and stopped.

"Can you tell me more about the exorcism?" Nick asked. A name came into his head, Father Nathaniel.

"We taped the session," his father said.

"Do you still have the tape? Can I listen to it?"

"I'm not sure it will help," his father said.

"Does the name 'Father Nathaniel' mean anything?" Nick asked. The question just popped out. The name went with the tall figure in black robes.

His parents' frowns mirrored each other. "No, why?"

"I remember a priest by that name."

"No, the priest was named Father Samuel, I believe." His mom sat up straighter. "It was long ago."

"I want to hear the tape."

His parents looked at each other.

"I'll have to find it," his mother said quietly, almost in a whisper. "Then you can listen."

Nick looked toward the clock on the stove and blurted, "I've gotta go." He needed to get away from them and think.

"But your breakfast!" his mother said.

"I'm not hungry." Nick stood and edged toward the door.

His mother frowned. "When have you ever not been hungry?"

He had never been in this situation before, that's why.

His stomach churned as he grabbed his backpack, stumbled out the front door and to the car. Inside, in the driver's seat, Nick willed his heart to stop jerkily galloping against his chest.

Oh, God, what was happening to him?

Chapter 13

Nick drove to school on autopilot, following the route in a daze of confused thoughts and confessions. He needed to see Cat. How did she know what she knew? And the disclosure from his parents was unbelievable. His parents! He banged his fist on the steering wheel. His midwestern, conservative, Methodist parents! Exorcism! He pounded his fist on the steering wheel one last time before getting out of his car, and started toward the school.

"Hey, Nick!" Gary was parked nearby and in the process of locking his car when Nick walked past. Gary whistled and called, "Wait up!"

Nick slowed.

"What's the matter?" Gary asked, struggling to put his backpack strap over his shoulder.

Nick mumbled something about his parents and quickened his pace. "Can you let Em know I've got to work on our project?"

Gary looked dubious but responded with, "Sure thing."

Nick quickened his steps. "Tell her I'll see her later."

****

Nick went to Cat's locker, but she wasn't there; only a girl he didn't know very well was reading through a notebook. "Do you know where she is?" he asked, putting his hand on Cat's locker.

"She headed toward the gym." She moved her chin in that direction.

"Thanks." He turned in that direction, walked the short distance, and stood in the double doors that led into the gymnasium, watching Cat dance. In a black leotard and pink polka-dotted leg warmers, her limbs seemed longer than before. She was one continuous motion of fluidity and grace. Her body moved in rhythm with the music coming from her phone. She was one sexy chick when she danced, and Nick's breath stuck in his throat, and his heart expanded in his chest. Her movements had that impact on him.

She had her back to him but said, "I feel you," without turning around.

He remained quiet until she finished her routine.

"You were watching?" She turned, coming closer, walking as a ballet dancer would: back straight, toes pointed.

He cleared his throat. "I'm sorry I snuck up on you."

"What do you want?" she asked.

"We need to talk." He wanted to study her perfect dancer body but instead cleared his throat.

"What do you mean?" she asked, her brows furrowing together. She went to her bag, took out a towel, and wiped her face.

"I need to know what you know and why you know it."

"Why? I thought you didn't believe?"

He cleared his throat and shifted his feet. "I...learned..."

"What?"

"Never mind that. Did you have dreams? Visions?" he asked.

Cat sat on a folding chair, removed her leg warmers, and put on boots. "Something like that. I started remembering things. A woman with long dark hair. I figured maybe she was my mother, my birth mother. I already knew I was adopted. Even my real parents weren't my parents, if you know what I mean."

"I don't." Nick shifted his feet again, as if the floor was uneven and he was losing his balance.

"I don't remember how old I was when I began putting the puzzle of my life together. I kept remembering people, faces, and places. Some were familiar, and I thought I knew who they were, but others I had no idea who they were." Cat struggled into her sweater.

"Let me help you." Nick guided her arm into the sleeve.

"Thank you." Cat stood facing him, her hand on his chest, studying him.

He pulled his gaze away. "Sorry, I interrupted you," he said, stepping back. "Tell me more."

"There was a note left with me at the orphanage, saying my name was Catherine Anne and my birth parents couldn't keep me."

"But you don't remember them?"

"No, I was about two, I think. I searched for signs of recognition on everyone I met, but nothing connected for me. Even here, in Laketon, I found you instead."

"How did you know me?" They moved to the door, and Nick leaned against the wall. "I could feel your vibes, and your eyes are familiar."

"Isn't anything familiar about me?" she asked, shivering as if she was cold, and rubbing her arms.

Cat's eyes were familiar. "Your eyes remind me of our cat."

She laughed. "I was once a cat."

He didn't want to even go there.

"I've been having visions and dreams about a boy named Jean Claude. He's my age, and I think it was World War II. I think he was fighting the Germans."

She inhaled noisily and covered her mouth. "Really?"

"My parents…" The bell sounded, making him jump, and his thoughts scattered.

"Your parents, what?"

"Let's walk to class together." He guided her away from the gym. "I found out something crazy from my parents. My conservative, ultra-Methodist parents."

"What?" Cat asked, concern creasing her brow.

"My parents had me exorcised when I was a kid because I was talking about being a soldier in France!"

"Oh my gosh." Cat stopped walking, and they accidentally collided. Nick caught her elbow so she wouldn't fall. He held her longer than necessary, feeling the urge to hold her.

A zing ran up his spine. "I know. I didn't believe it when they told me, but with the visions and what you shared, it makes more sense to me now."

"What are we going to do?" she asked.

He shook his head. "I need to think about this and listen to the tape of my exorcism. I'm having trouble believing this."

"I had some help in the remembering part," Cat said.

"How?"

"I went to a past-life therapist, and he helped me remember."

"That sounds kind of whoo whoo."

"It wasn't," she said. They stopped by the English room door. She nodded. "This is my first class. Later?"

He nodded dumbly.

"Nick?" Emily's voice. She touched his sleeve. "What's wrong?" Her eyes narrowed as she watched Cat in the doorway.

"Nothing."

She moved around to stand in front of him without taking her hand off his arm. "I can tell something's the matter." Her facial expression mirrored her words, showing her concern.

He moved his head toward Cat.

"I wish she'd never came to Laketon!" Emily retorted, stamping her daisy- and sequin-patterned sneaker.

"My life would be less complicated," he said after a ragged breath.

"So it's true?" Emily asked. "Is she a former girlfriend?"

Nick shook his head as the tardy bell sounded. "I don't know how you jumped to that conclusion?"

"She has that look."

Nick wished he knew what the "look" was. He sighed. "I've gotta go."

Chapter 14

The exorcism tape was all Nick thought about during school. He wanted—no needed—to listen. His mind conjured up all kinds of scenarios and images. Were any of the visions from the actual event or just his overactive imagination? Would his mother find the tape? He willed the school day to fly by so he could get home.

Once at home, he confronted his mother. "Do you have it?"

She didn't ask what; she only drew out a rectangular object from her pocket and handed it to him.

The cassette tape, still warm from her pocket, wasn't unusual looking except for the date when he was a little kid.

"We have an old cassette player in the garage you can use," his father said. "But are you sure this is a good idea?"

"I don't know," Nick said. "I just need answers. I want to understand what's happening to me."

"I bet it was a concussion when you fell out of the tree," his father said. "Or from football. They're doing a lot of research on how concussions can affect the brain."

Nick mumbled, "Yeah, maybe." But somehow he knew that wasn't the case.

He took the tape from his mother and went to the garage to find the tape player. Once back in his room, he dusted it off and set it on his desk.

Should he listen? He was a mass of contradictions. He wanted to, yet he didn't.

Nick took a deep breath, fit the tape into the machine, and hit Play on the antiquated recorder. He strained forward to hear his four-year-old voice, high-pitched with a slight lisp because of a loose tooth. He turned up the volume as high as it would go. Minnie entered his bedroom, mewing at the strange sounds, and Nick reached down and lifted her to his lap, stroking her silky fur as he continued to listen. He began to remember it all as if it had happened yesterday, every bit.

He was sitting in a darkened church with flickering candles highlighting a picture of the crucified Jesus. The man, wearing a robe, told him he'd feel better when they finished. The distinct smell of the candles seemed to waft out of the recorder and into his bedroom.

"Do you know what we're doing today, Nicholas?"

"Mon nom est Jean Claude." Nick put his hand over his mouth. He remembered! Nick continued listening as Father Samuel talked.

"I ask our dear Lord and Savior to make powerless the wicked and godless influences in Nick's life and pluck the evil eye from his soul. Where there was once bad, replace it with goodness and charity. Please guide Nick in your ways of goodness and not let him be poisoned by the dark forces of evil. May he be under your protection and know that you are his salvation and strength."

Then there was silence. The tape crackled. *Is that it? Wait.*

"How do you feel, Nick?" Father Samuel was talking.

"Okay." Nick heard himself answer.

The words stopped, and the tape whirled soundlessly, but Nick continued listening, tensing his jaw muscles even though the recording was clearly over. Minnie struggled to get out of his arms, so he let her jump to the floor. He reached to turn off the tape player and saw the deep gashes Minnie had scratched into his arm. Nick switched off the tape player when his mother stepped into his room. He heard her light footsteps but didn't turn to her immediately, giving his jumbled thoughts a chance to settle.

"You were listening?" he asked, rewinding the tape, hearing the whirl and click when it finished.

"Yes," she said, frowning at Minnie's scratches.

"I guess I held Minnie too tight."

They were quiet. Minnie meowed quietly for his mother's attention.

"I don't remember a thing," he lied.

His mother came around to face him. "You're crying, Nick," she said, touching his face lightly.

"I'm crying for that little boy." He swiped at his wet cheeks.

"That little boy was you." Her words a soft whisper.

"I know." His words were quiet, then stronger he said, "I don't remember those things—I don't remember that war." But the smoke from those long-ago candles remained in his nostrils.

"It was long before you were born." His mother

smoothed his hair. "I wasn't even born yet," she said, sitting on the edge of his bed with a creak and rustle.

"Then why would I say those things?"

"I don't know," his mother said with a sigh. She pulled a folded piece of pink paper from her pocket. "I found this. Your kindergarten progress report." She read: " 'Nicholas has a great imagination and good verbal skills. He has shared French with us, and his imaginary friend, John. He's a pleasure to have in class.' "

Nick sat quietly. "Am I going crazy?"

"Of course not."

"But that tape and now the report card?" He spread his arms helplessly. "What does it mean?"

"Your father and I think it might be good to have you see a psychologist or a counselor."

"So you do think I'm crazy?"

"I think your mind is playing tricks on you."

She got up, gave him a hug, and left the room.

He picked up his phone. There was only one person who could help him sort this out. He found her number and called. There was no answer, only the breezy greeting: "I'm busy and will get back to you!"

"It's Nick. Call me."

He set his phone down, and it immediately vibrated. He looked at the caller ID. Emily. He blew out a long breath before answering. "Hi."

"What are you doing?"

"Homework," he lied.

"Me too."

He heard a beep. Cat returning his call. "Can I call you back?"

"Who's calling you?"

"Cat."

"Fine! Talk to her!"

"Em. Don't be like that. I want a good grade, and she's my partner."

"Is that all?"

"It is. I'll call you later."

"Sure."

He switched callers. "Hey! Thanks for calling back."

"You sounded serious."

"I guess it is."

"What's wrong?"

He let out a ragged breath. "Remember I told you my parents had me exorcised when I was a kid because I told them I was a French soldier named Jean Claude."

He let the words sink in, and she remained quiet.

"They taped the session between me and the priest."

"So what do you believe now?" she asked.

"I don't know," he whispered. "It's crazy. Am I crazy?"

"No, if you're crazy, then I am. We'll be crazy together."

Chapter 15

Nick settled into bed, put his hands under his head and stared at the dark ceiling. Sleep seemed to have run away, but in its place, a vision of *brightly colored wagons circling Saumur before settling in a vacant field and closing ranks. Jean Claude*—yes, that boy again—*crept a bit closer, seemingly looking for a lost object.* Nick watched the scene unfold as he looked into the dark. *As I watched, I was transformed into Jean Claude. Even my skin felt different.*

I continued searching the ground, inching closer. I smelled the fire and cooking meat, sizzling over the flames, succulent and juicy. My mouth watered.

"Do you want some?" a voice asked from behind me.

Startled, I dropped my pretense of searching and whirled around.

The girl, about my age, was dark-haired with topaz eyes rimmed with more smokiness. She wore a white blouse with embroidery and a skirt with many colors and patterns.

"I was looking..." I stammered. "For my dog." We had no such beast. But how could I explain what I was doing in the forest surrounding their camp at this hour? "It does smell wonderful. Rabbit?"

She nodded.

"I'm Chaton." She gestured to herself.

"I'm Jean Claude."

"Come." Chaton led me to the fire in the middle of the camp.

None of the local girls would be so forward. Gretchen was prim and proper and didn't make my hands sweat—maybe a little. My heart hammered with anticipation as I followed Chaton eagerly toward the delicious smells and the large fire dominating the center of their encampment.

An old Gypsy woman handed me a bowl.

"Come," Chaton said with a laugh revealing her small white teeth, beckoning me. Her forefinger hooked around a jug of wine.

I followed her willingly back into the forest. Before we left, my eyes darted around the camp. It was a fairly large group of ten or twelve wagons, circled together with people moving around, stacking wood, shaking out blankets, and some were strumming instruments.

Chaton led me back toward where I had been searching for my pretend dog. She found a fallen log where we could sit. We sat, ate our stew, and shared the jug of wine.

"How long will you be here?" I asked, burning my tongue from the stew and taking a swallow of wine.

She shrugged. "I never know. We keep moving from place to place."

I hoped she would stay awhile so I could get to know her.

"Tell me about Jean Claude?"

"I'm a cadet at the Cadre Noir. We are training to be military leaders."

She shrugged. "Is that what you want to do? Lead an army?"

I settled my feet in a more comfortable position and took another sip from the jug and handed it to her.

"We just declared war on Germany." I hoped she'd be impressed, but Chaton remained quiet.

She sighed and said, "I think war is pointless."

"Hitler has invaded Poland, and who knows how long until he reaches our door?"

"Hmm."

"My father is fighting with the French Third Republic." I hadn't heard from him in many months. "Do you want the Germans in France?"

"We travel all over Europe." She shrugged and took a swig from the jug. "Germany? France? Poland? They are all about the same to us."

Now it was my turn to pause. "I guess you wouldn't understand the importance of defending country and home."

"I don't understand war or staying in a fixed location. Don't you long to wander?"

Yes, I guessed I wanted to see other parts of France and Europe—experience life. If I was called to fight, I'd see plenty. I sat up taller thinking of joining my father fighting to keep France unoccupied.

She nudged closer to me, resting her shoulder against my arm. "Do you mind?" She rubbed her arms. "The night air is chilly."

"No." I slipped my arm around her shoulders and pulled her closer. The wine had warmed my veins, and when she turned toward me, her face lifted and her eyes opened slightly. I leaned closer, and her lips touched mine. I hadn't kissed many girls, but this passionate exchange was different than kissing Gretchen. Chaton kissed me softly at first and then with more purpose,

finally biting my bottom lip before resuming her exploration of my mouth. I could think of nothing but her lips and the beating of my heart.

****

"Nick?" his mother called, and he fought his way through the darkness of sleep to her voice.

"You're going to be late for school." The school or the barn? His mind was in a tangle of images, thinking first of the large, sturdy barn that had housed the many horses of the Cadre.

"Do I have to clean the barn?"

Her brows came together in a V. "What did you say?"

Nick yawned and struggled to a sitting position. "I must have overslept."

"Are you still thinking about the exorcism?" His mother touched the tape recorder.

He inclined his head.

"Did you get any sleep?" she asked, opening the curtains to let in the light. She was dressed for work in slacks and a sweater.

He yawned. "A bit."

"We didn't have much time to discuss the tape." She adjusted the blinds. "We should have more time tonight."

He nodded and looked at his phone, noting the missed calls and messages from Emily and Gary.

—*WHERE ARE YOU?*— Emily asked. She must've called about five times too.

—*ARE YOU SICK?*— Gary had texted.

****

How Nick reached school was a mystery to him. It was as if he had lost the ten-minute drive to a black

96

hole in his head. The clock on his dash read 9:35. He had missed two classes. He went in to face the consequences.

The Laketon principal nodded and said, "Nick."

"Sorry I'm late." Nick shifted feet and moved his backpack to a more comfortable position on his shoulders. "I overslept."

"That can happen," the principal said, looking down at his computer before typing in Nick's name. "Since these are your first unexcused absences, and your grades are fairly good…" The principal frowned at the computer. "Your grades have suffered a bit these last few weeks."

"How?" Nick's breath caught in his throat. "How so?"

"You were at an A- in calculus, but now it looks like you're at a C-." The principal paused as if considering what to say. "I should give you detention, but I'll let these absences slide this time, but next time there will be consequences."

"I understand." Nick swallowed slowly.

A bell sounded. Nick looked around, confused.

The principal said, "Nutrition break." A twenty-minute break after second period so students could recharge and have a snack.

"Oh, right." His stomach did a little flip. He was hungry, but he wanted to find Cat. Nick left the office and plowed through the throng of students packed into the hallway by the junior lockers.

"Nick! Nick!" He heard Emily's frantic calls and slowed. She caught up with him. "Did you get my messages?" She positioned her body blocking him from continuing. "Where have you been?"

"I overslept."

"Is everything all right?" She placed her hand on his arm and frowned at Minnie's scratches.

He let out a sigh. "I guess."

"What's the matter?"

"Nothing. I can't discuss it right now. Later, maybe."

Emily frowned. "Problems at home?"

"You could say that."

"Oh, Nick! I'm so sorry." Her eyes teared up.

He reached down and kissed her. "You're the best thing in my life." He grabbed her hand.

She lost her concerned grimace.

Nick looked around. "I have to talk to Cat about something. Seen her around?"

Emily pouted. "Her again? We can't have nutrition break together?"

"How about lunch?"

"I've got a lunch meeting," Emily said, chewing her lip.

"After school?"

Emily froze, not answering him, her eyes a concentrated stare. Nick turned to see what she was focused on. Cat, dressed in a leotard and magenta-colored tights, was walking toward them, swinging her glossy black hair over her shoulder.

He gave Em one final kiss and the promise of meeting after school before going to Cat. "I'd like to talk to you," he said in a low voice just barely heard over the students herding into the cafeteria for snacks.

The halls quickly emptied of students.

She looked around. "Pretty deserted right now."

Nick swiveled his head to see if anyone was

listening. Satisfied no one was eavesdropping, he said, "I want to tell you about last night," Nick said, rubbing at the scratches Minnie left.

Cat took his hand and kissed his scratches. "All better?"

He gave her a weak, anemic smile. "I listened to the exorcism tape. And I remembered some things."

Cat moved her head back as if considering his statement. "For real? A real-life exorcism?"

"A priest prayed for me, to drive the evil spirits away."

"Interesting," Cat said, squeezing his arm as she talked. "What did you remember?"

Nick swallowed slowly. He was aware she was touching him, but he didn't mind. "Being a soldier." He looked up. "During the war."

"Our war?" she asked.

He gave a quick nod.

"So you believe me now?"

"I don't know what I believe," he said. "In a matter of weeks, my life has been turned inside out."

"I understand," Cat said, trying to grip his arm tighter.

"No you don't." Nick yanked his arm away. "There's a lot of pressure for me to do well in school and help with my father's ministry. Be a good citizen and live a Christian life." He swallowed the lump in his throat. "This goes against all that," he gasped in a strangled croak.

"Maybe I can help." She put her hand back on his arm and squeezed reassuringly.

"Anything," he said as the bell sounded and the hallway began to fill with students once again. "We can finish our conversation at lunch." They walked to World History together and sat in their assigned seats.

Bryan walked by and ran his fingers through Cat's hair, and in a flash, she dug her nails into his hand, leaving red welts.

"Ouch! The cat has claws."

"Keep your hands to yourself!" Cat said, flexing her hands and studying her long red nails.

Bryan gave a short bark of laughter. "Or I'll end up like the Reverend?" Bryan nodded toward the scratches on Nick's hand before sitting down.

Nick frowned. He looked over at Cat. "He's not...Is he from..." Nick lowered his voice even more. "...before?"

"I don't know," she said.

Now he was questioning everything he thought to be true. And who was he exactly if he wasn't Nick Dupont from Laketon, Michigan? Did the soul from Jean Claude move into his body at some point? How did that happen exactly? He needed answers, and he needed them now.

Chapter 16

Coach rapped on the board for their attention. "I'll give you the second half of class to work on your projects. Right now I want to turn your attention to how the Americans got into the war and the D-Day invasion."

Nick listened to the lecture.

"President Roosevelt was hesitant to pull Americans into another European war. To help our allies, we sent money, munitions, and out-of-commission WWI ships. We did send warships to guard our merchant ships in the area. But when the Germans torpedoed one of our ships on accident, we had a vested interest in the war. Nick?"

He jerked his head up. "Yes?"

"Would you like to share a bit of your grandfather's journal?"

Nick pulled out the journal and began reading. "Some of this is hard to read because it's water marked and smeared. But here's how it starts. 'May 20, 1944. I'm part of the 29th Infantry Division and we're training for a top secret mission. We understand it will be dangerous, but we don't know where our mission is and what we are to do. We know it's to stop Germany, but they are everywhere in Europe, it seems.' "

Coach held up his hand. "Okay, that's a good intro to my next topic. Who were our allies in this top secret mission?" Coach began talking about the British and Canadians.

They continued in this fashion until Coach stopped and let them work on their projects. Nick's mind began flashing pictures like an out-of-control PowerPoint presentation. Jean Claude wearing a uniform. The German army across the river. The old, dilapidated internment camp.

"I've been doing more research about the area." Nick's mind went to the research about the Cadre Noir cadets and the German Panzers.

Cat's expression encouraged him to continue.

"The military training schoolboys were able to keep the Germans at bay for two days."

"The boys of your school did that?" Cat asked, clearly impressed.

His school? He'd let that slide for now.

"Yeah, they were a figurehead cavalry unit for boys who would become officers someday. I'm not sure the Romas and the boys had anything in common except living in the same area."

"They have a connection to us," Cat commented.

"True. But to get a good grade, we probably should tie it together in some way. And I don't want to put anything about reincarnation in our paper. Understood?"

Cat smiled and rolled her eyes.

Nick drummed his fingers on the desk. "Both took place in 1940."

"Maybe they aren't connected," Cat offered, drawing circles on her paper as they talked. She shrugged. "Maybe we're connected."

"Possibly," Nick said, scrunching his mouth as an

image of a man falling off a motorcycle after being shot in the chest entered his mind. He tipped his head back and studied the ceiling. "I'm confused."

"How?"

"I'm not sure I know how the Romas and the school are connected. Can you tell me more about your people?"

Many seconds ticked past before she said, "My people are an old culture. We have been traveling around Europe for hundreds of years." Cat's voice took on a different intonation. Nick frowned at her speech pattern. A flatness and a hint of an accent.

She continued, "People were superstitious and thought we brought bad luck to the places we visited. Gypsies are nomads; we had no fixed place, like some American Indians."

Nick wrote *Gypsy* and *Indian* in his notebook.

As Cat talked, she tipped her head back and looked over his shoulder with unseeing eyes, remembering details. "Before the war, the French enacted laws to track us and make our way of life difficult. We were chased away from towns. Our wagons, automobiles, and boats burned."

Nick's mind went to a memory of a wagon on fire, running feet, shouts, and screams. An encampment in chaos. "So the persecution stuff started before the war?"

"Yes." Cat continued, "Our children were snatched away to be raised as proper 'European citizens' rather than in a caravan with loving parents and a tribal support system."

Cat paused and ran her red fingernail over the top of the table, tracing a scratch in the fake wood.

"My sister was one such prisoner. We stayed close to Saumur to keep watch on her."

Nick wrote *Saumur* and circled it on his paper.

"My little sister was named Adella."

A memory of a little girl bringing sugar for their tea ran through his mind. A beautiful cherub face with long curling locks and a pinafore over her dress. Was he remembering Adella?

The bell sounded. Nick jerked away from images of the girl with a demure face and defiant eyes. "I better get to my next class." Calculus. He fished his water bottle from his pack and took a long swallow of liquid courage.

Cat wrinkled her nose. "You're not fooling anyone, you know?"

"I don't know what you mean?"

"I can smell it."

"Oh." He tucked it away.

"You better be careful," she warned. He grimaced and followed her out of class.

"Nick!" Emily said, bouncing toward him and glaring at Cat. "Walk me to class."

"Hey! I can't. Calculus, remember?" Opposite Emily's class.

Emily pouted. "Oh, right."

"See you after school." Nick gave her a sympathetic smile before continuing down the hall with Cat. He could feel Emily's eyes on them as they walked away.

Chapter 17

After school, Nick met Emily on the bleachers before practice. He hopped up to where she was sitting. Tiny tendrils escaped her messy bun and danced around her temples. He studied her as he sat down. "I wasn't sure you'd be here."

She shrugged. "Don't you need to be with her?" She grimaced. "Cat. Research partner?"

"Em..." Nick put his arm around her shoulders and squeezed. "I didn't have a choice in partners."

"I guess not." She gave him a small, forced smile.

"Tell me what's new?"

She wiggled her feet, showing off her sneakers with pictures of cartoon characters on them.

"Besides those," he said with a laugh.

"Homecoming."

He frowned. "That's weeks away."

"It is, but there's a lot of planning for the dance, the floats. Everything."

As she talked, her feet moved, and he couldn't help but look at the characters and wonder where she found her shoes.

He grimaced, not realizing what all went into planning homecoming.

He opened his mouth to speak, but Emily continued.

"The lunch meeting didn't go well." Her hands

fluttered with her agitation. "I had the DJ all lined up," she cried. "And someone, I won't name names, hired a different one. Now we have two DJs!"

Nick tried to look attentive. Emily was stressing about a DJ, while he worried about his soul in another life.

"This will be a real mess to fix," she said.

Nick listened in sympathy, knowing there wasn't a fix to his mess.

****

Nick arrived home to his father's red-hot chili for dinner.

His parents were having wine, and Nick looked longingly at the burgundy liquid, wishing he could have a drink too. The alcohol might take the edge off the weird vibes from his dreams and visions and even give him more energy to do his homework later.

"We didn't get a chance to talk about what you thought after listening to the tape last night," his mother said, picking up her drink and studying the contents before taking a swallow.

His parents leaned forward expectantly, waiting for his reply. *Tell the truth or fudge.* In seeing his parents' fatigued faces from running back and forth to check on Grandma, he decided to fudge a little to not add to their worry. "I honestly don't remember it."

And as much as he wanted their help, this was something he had to do himself. It was his problem, not theirs.

"That's what I thought. It was from the concussion," his father said, flourishing his spoon over the chili.

Nick pushed a few remaining beans around his

bowl. "Coach harps on us about wearing helmets."

"Scary stuff." His father shook his head.

"So what about that girl?" his mother asked.

Nick chose his words carefully. "She's had a hard life," he said and paused. "When she was little, her parents left her at an orphanage because they couldn't take care of her."

"That must have been terrible."

"She said her adoptive parents are good to her."

"And…What about knowing each other before?" His father leaned over a bit as if stretching out his words.

"I'm not sure where that came from."

"Does she know you were talking about a boy who lived in France when you were younger?"

"Yeah, I told her."

His parents waited for him to continue. He pushed away his bowl, full and satisfied. "She said something about how little kids fantasize about stuff like that." That wasn't exactly what she said, but they didn't need to know the full extent of their conversation. He decided to switch the topic. "How's Grandma?"

"Much better." His mother smiled. "She asks about you, you know? But I told her how busy you were."

"I'll try to see her soon."

"She'd like that."

Nick pushed back from the table. "I've got homework. Thanks for the chili, Dad. It's the best." He fanned his mouth, indicating it was beyond hot.

His father grinned.

Once in his room, when his homework was finished, he had a chance to sort through what he knew: One, he thought he had been a soldier named Jean

Claude when he was a kid. Two, his parents were concerned enough to have him exorcised by a priest. Three, he remembered bits and pieces of dreams and visions about Jean Claude. But did that prove anything? Four, Jean Claude Rousseau was a real person, a famous movie director, so he could have heard that name or read about him somehow. Five, Cat remembered he left her to die. He wasn't entirely sure about this reincarnation or rebirth stuff, but he knew to his very core he wouldn't have deliberately left someone to die. Many innocent people died during wars.

A rap on his bedroom door. "Night!" his parents said in unison. After his parents went to bed, Nick snuck downstairs, uncorked the cabernet, and gulped some from the bottle. He waited for the warmth of the French wine to spread through his body before going upstairs to bed and slept dream-free.

Chapter 18

The next morning when Nick arrived at school, Cat was conspicuously absent, and Nick was kinda glad. Emily was waiting by his locker, bouncing from foot to foot on pink-and-white-swirl sneakers, a habit she had when excited.

"Guess what?"

He hoped the DJ problem was solved so he didn't have to listen to it again.

Emily gave a little squeal, and Nick couldn't help but smile at her. "What?"

She held his wrists and shook them. "We've been nominated!"

Momentarily he couldn't think why she would say that.

"Homecoming." Her face fell. "Remember? Junior Princess and Prince!" She gave his wrists another half-hearted shake. "Gary and Tiffany too!"

"Oh." He remembered his English teacher passing out the ballots and gave Emily a tight smile. "That's great!" He secretly hoped Gary and Tiff won so he wouldn't have to wear a dopey crown or anything.

"I've got to start looking for a dress!" Emily said. "Gotta go!" she squealed. "I need to talk to Veronica! She knows the best places to shop."

Nick shoved his backpack inside, slamming the locker shut. He looked at the clock and headed for the cafeteria for some coffee. Immediately he spotted Tiffany and Gary.

Gary gave him a tweet-whistle. "Where's Em?"

Nick shrugged. "Something important to discuss with Veronica."

"Probably how to style her hair," Tiffany said. "Or where to find a dress."

"Really, girls talk about that?" Nick asked.

Tiffany gave him an exaggerated grimace. "Of course! That's what we do."

"How are you going to style your hair, Gary?" Nick asked.

"I'm thinking about shaving my head," he said, running his hands through his curly blond hair.

"No!" Tiffany pushed him. "Don't shave it all off!" She touched a curl behind Gary's ear, causing him to lean away, laughing and shrugging off her hand.

Nick concentrated on his coffee.

"How's your research paper coming?" Gary asked.

"I'm not sure where we're going with it," Nick said. They had been so busy talking about the reincarnation stuff, they hadn't even discussed what they wanted to cover on their paper about the Saumur internment camp and military school.

"Yeah, ours—kind of boring too," Gary said. "You know how I hate writing papers."

Just then the bell rang.

When Nick got to World History, Cat was already seated. He hadn't seen her until now.

"Hey! Did you just get here?"

"Chiropractor's office," she said, rubbing her lower back.

"What's wrong?"

"Fell during a dance number, and now my back's been bothering me."

"Oh."

Nick stopped talking just as Coach began speaking. "I'd like to meet with each pair on their progress and answer questions they have about their topic so far," Coach Sullivan said.

Grumbling from the class. "But we've only had a week," came a response.

"Settle down." Coach Sullivan waved his hands. "I just want to help you get—and stay—on track."

"Shit!"

"Excuse me?" Coach Sullivan raised his eyebrows. "Can I start with you, Nick and Catherine?"

Nick flipped open his notebook. He had written down some facts about Cadre Noir.

Coach moved a chair near their desks and consulted his notes. "You two are reporting on the Gypsies during World War II, I believe?"

Nick squinted at the words written on his paper. "We might be broader than that. Focusing on what happened in Saumur during WWII."

"And what was that?" Coach asked.

"The boys at the school fought off Hitler's Elite Panzer Division for two days."

"Oh, yes!" Coach wrote something on his clipboard. "Cat?"

"Our paper will cover the Roma's persecution during the war." She looked pointedly at Nick for his reaction. "Mainly how they were rounded up and killed, many starving to death in the internment camps. There was one in Saumur."

"So you'll be covering two different factions and

their activities during the war?" Coach asked.

They nodded in unison.

"Interesting." Coach shook his head, and his eyes conveyed his interest.

Coach Sullivan wrote something on his clipboard and said, "Sounds like you two have a plan." He went to the next pair.

Suddenly the topic was becoming more interesting. "So they were put into this camp and then what?" Nick asked.

"Back up," she said. "I think we should talk about their nomadic ways and a little about their culture. Then we should discuss the camp and what happened afterward to those still living." As Cat talked, she tapped a finger on the desk. "So as not to make Gypsies seem strange and weird, I think we should include some famous people who were—and are—Roma."

"Like who?" Nick asked.

"Charlie Chaplin, Michael Caine, and Mother Teresa."

Nick was beginning to feel better about their paper. Mother Teresa put a whole new spin on Gypsies. They had a plan for their paper.

****

Later, at home, Nick switched on the study lamp and spread out his books on the desktop, preparing to get his homework done. The light glowed over a picture of Nick with his parents and grandparents at his church confirmation and a small green plastic soldier figurine he had played with as a boy. He picked up the toy and fingered it, turning it over in his palm. Were his play wars as a kid part of the reason for the thoughts about Jean Claude? There had to be an explanation other than he had been reincarnated from another time.

His cell phone vibrated on the desk. So much for little green men. He looked at the caller ID. Emily. He answered, "Hi there."

"I just wanted to let you know I found my dress."

"Your dress?" His mind drew a blank. Then he remembered a multicolored skirt puddled on the ground.

"You know, the homecoming dance."

Of course. How silly of him to have forgotten.

"What color corsage?" he asked, knowing from previous dances with Emily that the corsage couldn't clash with her dress.

"Let me think about it," she said.

Just then he had another call coming in. "Can I get back to you? Another call."

"As long as it's not Cat!" Emily said.

In fact it was Cat, but Nick said "Gary" to keep the peace.

"Oh, sure."

Nick answered Cat's phone call. "Hey, what's up?"

"Just wondering if we should spend some time after school tomorrow doing more research."

"I thought you already knew everything?"

"Not everything."

"I guess it would be okay to go after football." Nick put a fist to his forehead, trying to remember something else. "I've got to make a quick trip to see my grandmother."

"Would you like me to go too?"

Nick studied the ceiling as he thought that over. Grandma and Cat? "What the heck."

"I'd like to meet your grandmother." He heard the

smile in her voice. "I've never had one."

What harm could there be in introducing Cat to Grandma? Grandma might like meeting someone new.

After football practice the next day, Nick found Cat waiting by his car. "Hop in. We can't stay long, because I've got a ton of calculus."

Cat shrugged. "Sure."

They arrived at the hospital and went to Grandma's room. "Knock. Knock. Grandma?"

"Nick!"

Grandma's eyes widened when Cat followed him into the room.

"Who's this?"

"My research partner, Cat."

"Nice to meet you," Cat said.

"Cat," Grandma said slowly. "Is that your real name?"

"No, it's Catherine, actually."

"Do you go to school with Nick?"

"Yes."

"Are you one of the cheerleaders?" Grandma asked, peering closer at Cat.

"No, I'm a dancer."

"Hmm."

"She's good," Nick added, shifting from foot to foot. "You should see some of her moves!"

"It's kind of crowded in here," Grandma said, moving her chin to a small area next to the bed.

Cat rose up on her toes and twirled around, then bent at the waist, making her hair fly out like a black cape, before taking a dive to the floor and sliding on one knee.

"What kind of dancing is that?" Grandma asked,

frowning.

"Modern," Cat responded.

"Do you do ballet or tap?"

"No, I prefer modern."

"Um."

"We're on our way to the library to do more research," Nick said.

Grandma pouted. "You can't stay?"

"Afraid not." He bent over and kissed her cheek. "I'll come this weekend."

"Nice to meet you, Cat." Grandma raised a hand from the blanket.

"And you," Cat said.

They left and got back in Nick's car.

"So that's a grandma, huh?" Cat asked.

"She's sweet. An important part of my growing up. Her and Grandpa."

Nick yawned. He was tired, hungry, and didn't feel like researching tonight. "Why don't we grab a burger and call it a night? I'm beat."

"I thought we were going to the library?"

"I've got calculus homework. Maybe some other time?"

"Fine," she said. "Drop me off at school so I can get my car. I'll skip the burger."

Nick dropped her off in the parking lot and drove to the nearest hamburger joint and ate while he drove home.

Chapter 19

Nick tossed and turned in bed, scrunching the pillow into a more comfortable shape. His mind ran through a collage of images. He punched his pillow in frustration. He needed sleep and not to think about the exorcism or Jean Claude. Finally blackness closed over him, and he slept and dreamed.

"Wake up, you lout. We've got work to do."

My childhood pal Louis was my partner. The only two boys from Montreuil-Bellay to be at the Cadre, we were the envy of the town. We both worked extra hard to earn a spot at the school.

"We are to clean the barn," Louis said.

"Bah! I hate cleaning horse shit!"

"You are horse shit!" Louis said.

We both laughed, heading for the barns.

"I have a message from Gretchen for you." Louis fished a crumpled paper from his pocket.

"When did she give you this?"

"I was in town for supplies, and she stopped me."

"Oh? What does she want?"

"I don't know!" Louis snorted. "I didn't read your note!"

I quickly read her message. She wanted to see me tonight. But I wanted to see the Gypsy girl Chaton, not Gretchen.

"Are you sneaking out later to see her?" Louis

asked.

"No!" My face flushed.

"I see you sneak away."

"The pub." Did Louis guess the real reason I left? Chaton was so much more fun than proper and careful Gretchen.

Chapter 20

Nick awoke bleary-eyed and tired, rubbing the sleep from his eyes, scrubbing away the dream of kissing the Gypsy girl—Chaton. As he readied for school, he decided he wanted to talk to Cat about his vivid and detailed dreams.

He entered the school through the big double doors. He had seen the foyer hundreds of times, but today, his mind superimposed another image—a long hallway lined with pictures of men with handlebar mustaches, wearing uniforms decorated with rows of metals and pins, the plaques by each picture etched with the names of these men and the year. Nick blinked, but still the image stayed. *Holy Cow, there were dates from 1902, 1865, and even farther back!* The glass cases held trophies and ribbons for horsemanship. Was he looking at Laketon's cases filled with football, basketball, and baseball trophies? No, this was Cadre Noir. Horse heads adorned most of the trophies.

He stood there, rooted in place until the hallways began filling with students. The Cadre Noir displays were significantly more impressive and told the story of the men and boys who worked and learned here.

Someone bumped him. He turned, expecting to see Bryan, but whoever it had been blended in with the crowd rushing by.

As much as he tried pushing the images away, they

stayed with him until World History. Nick fidgeted and daydreamed, his heart pounding when he thought of Chaton with the fancy skirt, wondering why he had seen it puddled at her feet at one point. Had they made love? His palms began to sweat, and he rubbed them on his jeans.

He was relieved when it was time for World History. "Tell me how we met," Nick whispered as he slipped into his desk next to Cat's.

She didn't seem surprised and tilted her head in response. "We met when you were a student at the cavalry school. My family group was camped on the Loire River."

He remembered a line of wagons encircling a bonfire in the middle of the camp.

"We called ourselves *tsiganes*, or as you say, Gypsies, or Romas. We came from Romania many centuries before." She paused when Bryan passed them, banging his leg into Nick's desk.

"Oh, so sorry, esteemed Reverend."

Nick rolled his eyes as Bryan took his seat. Even Bryan couldn't bug him today, and Cat continued.

"My people picked up and moved from place to place."

Cat's voice was low. Nick leaned closer to hear.

"We needed money to buy food, so we were entertainers, musicians, and dancers, with a few mystics and healers thrown in. My mother was one such healer."

A red skirt, hair flying in the wind, a raven caught in the undercurrent. Laughter. Exhilaration. A multicolored skirt flowing and flaring around bare legs.

"You were looking for something the first time we

met, but you stayed to eat," Cat continued.

"A dog?" Nick asked. "I was looking for a dog?"

"Yes," Cat affirmed.

As Nick listened, he felt a chill run up his spine. The dream, the one he had last night, was real.

"We had rabbit stew," he answered, still recalling the savory meat and vegetables, mushrooms swirling in the eddies of the roiling broth.

"*Du ragout de lapin, oui*?" Cat questioned.

"*Je me rappelle*," he answered. *I remember*.

He gasped, his breath strangled with realization.

"Nick?" Coach Sullivan asked. "You all right?"

He coughed behind his hand. "Yeah. I just need some water."

Coach waved his arm toward the door, and Nick hurried out to the drinking fountain. He drank deeply and slapped some on his cheeks.

He came in and took his seat again. "Maybe we should talk later."

She nodded.

The coach started his lecture, and Nick sat motionless, his body still, his mind racing. He needed to act normal. And what was normal exactly? He looked the same on the outside, but on the inside, he was becoming a different person. He didn't know how to act. The "new" Nick scared yet fascinated him.

****

At lunch he sat with Em, Tiffany, and Gary while Cat sat at a far table by the window, only Veronica going over to say hello to her. Should he invite her to sit with them? He glanced at Emily, who was telling Tiffany about shopping for shoes. He cleared his throat and motioned toward Cat. "Should we invite her to sit with us?"

No one said anything, and Emily looked stricken.

"I'm just asking," Nick said.

Emily hung her head. "If you want."

"No, what does the group want?" Nick asked.

Gary shrugged. "I don't care. She never talks to anyone except you and Veronica."

Tiffany glanced over at Emily. "I don't think it's such a good idea."

"Em?" Nick used his forefinger to lift her chin. "I'm just trying to be friendly. It doesn't mean anything."

She sniffed and gave him a minuscule nod.

He walked over to where Cat sat. "Would you like to sit with us?"

"No, I don't think that's a good idea. Your girlfriend doesn't like me."

"She doesn't know you."

"Thanks—" Cat smiled. "—but maybe some other time."

"If you change your mind…" He walked backward for several steps before turning and rejoining his friends. "She wants to be alone," he said as he plopped down.

Tiffany clasped Emily's hand. "Finish telling me about shopping for shoes with your sister."

Emily blew out a sigh. "It doesn't seem so funny now."

Chapter 21

The gymnasium was abuzz with voices, stomping feet, and the twang of the antiquated PA, hissing and balking at being used.

"Can I have your attention?" the principal yelled over the din.

The noise level dropped but didn't go away.

Nick sat with Emily, Gary, and Tiffany. While they waited for the gymnasium to fill, Nick drank from his fortified water bottle.

Emily wrinkled her nose. "What are you drinking?"

"Vitamin water." Already he began to feel the warmth spread through his body.

"It smells strong," Emily said with a frown. She leaned closer for a better smell, but Nick stowed it in his pack.

As people walked by, they were jostled and poked. One poke was harder than necessary, and he turned to see Bryan.

"Sorry, didn't see you," Bryan said with a fake look of sincerity.

"I'm sure you didn't," Nick said.

Emily took his hand and squeezed.

"Everyone, take a seat!" the principal urged. "Let's get started."

The cheerleaders took the floor and began a chant.

"Go Laketon! Go Laketon! Beat River View!"

Emily clapped along with them and stamped her feet. Today she was shod in red-sequined sneakers and mismatched green and turquoise socks.

"Go! Go! Victory!" She pumped her fist in the air. "Come on!" she urged Nick. "Get in the spirit!"

The pep band played along with the cheerleaders. They were barely audible over the din in the gymnasium.

Nick and Gary bumped fists and managed a few claps before the principal said, "I'd like to introduce the senior class president, Marco Berg! He'll take it from here."

Marco had been standing to the side and ran to the principal and took the microphone. "Let's make some noise, Laketon High!"

Tiffany screamed and jumped up. Emily too. Nick and Gary looked at each other with raised brows and remained seated.

"How come they don't cheer this loud for the football team?" Gary asked, adding his customary tweet-whistle at the end of his question.

Nick shrugged. "Beats me."

"Homecoming candidates." Marco took a piece of paper from his pocket. He read the names of the freshman candidates, and they came out of the bleachers and joined him on the floor. "Now the sophomore candidates." They too stood, waiting. "The junior candidates."

All Nick heard was their names—he and Emily had been nominated, Gary and Tiffany too. Fortified somewhat by the vodka, he stood and pumped his fist in the air as he followed Emily to the gymnasium floor.

Nick looked up, sweeping his eyes over the mostly familiar faces until he saw Cat. Even in the crowded bleachers, she sat alone, about halfway up with her back to the wall, but her head turned, facing them, a shadow in the light.

He thrust his hands deep into his front pockets and looked away.

Emily's eyes sparkled, and she grabbed his arm and smiled. "Aren't you excited?"

He nodded. "Of course." But his words were overtaken by the roar and clapping from the crowd.

When they returned to their seats, Bryan was holding Nick's water bottle and was unscrewing the top. "Whoa! Reverend. That's some strong shit in there."

Nick grabbed the bottle back. "Did you go through my backpack?" He shoved Bryan, making him stumble.

Bryan jumped up, his fists ready to punch.

"Nick?" Emily asked, "What's going on?" She maneuvered her way between Nick and Bryan.

"Nothing! He had no right to go through my things."

But already several teachers were heading toward them. Nick tried to put the bottle away when the principal started climbing toward them.

"Nick? Bryan?" the principal asked. "Problems?"

"I think you should check his water bottle," Bryan said. "I smell alcohol."

"Is that true?" the principal asked.

"Just some vitamins I put in my water," Nick said, feeling a flush creep up from his neck to face.

The principal held out his palm for the bottle, and reluctantly, Nick handed it over.

The principal unscrewed the top and sniffed. "I think we should finish this in the office." And with cement-leaded feet, Nick trudged toward the office.

What he wouldn't give to pop Bryan in the mouth right now.

Once in the office, the principal indicated Nick should sit. "Now tell me what happened."

"Excuse me!" Cat said, trying to ease around the secretary who was standing at the principal's door.

"You can't just barge in!" The secretary huffed.

"But that's my water bottle," Cat said. "Nick was holding it for me."

"Yours?" He turned toward Nick. "Who's telling the truth here?"

"I am," Cat said.

"Are you sure that's your bottle?" the principal asked, frowning at Cat. "You're fairly new here, aren't you?"

She nodded.

"I hate to do this, but I'm suspending you for two days, and I'll need to have a conference with your parents."

"Sure!" Cat said, her eyes downcast, studying the floor.

"Nick, you're free to go."

"But…"

"No, I'll handle it from here," the principal said and closed his office door.

Nick stood in the office for a few beats, unsure of what to do now. It wasn't right for Cat to take the fall for him. Why did she do that?

Emily waited for him by his next class. "What happened?" She peered up at him.

"Cat said it was her bottle."
"She lied for you?"
Nick remained quiet.
"That bitch!"

Chapter 22

Cat was absent for two days. On the day of her expected return, Nick went by her locker, but she wasn't there. He found her in the gym, dancing with her earphones on. He knew she couldn't hear him, but he saw her back straighten slightly when he stopped in the doorway. When she finished, she slipped the earphones off and twirled around.

"How did you know I was here?" he asked.

"I felt you."

"You know you didn't have to stand up for me like that," Nick said. "I'm the one who should have been suspended."

Cat shrugged. "No biggie."

"Why?"

"I didn't want you to get in trouble." She did a quick shrug. "You're a leader, and I'm a nobody."

"Don't say that!"

"I am," she said. "And I'm okay with that."

Nick looked at her long and hard and then stepped closer to hug her and whisper, "Thank you."

"And besides, you took care of my sister."

Momentarily Nick was frozen and unsure. "Your sister?" Nick scratched his chin. "I didn't know you had a sister?"

"Before. Not now."

"Oh."

****

Later, in World History class, Coach Sullivan passed around a worksheet for the main ideas of their research projects. Nick looked at his sheet and mentally checked through what he knew about Saumur so it coincided with the Gypsies being put in the internment camp. The ant-like words marched into a recognizable form. *A line of Nazi soldiers, waiting. Jean Claude with his rifle, while fatigue and worry etched on his young forehead.*

Cat was hard at work already and had a couple of paragraphs finished by the time he picked up his pencil.

He watched her hand and pencil move quickly across the page.

Coach Sullivan stopped at their desks. "I see you're busy, Kate. And you, Nick?"

"Cat," she corrected.

Nick shook his head. "I'm thinking about what to write." He tapped his temple with his forefinger before deciding he wanted to make a timeline of the events happening in 1939.

Cat explained, "We're researching the social and economic conditions that led the Gypsies in France to be interned in Saumur. We'll start with their migration from India to Romania and the rest of Europe. Examine the nomadic ways of the tribes and loose families they organized," Cat said as if reciting a poem or recipe she had memorized. "And the social norms of the time and why the Romas were feared and then interned and forgotten."

Nick jerked his head up.

"Nick?" Coach Sullivan asked.

"I'm looking at other events that were happening in

France and Saumur in the autumn of 1939."

"And," Cat continued, "how the internments have affected current Roma families in France. And how their treatment has changed."

Coach Sullivan put a mark on his clipboard and moved to Bryan's desk.

Nick turned to her. "How do you know this stuff?"

"I've been doing research too."

"I thought you didn't need to learn about it?" Nick touched his forehead. "All in your head."

"I was a little angry at first."

"A little angry?" He remembered the first time he had seen Cat in the cafeteria. "Whoa! If looks could kill…"

"I know. I guess I was upset about moving to Laketon."

Understandable.

"But when I saw you, I figured I had found Jean Claude again."

"My eyes, right?" Nick asked.

"Yes, the eyes gave you away."

"Did you love Jean Claude?" Somehow that was important to him.

She nodded.

"Did he love you?"

"I think so, but I can't be sure, with the way it turned out."

"I thought someone helped you remember," Nick said.

"I did see someone, but we only went so far. And then the memories stopped."

"Why?" Nick asked.

"I'm not sure. Some of the details are fuzzy. Would

you go to a past-life therapist with me if I can find one locally?" Cat asked. She tucked her worksheet into her World History folder.

"Maybe." He chewed his bottom lip, undecided. "What happened during your appointment?"

Cat looked toward the ceiling. "He talked me through steps to relax my mind and body and began asking questions about what I felt or saw."

"Were you hypnotized?"

"No. He didn't suggest I bark like a dog or stop smoking, if that's what you mean! Would you see someone if you didn't have to cluck like a chicken?"

"I don't know. Let me think about it."

"Some of your questions might be answered," Cat said.

Nick paused and thought about her words. Did it really matter? Or would he go just to dispel the notion his soul had lived before? Would he be betraying his parents by finding out about something they didn't believe in? Maybe he wouldn't have to tell them. And after all, they had him exorcised—another thing the church didn't believe in.

Chapter 23

So on Saturday, Nick picked up Emily, and they drove to where Grandma was relearning to walk again. Then they would meet Gary and Tiffany at the movies.

"You don't mind stopping by to see Grandma?" Nick asked.

"Of course not. Your grandma's so nice!" She leaned into him.

"She loves you—especially when you said you wanted to be an elementary teacher."

Emily smiled and took his hand across the cup holder and gear shift of the Subaru. Once at the hospital, they parked and found Grandma finishing dinner and watching television.

"Emily! Nick! So good to see you!" Grandma pushed away her tray. "I miss your mother's cooking! She learned from the best. Me!" The old lady laughed at her own joke, and Emily giggled by his side.

They each hugged her and pulled up chairs to sit next to the bed.

Grandma nodded to Emily's sneakers. "I think I need some like that! Zebra print with purple socks! Just the trick when I get back to Bunco!"

Emily held up her feet and moved her ankles around. "I'm glad you like my shoes. I've been collecting sneakers for a couple of years. I have a bunch. My mom's threatening to get rid of them."

"So tell me what's happening!" Grandma said, sitting up straighter. "I'm tired of hearing about everyone's aches and pains, including my own."

"Well," Emily began. "Homecoming's in less than two weeks, and Nick and I were nominated as Junior Prince and Princess!"

"I hope I'm out of here by that time! If I'm not"—Grandma scowled—"tell your mother to take lots of pictures!"

"I will, Grandma," Nick said.

"When I'm better and you've finished your teacher training, I can help in your classroom," Grandma said to Emily.

"Thanks, Mrs. Chesterfield, I'd like that." Emily grinned. "But let me finish high school first."

"It'll happen before you know it." Grandma tried to snap her fingers. "Time seems to race by now." She rubbed her hands.

"Can I put some lotion on your hands?" Emily reached for the bottle by the side of the bed.

His grandmother held out her thin, vein-crossed hands, and Emily massaged the lotion while Grandma sat back and closed her eyes. "That feels wonderful. Thank you, dear child! I like Emily so much better than that Cat girl with her dance moves."

Nick saw Emily stop rubbing, and Grandma's eyes snapped open. "Are you finished?"

"You met Cat?" Emily asked.

"We stopped by before the library," Nick said with a shrug.

Emily's mouth formed into a thin line.

"I didn't like all that black gunk on her face," Grandma said. "I think she might be pretty if she didn't use that stuff."

"I agree," Emily said.

"But Emily's a keeper, huh, Nick?" Grandma winked.

"Certainly. Everyone loves Em." Nick looked at her, but she refused to meet his gaze.

"Make him treat you right!" she admonished when Emily put away the lotion and they prepared to leave.

He'd be disowned if he ever broke up with Emily, but she might disown him tonight if he couldn't explain what happened.

They left the hospital and walked silently to Nick's car.

"Em…" He tried to take her arm, but she pulled away.

"I don't want to talk about her right now!"

"Fine."

"I wish she'd never enrolled at Laketon," Emily retorted, fastening her seat belt and looking out the side window and not at him.

"Do you still want to go to the movies?" Nick asked.

Emily blew out her breath. "I guess. Since we promised Gary and Tiff we'd be there."

Chapter 24

At school on Monday, Nick found both Cat and Emily waiting at his locker. They weren't talking, and Emily was turned with her arms folded, as if miffed at finding Cat there too.

"Hello, ladies!" His voice came out a higher pitch. This couldn't be very good.

"I've got something to discuss with you, but it can wait until World History," Cat said.

Emily remained quiet and tapped her foot.

"All right." Nick raised his eyebrows. "We'll talk in class."

Cat left in the direction of the gymnasium, leaving him and Emily alone. He turned to her, taking note of her defensive stance.

"Why is she always hanging around?" Emily asked.

"You know why." Nick opened his locker. "The research project."

"I don't see my partner outside of class," Emily accused. "Can't she talk to you there?"

"She said she would." Nick shoved his backpack on the small shelf. "Now, what's up?" He slammed the locker closed.

"Does anything need to be up?" she said more sharply than normal.

"Come on, Babe, don't be mad. You know I love

you." He turned her toward him and put his hands on her shoulders, rubbing until he felt them relax. "Let's go to the cafeteria and get something to drink."

He slung his arm across her shoulders as they walked to the cafeteria and stood in line.

"I'm sorry to be such a bitch this morning, but she's always hanging around. She has that look."

Nick wasn't sure what "that look" was exactly, but Em was bothered by Cat's.

"She's on the prowl, and she has you in her sights," she huffed.

He laughed and nuzzled her ear. "Only you do it for me, baby."

She looked at him with a tilt of her head, evaluating his sincerity.

"I'm lucky to have you," she finally said.

"No, I'm the lucky one!" he declared as they reached the cashier and paid for their drinks and sat down.

****

"So what did you need to tell me this morning?" Nick took his seat by Cat in World History.

"I've found a past-life therapist in Grand Rapids." She paused, waiting for his response. None came, so she sighed and pressed more. "Have you thought about it?"

He hadn't. "No."

"Would you go with me after school on Wednesday?"

"I'd have to skip football practice."

"Can't you skip just once?" Cat scowled.

He could, but he wasn't playing his A game yet, and he knew Coach was growing concerned. But try as he might, Nick couldn't get upset. Maybe he wasn't meant to play pro football or college football for that matter. Wow, that was the first time he'd ever thought that.

"I guess I could skip this once." What in the hell was he getting himself into? More stuff to mess with his head?

She tilted her head and raised her brows.

"You're going to have to tell me more," he said, intrigued but a little concerned.

"It's not scary, if that's what you're worried about."

"What if I find out bad stuff about myself?" Nick chewed a nail. "Like I was an ax murderer or something?"

"Don't you want to know why?" She frowned at him.

He blew out a sigh. "Not really."

"Forget it, then!"

"No, I'll go." *Morbid curiosity.*

"You sure?"

"I said I would, and I will." He knew he was going to regret it.

****

Later still, his mother took note of his silence.

"What's up, Nick?" his mother asked. She was sitting on the couch, scrolling through her e-mails for work.

"Nothing."

"Give!" she said with a laugh.

Mothers had a sixth sense about stuff like that. "School. Football. Homecoming," he said in a singsong voice. The usual suspects for a stressed kid in high school. And not to mention, Past-Life Regression session. He'd let his mother take her pick from school, football, and homecoming.

"Research paper?"

"Coming along."

His mother didn't press further. "Football?" she asked.

"I can't seem to get my groove back this year." He let out a long sigh.

"A slump?"

"Sort of." His mind went back to the past-life session.

"Homecoming is fun," she said. His mother closed her laptop.

"Em and I are nominated for junior prince and princess. Gary and Tiff too."

"That's great!" She leaned forward for him to continue. "I always liked Gary. He's like a big sheepdog."

That made Nick crack a smile. Gary was big and goofy at times.

Nick hoisted his backpack, saying, "I've got homework."

His mother nodded before reopening her laptop. "You'll get things figured out."

He grunted noncommittally and took the steps two at a time to his bedroom and closed the door. He leaned against it for a moment and caught his breath. He had never been winded from running up their flight of steps before. Maybe he should lay off drinking for a bit. When his breath normalized, he went to his computer and typed in *Past-Life Therapy* and waited.

Past-life regression uses hypnosis to recall

memories of past lives. During hypnosis the therapist asks questions to help the patient recall alleged past lives. It is believed that experiences, attitudes, aptitudes, and relationships from prior lives follow into the current lifetime. Regression can be used as a way to discover a person's purpose in life. The technique has been refuted when inaccuracies of the recalled events have been proven false. There are more skeptics of the practice in the West than in Eastern cultures.

Nick scratched his chin and reread the definition. There wasn't anything to prove rebirth or reincarnation was a real thing. He would keep an open mind on Wednesday but discount anything that was suggested to him during the session.

Chapter 25

June, 1940: *I shivered in the cold night air as I crawled and wiggled away from the Cadre Noir. When away from the school, I stood and listened before hurrying to the river, now quiet in the night. Only an occasional stir and shift of the water from the wind or river otter.*

The villagers were wrong about the Gypsies. They were artisans, entertainers, and healers. They were happy and carefree people.

Chaton waited by a tree, wearing a thin blouse and the flounced skirt I liked. The moonlight highlighted her hair with ribbons of gold.

"Come! The music is about to start, and we have a pig on the spit." She took my hand and guided me into the center of the encampment before I could think further about where they had found a pig in the time of rationing.

We sat on a log by the fire. Chaton's father sat nearby, watching us through the glow of the fire.

"Tell me about the war?" he asked.

I sat up straighter and grimaced. "We are a country divided after signing an agreement with Germany to surrender. They still invaded."

"Baah!" Chaton's father said, spitting a wad of tobacco into the fire. "The French are a spineless bunch."

139

"The French Third Republic fights on," I responded, *thinking of my father.*

"And what have they done?" Chaton's father said, poking a stick at the fire, making it spark and glow.

I chewed on my lip. "My father is off fighting with the French, the resistance."

Chaton's father's face softened some. "Good. Your father is a brave man."

Now it was my turn to poke at the fire and watch the sparks snap and dance in the air. "Yes. Yes, he is."

"Will the Germans get to us?"

"Not here, not in Montreuil-Bellay," I said, reassuring Chaton's father.

"Bah!" The man spit into the fire again. "Many wars fought on French soil." He motioned with his head in the direction of the Cadre Noir. "Have you learned nothing in that fancy school of yours?"

We had learned some military history, the majority of our time spent riding horses in straight rows, making our mounts rear at precisely the right time to show their precision, and little else. But horses were useless against the Germans' tanks and machinery.

"Papa!" Chaton scolded. "He's our guest."

"Chaton, my sweet child. War is coming. Things are going to get bad. We'll need to move on."

I sat up straighter, hoping I looked confident and brave. I didn't want the Gypsies to leave the area.

"No, Papa, I like it here. Please, can we stay?"

"The war will soon be here," her father said.

"No!" Chaton cried.

I shifted uneasily on the log, feeling it jab into my hip. I felt the same way as Chaton's father. Germany had overtaken Belgium, Netherlands, and Luxembourg. Soon, they would be in France.

Chapter 26

A past-life regression therapist? Nick had no idea what to expect from such a person. He didn't tell his parents or even Emily what he was doing. He had no one to confide in except Cat.

On Wednesday after school, Cat led Nick from the school to her car, a green Jag she had parked away from the other vehicles.

"This Jag is yours?" Nick and his friends had seen it in the parking lot and admired the sleek, compact design but didn't know who the owner was.

"A gift from my parents," Cat said. "It's five years old." She unlocked it and said, "Get in."

It smelled of leather and polish and still had the new-car scent.

They drove out of the parking lot, the engine purring down the highway, so unlike his mother's hand-me-down Subaru.

"I'd like to drive this sometime," Nick said, looking around and appraising the leather interior. "This is a great car."

Cat responded with a laugh and hit the gas. They ate up I-96 in no time, heading for Grand Rapids and their appointment with someone named Dr. Sims.

As the car hurtled toward their appointment, Nick's mind conjured up images of a man smoking a pipe, wearing a tweed jacket, looking very distinguished and aloof, telling Nick he had a "mother" complex or something. He felt a pinprick of sweat on his forehead and pulled out the flask from his pack and took a sip.

"What are you doing?" Cat asked.

"Liquid courage. Want some?" He felt a flush from his neck up to his face. "Sorry. I forgot."

"I'm not going to rescue you next time," she said, making a face and shaking her head.

They arrived at the therapist's office, which was located in a tall, rectangular building, with Dr. Sims's name one of many on the listing of counselors, dentists, and accountants.

They took the elevator to the seventh floor and found the correct office. They stood in front of the door, neither reaching for the knob. Nick took a deep breath, and Cat said, "Ready?"

"I guess." He opened the door, and they stepped inside to the reception area.

Dr. Sims, a woman without a pipe, wore khaki pants and a jacket, and looked every bit a professional woman. "Hello, I'm Dr. Sims," she said and motioned for them to follow her into her office.

Nick relaxed a little.

She shook their hands and motioned for them to sit. "I'm pleased to meet you, Nick and Cat. So how can I help you?"

Nick wanted to know more about her, not the other way around.

"Er, how long have you been doing this sort of thing?" he asked. His eyes scanned her degrees and certifications on the wall.

Dr. Sims followed his gaze. "You're wondering if I'm genuine and not some quack, correct?"

"Not a quack, but…"

"Fair enough. I've been doing this for fifteen years, after having stumbled on my own past lives. In that search, I found my true calling. I help people find answers and make connections from the past to their present situation."

Nothing alarming in her statement.

"And you two?" Her eyes went from Nick to Cat.

Nick moved his chin toward Cat. "We met in class."

"I'm assuming you think you knew each other before?" Dr. Sims asked.

"Yes," Cat said, her eyes steady and unwavering. "We were lovers during the war. World War II."

Cat turned to look at him, raising her brows for him to say something.

He gulped and began. "When I was a kid, I told my parents I had been a soldier in France in World War II."

"I see," Dr. Sims said, like it was the most natural thing to say.

The images continued flashing before him. Chaton, Jean Claude, and a school far different from Laketon High. A small village—something out of a history book, with small shops, and produce spilling from baskets onto the walkways. A town far different from Laketon. Laketon with the Hometown Grocery and Rx-Drug Store, neither with baskets of food on the sidewalks. No, he was envisioning Saumur. He reached up and massaged his temples.

"Cat." Dr. Sims looked over to her. "Why do you want to discover your past life?"

"I remember many things." Cat smiled and winked at Nick. "We're mainly here for him." Cat patted his leg, and Nick meekly smiled. "I want him to know." Cat patted him again.

"Do you want to know, Nick?"

"I guess, but it goes against my religion," he said, rubbing his knee.

"Ah," Dr. Sims said. "Yes, religion. Western religion is very closed to the concept of reincarnation, whereas Eastern religious texts embrace the idea we may have lived before."

"I'm only familiar with Western religion," Nick said, thrusting out his chin stubbornly.

"I understand. Most of my clients feel that way. Do you want to learn more?"

Nick looked over at Cat, but she kept her gaze on the bookshelf behind Dr. Sims. Did he want to learn more? His dreams were becoming clearer, and he could remember more and more of them.

"I'm curious," Nick said. "And skeptical. My father's a Methodist minister, and he wouldn't approve of what I'm doing."

Cat cleared her throat. "Tell her what your parents did when you were younger."

Dr. Sims raised her brows and leaned forward.

"They had me exorcised because I was speaking French and calling myself Jean Claude and telling them I had fought in the war."

"World War II," Cat clarified.

"That seems out of character for a Methodist minister," Dr. Sims said.

"He wasn't a minister at the time."

"So your parents were concerned about what you were saying?"

"Yes."

Dr. Sims put her hands on her thighs. "Let me tell you how I usually run my sessions. The first time we meet, like now, we might just talk and get to know each other, but if you're ready, I can do a regression on each of you individually."

"We'd like to do everything today," Nick said.

Dr. Sims looked at the clock on her desk. "It might take about three hours for us to finish." She paused, letting that sink in. "Are you still good with that?"

"I think so," Cat said, looking at Nick, brows raised, whereas he shrugged.

"Now I need to ask, are you eighteen? If not, I'll need parental permission."

"We're both eighteen." Cat spoke for both of them, even though they were only sixteen.

"Good, then that's not an issue," Dr. Sims said. "Are you okay finishing around six?"

They would be back in Laketon around seven o'clock, the same time Nick usually got home from football practice.

"Now I need to ask you the inevitable question on how you're going to pay for these sessions," Dr. Sims said.

Cat drew out a credit card from her backpack. "Charge my card."

Nick raised his brows at her. First she drove a Jag, and now she had her own credit card.

"Let's start. The first thing I want to know about each of you is your life currently and what you hope to find out as part of a regression."

"We want to know about our past and how it's impacting our current lives," Cat said.

"Fair enough." She paused and waited. "Nick?"

He shook his head in agreement.

Dr. Sims put her palms down on the desk. "If you don't have any questions, we can get started. Who wants to go first?" Her eyes darted between them. "Nick, would you like to begin?"

"How do you get us to relax?" Nick asked, his fingers tightening around the arm of the chair.

"Visualization." That didn't sound too creepy.

Nick searched his mind for more questions but came up empty.

After a long stretch of silence, Dr. Sims looked at Cat. "I'll go," she volunteered.

He left Cat and Dr. Sims in her office and sat in the waiting area. He picked up a magazine but put it down and stood, looking out the window. Nick stretched, and his phone buzzed in his pocket, signaling a message from Emily wondering where he was. He responded with "Docs"—Dr. Sims said she was a doctor, so technically, it wasn't a lie.

Nick trudged around the small waiting area. He made one circle, then two, stopping at Dr. Sims's office door to listen, pressing his ear to the wood. He heard nothing and continued his restless wait.

What was Cat telling Dr. Sims? What was she remembering? He would have liked to be in there, listening. But he didn't want her in his session, so he guessed it was fair he was waiting.

An hour passed, and Cat came out, blinking at the light, her pupils large and black.

"How was it?" he asked.

She shrugged. "As I expected."

Dr. Sims came out and motioned; it was Nick's turn to find out what he remembered.

He followed Dr. Sims into her dimly lit inner office and sat on the couch as indicated.

"Get comfortable," Dr. Sims said. "Most people like to stretch out."

Nick lay flat on his back and propped his head up with his hands behind his neck.

"Now I want you to take some deep breaths until you feel relaxed, and close your eyes. I want you to imagine your special place to relax."

Nick conjured up an image of lying in a hammock on the beach with a soft breeze. The tropical beach, an ocean—not Lake Michigan. It was unfamiliar to him but comforting all the same.

"What are you feeling, hearing, smelling in this favorite place?"

Nick smelled the salt water, heard the gentle rustle of the palm leaves rubbing together in a soft whisper, and felt a coolness washing over his face.

"I'm going to use guided imagery now," Dr. Sims said. "Let's start by having you relax the muscles in your face and neck." She paused, and Nick willed his face to settle into a comfortable neutral expression. "Now your shoulders." After a long wait, she said, "Your chest and arms. Let them fall heavily by your sides."

Nick put his arms at his sides and moved them into a relaxed position.

"Do the same for your stomach and legs. Relax some more. The more relaxed, the deeper you will go."

Nick felt the urge to yawn but kept his eyes closed and his face expressionless.

"Are you comfortable?"

"Umm hmm."

"I want you to find the long dark tunnel in front of you. Do you see it?"

A long black tunnel stretched out before him, a subway of sorts without the cars. "Yes."

"There's a small white light at the end. Do you see that?"

As he moved closer, he saw the light. "Umm hmm."

"The light becomes bigger and brighter as you move toward it. Is the light brighter now?"

"Yes." His eyes watered at the glow.

"Tell me when you have reached the light."

Nick moved forward, drawn to the glare. "I've reached it." The light hurt his eyes, and he closed them tightly.

"You'll get used to the light, Nick. Relax your face again."

He did.

"Can you see better now?" Dr. Sims asked.

"Yes."

"Imagine the light streaming into your head and filling your body."

The glow surrounded him. It filtered through his mouth, eyes, and ears, filling him with lightness and a buoyant feeling.

"Are you filled with light?"

"Yes."

"I want you to float up on the light away from the tunnel. You will soar high in the sky. What do you see?"

"I see a large school." He paused. "Yes, it's a school. I see the sign over the fence. École de Cavalerie."

"Is that French?"

"Yes. I attend the school. I am a student. I'm wearing a black uniform and tall black boots."

"And who are you?"

"I am Jean Claude Rousseau." He remained quiet as he turned the familiar name over and over in his head.

"And can you describe the school?"

"Yes." He paused to study the building. "Rectangular, with many windows, with two wings forming a courtyard."

"Is it very large?"

"Yes, massive."

"What else do you see?"

"Boys working horses."

"How are they working them?"

He concentrated. "They are practicing riding. Around and around. Around objects. Walking backward. Jumping."

"Good. Let's skip forward a bit. What do you see?"

"I'm in the forest."

"Can you tell the season?"

"It's definitely not winter, but maybe spring? Buds on trees and small grapes on the vines."

"What are you doing?"

"I'm watching a caravan set up in a vacant lot. And I am looking for something on the ground."

"Did you find what you were looking for?"

"I think I'm pretending to search, but I'm also looking. I see a girl through the trees."

He concentrated at the fleeting figure of the girl. Seeing a patchwork skirt made of scraps of multicolored material, then long hair, and hearing her laughter. He put the images together into a beautiful dark-haired girl with brown, serious eyes that seemed to waltz around the fire in the middle of their camp.

"I'm not supposed to be with this girl. They say she's bad, but they're wrong about her. She's a Roma— a Gypsy—and they are good people."

"Are you with her now?"

"She is coming for me."

She surprised him, walking out from the trees, startling him.

"What are you seeing now?" Dr. Sims continued.

"Her name is Chaton." He knew what the word meant. "It's French for 'little cat.' A kitten."

"What are you doing now?"

"We're eating rabbit stew, I think. Yes, rabbit." He paused, scanning the scene before him. "There is singing and dancing. Everyone is happy."

"Are you happy?"

He thought about her question. "Yes, I'm very happy. Happier than I've been my whole life."

"Why?"

"The Gypsies are fun. There is singing and dancing. I wish I could stay longer."

Dr. Sims waited for him to finish before saying, "Can we move forward a few weeks?"

Things went dark for Nick, and when they cleared, he saw people running. "Er, people are running, and there is a lot of excitement."

"Can you tell me what's happening?"

"I think the war started." He thought about those words and what he felt. "France is being invaded by the Germans, and some people want to fight and some want to collaborate."

"What are you doing?"

"We're going to fight."

"And what about Chaton and the Gypsies?"

Nick concentrated. "I think they've left." *No, that wasn't right.* "They've been forced into a camp."

"Can you describe the camp?"

Nick willed himself to move closer to the camp surrounded with a fence and barbed wire. Not a nice place to be. Nick felt cold and shivered.

"Are you cold, Nick?"

"Yes, it's bitterly cold. There is no protection for the people here. They are freezing and hungry."

"Do you see Chaton?"

He frowned in concentration. "No, she's someplace else."

"Do you want to continue looking around the camp?"

He hunched his shoulders. "I'd like to move on."

"All right. Move ahead."

After the blackness cleared, Nick saw an army on one side of a river and Jean Claude and the cadets on the other side.

"Can you describe what's happening?" Dr. Sims asked.

"I'm helping blow up a bridge."

"Why?"

"To slow down the Germans."

The bridge exploded before his eyes. "The bridge is gone, and everyone is waiting."

A shot rang out, and a Nazi soldier fell off his motorcycle. Both sides began firing. The cadets were hidden behind monuments, trees, and buildings, whereas the Nazis were out in the open. "I've shot a man."

"And how does that make you feel?"

"I don't...feel anything," Nick said plainly. "The Nazis are bad and deserve to be shot."

"Let's speed it up. What do you see now?" she asked.

"I'm running away. Someone is after me. He doesn't like me."

"Is he a Nazi?"

"No, one of us. I shoot him, and he shoots me. I'm trying to do something, but I'm not sure what. I'm also running toward someone, but I don't know who."

"What else can you see?"

"I'm starting to float away."

"Where are you now?"

"I'm over the river. There are dead men and blown-up tanks and trucks. A real mess. Everything is covered with thick smoke. But the Germans are fording the river in rafts, and we keep shooting."

"Would you like to return now?" Dr. Sims asked.

He wanted to get away from the war and the blood. "Yes. Yes, I would."

"Do you see the light by the tunnel?"

He did.

"Float down to the light and let the brightness leave your body, and walk through the tunnel."

Nick did as he was told before shifting and moving his body from the swaying hammock at the ocean to the couch in Dr. Sims's office, reluctantly leaving the relaxed feeling before opening his eyes.

"What did you think of your regression?"

"It was interesting, like I was watching a movie."

"Do you believe you were watching yourself?"

"Yes, I was Jean Claude." Jean Claude was imprinted on Nick in some way. "But I don't know the whole story. I think I've missed parts."

"Probably, but you may start to remember or dream about more of your life as Jean Claude."

"And Cat? Is she the Gypsy girl, Chaton? She felt familiar."

"Only you can recognize her."

"Yes, Cat was Chaton—the little kitten."

They returned to her car and drove home. Nick couldn't explain what he was feeling with images jumping around his head and feeling as if someone had poured fizzling soda into his veins.

"How are you feeling?" Cat asked.

"I'm just confused." He leaned forward, his arms and hands hanging limply. He felt drained and tired. "And I don't know what to believe."

She laughed softly. "I remember my first time. Trying to keep an open mind and be skeptical too."

"I was Jean Claude." *I am Jean Claude.*

Nick paused and tried to collect his scattered thoughts. "Or was I making it all up in my head? You know, the power of suggestion?"

Cat remained quiet, her right hand splayed on the wheel. Her blue-stone ring caught the fading light and winked at him.

"Do you think you were making it up?" she asked.

He shook his head wearily. "It would be easier if I was."

"Why is this so difficult for you to accept?"

He turned toward her, as far as the seat belt allowed. "Do you know what it's like being the son of a minister?" It was then that the fizzing inside turned caustic, and he caught his breath.

"No, I don't," she said.

"It's damn hard. I have to follow the Bible, be nice and polite to everyone, and reflect positively on my father."

"That sounds like a heavy responsibility."

"It is!"

Cat drove for several miles, with Nick looking out the window at the acres of farmland and orchards, before continuing, "My father thinks I have a concussion. He doesn't believe in past souls or reincarnation." Nick banged his fist against his chest. "None of that. If I accept this, I've lost my family!" A strangled gasp escaped. "I'm afraid."

Cat gripped the steering wheel, and they traveled the rest of the way in silence.

****

Thirty minutes later, they pulled into the mostly deserted school parking lot. Football practice had just finished, and the team spilled out from the field into their cars and trucks.

"Hey, Nick!" Bryan waved to him. "Nice of you to show up!"

Nick eased out of Cat's car. He was in no mood for Bryan's bullshit tonight.

"Nice wheels!" Bryan ducked down to look at Cat and the car's interior.

"Yeah, she's a beaut," Nick said, closing the door.

Bryan still had his hand on the door when Cat drove off, making Bryan pull away in surprise.

"Are you talking about the car or Cat?" Bryan asked, adding a whistle to his question.

Nick just shook his head and snorted.

"So," Bryan said slowly as they watched the green Jag round the corner. "You and Emily over?"

Nick rubbed at his chest. "No." His feelings for Emily were solid. Weren't they?

"Well, what's with that?" Bryan flicked his hand toward the flash of Cat's taillights.

"Working on the project together," Nick explained with a shrug.

"Yeah. Right." Bryan smirked. "Project." He air quoted. "I might have to give Emily a call…"

"Shut up, Bryan! I told you I'm working on a project."

Coldness tightened around his heart at the thought of Emily—sweet, innocent, wonderful Emily—going out with a sleazebag like Bryan.

Bryan punched Nick playfully in the arm but with more force than necessary, and Nick shoved him back with equal force. Bryan stumbled, and just as they both clenched their fists, the rest of the team surrounded them, giving Nick a look of concern and disappointment.

Bryan spit on the ground. "You're a piece of shit!"

"Back at you," Nick mumbled as he unlocked his car and got in. He was still fuming when he got home and banged into the house. Slamming the door jarred him from his thoughts of knocking Bryan's teeth down his throat.

"Nick? That you?" his mother called from the basement where she was doing laundry. He heard the telltale thump of the machine as it flipped the clothes from inside the rotating drum.

"It's me!" He grabbed some cookies from the kitchen and went down the steps to the basement. He had been afraid of this dark, creepy space that held the washer and dryer and the funny-sounding water heater. He shook away the creepy feeling. Even at sixteen, the musty space felt scary to him. *A vision of a cave flashed through his head.* A cave smelling of vinegar and eggs.

His mother gave him a kiss. "Coach called and wanted to know how you were feeling?"

"Uh…yes, I was…you know…working on my report." The basement reminded him of something, and a creepy feeling caused him to twitch his shoulders.

Then he remembered. *The limestone caves by the Loire are perfect hiding places. I played in them as a boy, always careful not to disturb the mushrooms that grew on the walls and floors. The monks, at one time, had stored their barrels of wines and spirits in the caves for safekeeping and for the constant temperatures deep in the caves. They were little used now and rarely considered for hiding places after one had collapsed many years ago, killing a monk and a local laborer.* Was the cave a memory or just his brain conjuring up a scene, an overactive imagination?

His mother turned to face him. "You don't sound very sure."

I hadn't visited the caves since boyhood. He rubbed his neck. "It's been a long day."

"Oh?" His mother raised her brows. "Is everything all right?"

"Sure. Sure." He looked at the pile of laundry his mother was sorting and began to help fold the bathroom towels. "Where's Dad?"

"Visiting Mrs. Kady from church and checking on Grandma. They're both at the same hospital."

"Dinner?" He needed out of their dungeon

basement and to get some air.

"A plate in the fridge for you."

"Thanks!" He kissed her again. "Love you, Mom." He gathered up an armload of towels and took the stairs two at a time.

"Love you too," she called after him.

His phone buzzed in his pocket as he went into the kitchen to reheat his dinner.

"Hi! Missed you after school," Emily said, a hint of an accusation in her voice.

He cradled the phone against his neck as he pulled out the plate and put it in the microwave. Leftover pork chops from the looks of it.

"At a doctor appointment."

"Oh? Someone said they saw you drive away with Cat."

"Umm hmm. They must have been mistaken."

"Can I come over and show you my dress for the dance?"

Nick cut into his chop. He knew it was rude to talk and eat at the same time, but he was starving.

"What are you doing?" Emily asked.

"Eating dinner," he mumbled through some mashed potatoes.

"Oh, maybe I can show you at school tomorrow?"

"Sure. Sure." Nick shoveled more food in his mouth. "Tomorrow is better."

"Love you."

"You too!" he choked out.

He didn't care about the color of Emily's dress. What he needed was a drink to steady his nerves. He paused and listened for footsteps on the basement stairs.

All quiet. Maybe he could sneak some Jim Beam while his mother was busy and his father gone.

Chapter 27

No, Jim Beam didn't help tonight as *Chaton took my hand and led me to the fire in the middle of her family's encampment. I knew I shouldn't be here, but I couldn't help myself. I looked sideways at Chaton, so different from Gretchen. I've known Gretchen all my life, and it was only a year ago she let me take her hand. Chaton was bold and expected to be kissed. Gretchen hung back and turned her head when I tried to sneak a kiss. Gretchen was good and chaste, and Chaton was more like a flame, hot and beckoning.*

"Jean Claude," Chaton said and indicated a place on a nearby log to sit so I wouldn't get my uniform dirty.

She poured some wine and sat next to me, tucking her legs under her skirts, only her bare toes visible.

"So, tell me about your uniform." She pointed to the badges on my tunic for each level of horsemanship and skill.

"We are the best horsemen in all of France," I declared. Although my skills were average, attending such a school was an honor, one I had worked hard to achieve.

She laughed, a bell tinkling on the air.

"Will you fight if there is a war?" she asked.

"Oui, that is our duty. But..." I lowered my voice. "We aren't trained for fighting."

"No?" she asked, confused.

"We are training to be officers, to lead, but not to fight."

"Don't you need to do both?"

"Perhaps." The lack of training bothered me, but my father was fighting with the resistance movement against Germany, and he was a merchant until the war.

Chaton put her cup down and said, *"It's been difficult to find places to camp."*

The war would make it even more so. *"Where will you go?"* I asked, hoping it wouldn't be far so I could continue my visits.

"We don't know. We may have to split up into small groups."

"Yes, small is best," I agreed. Large groups of people drew attention; smaller would be better. The same was true for armies in war.

She slipped her hand into my pocket and moved closer. *"Do you mind if I warm my hand in your pocket?"*

"No." A ploy to get closer. I placed my hand into the pocket and squeezed her fingers. I liked the smallness of her hand in mine.

Gretchen allowed me to kiss her behind a tree when no one was looking. Her lips stayed closed, and although the kiss was nice, it wasn't satisfying. When Chaton had kissed me, it sent quivers up my spine. I longed to kiss her again and again, but she looked into the fire.

We drank our wine and watched the activities begin. With the dark closing in, I needed to get back to my dormitory for the night.

"I must go now."

"So soon? There will be dancing later." She *slipped her hand from my pocket and placed it on my thigh. The pulse in my neck beat erratically.*

"I'll come again." I *shivered—not from the cold but from the pressure of her hand.*

She walked me to the edge of the encampment and waved her fingers. No kisses tonight, *I conceded glumly before turning away and trudging back toward the Cadre Noir and my narrow cot.*

Chapter 28

The next morning, after Nick had stowed his backpack in his locker, Emily took his hand and led him out to the parking lot. "Close your eyes," she commanded.

"Where are we going?" Nick asked, covering his eyes with his free hand. The toe of his sneaker caught the lip of the doorway, and he stumbled behind her.

She pouted. "My dress?"

Oh, yes, the dress.

They got to Emily's light-blue, late-model Toyota, when she stopped abruptly and screamed. "My dress! Where's my dress?"

Nick's eyes flew open, taking in the open car door with the hanger and plastic cover on the seat. The dress was gone.

Emily began crying and pounding her fist on the hood. "Why? Why would someone take my dress?"

Nick looked around the interior and on the floor. No dress. He opened the trunk. It held a snow scraper, tangled jumper cables, and several school notebooks but no dress.

Nick gathered her close. "We'll find it, Baby. Maybe it was taken as a joke."

She hiccupped. "Do you think?"

"Maybe." *But probably not.*

"How could anyone do that to me?" she wailed into

his shoulder.

Several students stopped.

"What's wrong?"

"Someone took Em's dress," Nick said, motioning with his hand toward the car.

"Oh no!" Tiffany said with a gasp. "Was it that bitch Carmen?"

"I don't know!" Emily pulled away and wiped her nose on the back of her hand. "What will I wear?"

"I've got one you can borrow." Tiffany rubbed Emily's arms. "You need to report this to the office."

Nick kept his arm around her as they reentered the school, and Emily told the principal about the missing dress.

"Was there any damage to your vehicle?"

"No, my car wasn't locked."

"I see." He cleared his throat. "You should always lock your vehicle."

"We never had to before," Emily said with a sniff, and a fresh batch of tears welled in her eyes, threatening to roll down her cheeks.

The principal made an all-school announcement. "There has been a theft of a blue prom dress from a car in our parking lot. If anyone has seen the dress, please come to the office. And students, please lock your vehicles in the parking lot."

As they waited, Bryan appeared. He glared at Nick and patted Emily's shoulder. "I saw who took your dress."

"Who?"

"Cat."

"Cat?" Nick gasped. *Why would Cat steal Em's dress*?

"Cat?" the principal said with a frown. "Who's that?"

"Her first name is really Catherine. Catherine Thomlinson," Bryan said.

Cat was called to the office. Nick tightened his arm around Emily while they waited for Cat. He imagined this would be a screaming match, with Emily unleashing all her pent-up anger.

Once at the office, Cat stopped in the doorway and looked at Nick, then at Emily's tear-streaked face, and finally at Bryan. "What's going on?" she asked.

"Bryan saw you take my dress!" Emily lunged at her. Nick grabbed Emily and held her firmly, while Bryan just looked on with an amused uplifting of his lips.

Just then the custodian came in holding a scrap of blue fabric. "Is this the dress?"

"Yes!" Emily shrieked. "That's my dress!" Emily pointed at Cat. "You ruined it!" She broke away from Nick and pushed Cat.

"I didn't touch your dress," Cat said, sidestepping Emily.

Nick grabbed hold of Emily's arm and held her back.

"You did too. Bryan saw you!" She twisted in Nick's arms.

Bryan chuckled, covering his mouth.

"I did no such thing!" Cat said, turning and folding her arms.

"I saw you take it," Bryan said.

In a flash, Cat whipped around, confronting him with fury in her eyes. "It wasn't me! For all I know, you did it, Bryan! You've always had it in for Nick! You wanted to date Emily, but she chose Nick!"

Bryan laughed, but his neck was red. "You're one crazy chick, you know?" He waved a finger in her face. "You've only been here for a few weeks! What do you know about Nick, Emily, and me?"

"I know plenty." Cat breathed hard, her nostrils moving in and out.

"Did Reverend tell you that?"

"No, it's written on your face as plain as day."

"Let me get everyone's statement." The principal yelled and waved around some paper. "Bryan, Cat, and Emily!" The principal clapped. "Your statement—not rumor or gossip—please." The principal led Cat to his office, pointed for Bryan to go to the conference room, and Emily to a chair outside the office.

"Nick? Did you see anything?" the principal asked. Nick shook his head *as he saw a vision of Jean Claude holding a lumpy sack, stealing food for Chaton's family. Food to keep them alive.*

"They have to eat," he blurted.

The principal frowned. "What did you say?"

"Sorry." He willed his mind to think clearly. "No, I didn't see anything. Just here for moral support." He held his arms at his side.

"I think you need to go to class. I'll handle this," the principal said.

Nick went to class, where Gary poked him and asked, "What's going on?"

"Someone took Emily's dress."

Gary gave him a confused look.

"For the dance," Nick clarified. "Bryan said Cat took it."

"Oh, man." Gary ran a hand through his hair. "I bet

Em was upset."

"The janitor found it," Nick said, trying to keep his voice low.

"Is she happy?"

"No, the dress is ruined." Nick turned back to the front of the room.

Gary's mouth hung open. "I bet Emily's pissed!"

"Big-time!"

****

At lunch, Nick found Emily surrounded by her posse of girlfriends, commiserating about the dress. Plotting their revenge, no doubt.

"Nick!" Emily exclaimed.

"How are you doing?" He put his hands on her shoulders. She leaned back into his chest.

"Better. I'm going to borrow a dress from Tiffany."

He nodded at Tiffany, mouthing "thanks" over Emily's head. "Did Cat get suspended?"

"I don't know." Emily sat up and quickly turned around. "That bitch. I wish she never enrolled."

Nick nodded. *Change the subject*, he told himself. "You'll look beautiful in Tiffany's dress." *She would*, he thought. *Honestly, she'd be beautiful in any dress she chose.*

"You're so sweet!" Emily said, and her friends responded with kissing noises. Emily pretended to be embarrassed, but Nick could tell she was happy.

It was good to see her smile.

Chapter 29

Even with the dress incident, life went on as usual at Laketon High.

But even so, Nick was surprised to see Cat in World History.

"Hey!" he whispered when he sat down. "Were you suspended?"

"No!" She folded her arms and kept her eyes lowered. "And I didn't take the stupid dress!" Cat's eyes flashed when she looked at him. "Why would I do that?"

Jealousy. "I dunno. Bryan said..."

"Bryan's a jerk," she said as he walked by. "He did it! I know he did."

Bryan raised his brows at Cat when he walked past them to his seat. "Did you call me a jerk?"

"Whatever," Cat said.

Bryan sat down, but not before giving them a grin. Nick wanted to smash in his teeth, but he remained seated.

Cat's hand crept into his view, and she wiggled her fingers at him.

Nick cleared his throat. "I'd like to talk about our session with Dr. Sims sometime, but not at school," he whispered as his eyes moved around the classroom. Most students ignored them, but several of the girls shot dagger eyes at Cat.

The world map was pulled down, covering the board, which could mean a pop quiz or information Coach wanted to include in his lecture.

Bryan turned to them. "Where did you two go Wednesday night? A motel?"

"Bryan," Coach Sullivan said. "Pay attention."

"Sure thing, Coach, just checking to see why Nick missed practice." Pause. "Again."

All eyes turned toward them. Nick looked down at his notebook, but he felt the tension in the room and warmth creeping up from his neck to his forehead.

"I'm sure he has a good reason," Coach Sullivan said. "Right, Nick?"

Nick remained quiet.

Coach Sullivan said, "Okay, let's get on with class." He pulled up the map and began his lecture. No pop quiz today, and for that Nick was thankful.

****

Emily waited for him in the hall when World History was over. Cat turned the other way, leaving them alone. Emily's face was red with blotches like she had been crying.

"Are we still going to the homecoming dance?" she demanded.

"What? Of course! Why would you even ask?" Nick's eyebrows shot up.

"I heard a rumor," she said with a sniff.

"About what?"

"You and Cat. Are you really sleeping with her?"

"No! I—" he started.

"But Bryan said…"

"Bryan!" Nick threw up his hands. "Bryan doesn't know what he's talking about! You know him as well as I do. He's all talk and no facts!"

Her face brightened as she took off her glasses and wiped the lenses before putting them back on, the red blotches on her cheeks fading some. "I was hoping that was the case." She sniffed.

He hadn't thought much about homecoming. "Of course. I wouldn't let you down!" Nick tried to put on some fake cheer. But he *had* let her down. He could feel a small chasm between them, and it was his fault.

"I haven't seen much of you since we started our research projects," Emily pointed out.

"Let's go to the movies this weekend!" Nick suggested. The new James Bond was out, and Nick wanted to see it. "Date night?" Nick asked, hesitation in his words.

Emily nodded. Things were right between them again for the moment.

"See you later?" She looked hopeful.

"After school." He squeezed her hand before turning toward his next class.

****

At football practice, while he changed into his practice uniform, he was ribbed by the rest of the team.

"Dude, where have you been?" they chided, clearly happy to see him. "We need you for the game." Nick followed them onto the field, his enthusiasm leaking away—dreading football. Football had been his life, and now it was not.

"Things have been crazy." Nick shrugged. "My grandmother is in the hospital again," he said.

They all seemed sorry to hear it—everyone except Bryan.

"Grandmother, my ass," Bryan whispered.

They began their on-field warm-up and stopped talking.

Bryan's comment hit a nerve. Nick was entangled with Cat and hadn't been worrying about his grandmother's health, really. He hadn't been worrying about Emily either.

While practicing their plays, Nick put his left shoulder down and plowed into Bryan. There were no more comments about his grandmother for the rest of practice, only a grunt from body impact.

After showering and dressing, Nick decided to go to the rehab hospital to see his grandmother. He had neglected seeing her. *At least Bryan was good for something*, he thought.

When he knocked on her door, she greeted him with, "Nick! I've missed you!"

"I've missed you too, Grandma." Nick meant it. "Sorry, I haven't been here much. It's hard with football practice and the research paper I'm writing."

"No need to apologize. I remember how busy your mother was in high school."

He pulled up a chair next to her bed. She was propped up, alternately looking at a magazine and the television.

"What's new?" she asked.

"Not much." *Nothing to tell you about anyway*.

"Here either." Grandma waved her hand around. "I'm anxious to get home! Have you remembered to water my plants?"

"I did." Nick stood and gave her a kiss. "I'll go again on Sunday."

****

After he got home, his father looked at his watch.

"Where have you been? It's almost eight o'clock. We've been waiting on dinner."

"I stopped at the hospital to see Grandma."

His mother's face softened. "How is she?"

"Good, but she wants to go home."

"I wish you would have let us know," his mother said.

"Sorry."

"Let's eat." Dad waved her off.

Something was bugging them, and it wasn't his lateness for dinner.

As they all sat at the dinner table, Nick's dad cleared his throat.

"Son, I've heard several rumors about your history partner," he said. "Cat, right?"

"Umm hmm," Nick mumbled through food.

His father paused to consider his question. "It's been suggested she's a bad influence on the school with the dress incident."

Now the church was involved? Nick wanted to grimace and make a face but willed his mouth to stay neutral.

"I don't think it was Cat that took the dress. Bryan is trying to stir up trouble."

Nick wished people would mind their own business. Why were they telling his father about something that happened at school? Some of those busybodies needed to get a life.

"Really?" His mother leaned forward with a frown. "Bryan seems like such a nice boy."

Nick rolled his eyes. Bryan would put on an act for Nick's mother.

"He's not such a nice guy at school."

"We'd like to meet Cat and form our own opinion about her. Would you invite her to dinner?"

"Sure. If she'll come." He pictured a black, aloof Cat when his mother served meatloaf and mashed potatoes and informing his parents she was an atheist or a Buddhist. *Dinner would be a disaster.*

Chapter 30

Before Nick went to school the next morning, his mother said, "Remember, we'd like to meet Cat."

"I'll ask if she wants to come over," he grumbled, piling books into his backpack and putting on his jacket, preparing to leave.

Then his mom asked, "Would Emily like to come too?"

"No!" Nick waved his hands. "Emily doesn't like Cat."

"Really?" His mother set her cup down.

"Yes, remember Emily thinks Cat took her dress for homecoming," Nick explained. "Anyway, there's bad blood between them."

"So, no Emily, then," his mother said, although she looked concerned. "That's out of character for her, isn't it?"

Nick rolled his eyes. "Girls can be vicious and mean when they think someone is out to get them." He paused.

"That's pretty strong."

"It started the day Cat checked into school, and it's been intense ever since."

"Oh, I see." *But she didn't.* "We'd still like to meet Cat even if Emily doesn't like her."

****

At school, against his better judgment, he said to

174

Cat, "My parents would like to meet you." They had just finished World History and were waiting for the bell to release them.

"Why do they want to meet me?" Cat asked, stretching in her chair, bending from side to side.

"Get to know you, that's all." The bell shrilled overhead. And evaluate if Cat was a bad influence on the school and in particular their son.

Cat laughed as she stood. "For the fun of it?" They stepped out into the crowded hallway.

"I guess." He raised his voice to be heard over the din.

She laughed again.

He wasn't sure dinner would be a laughing matter.

"They've invited you to dinner," Nick said.

"How nice," she replied in an offhanded way. "When?" Her eyes narrowed.

"Whatever is good for you."

They moved through the crowded hallways to their lockers. They stood before Cat's as she opened it and took out her book for the next class.

"My mother is a great cook," he added. Cat could use a few extra pounds.

"I'm sure," she said, closing her locker and eyeing his broad shoulders. "You haven't always been so...so muscular."

"That's another thing. Play down the past-lives thing. They don't believe in that," Nick warned.

"The same parents who had you exorcised because you talked about your 'friend'?"

"Doesn't make any sense, I know." He flopped his hands to his side.

"What do I tell them if they ask?" She waited for

him to reply, and when he didn't, she added, "Are they always so closed-minded?"

Nick thought for only a moment, then smirked. "Yes."

Cat laughed again. "I'd love to meet them! How about tomorrow?"

"I'm sure that's fine."

****

The next night, before football practice, Nick sat with Emily on the bleachers.

"I hardly see you anymore," she said with a little pout, peering up at him from under her bangs.

"I know. I'm sorry," Nick apologized. "I miss you."

"We have to discuss homecoming!" She swatted his arm. "It's such a busy time! All kinds of things to get done! How about I come over for dinner, and we can discuss and plan?"

Nick's mind froze. Tonight? Emily for dinner. No, that would be a disaster. Emily and Cat. He didn't want to think about what might happen.

"Um…I don't think tonight is good. I might be late from practice. I think we're having leftovers. How about some other night?"

"Oh…Well." She gave him a doubtful look.

"We'll talk later, I promise." He squeezed her fingers. "Later, okay? Don't worry."

She gave him a tentative smile.

He gave her a quick kiss and headed to practice.

After practice, Nick anticipated Cat's visit with his parents. As he showered and changed, he imagined the good, the bad, and the ugly. His dad preaching about what the Bible said about one body, one soul, his mother crying, and Cat leaving in a huff. Cat had her notions, and his father had his.

Well, he gulped, *it's now or never*. He went out to his car.

"Rev!" a voice growled.

Nick had been engrossed in his thoughts, and he hadn't seen Bryan lurking behind a tree.

"Bryan." A statement of fact and resignation.

He surveyed the parking lot. There were only four vehicles left: Nick's Subaru, Bryan's truck, a sedan, and the coach's SUV.

There wouldn't be any help this time. Gary was gone. Nick opened his car door and put his backpack on the passenger side and turned back to Bryan.

"What is it with you, Bryan?" He took a step forward. "You have to solve everything with a fight?"

Bryan smirked at him.

"Hey! I'm sorry for what happened when we were in elementary school. There! Can we stop this?"

Nick truly regretted teasing Bryan about the water fountain malfunction that sprayed his crotch, making it look like he had wet his pants. But they were in third grade! *Get over it!*

"You think a lame apology can fix everything?" Bryan chuckled and flexed his hand. "Are you afraid, Preacher Boy?"

Nick would have to fight Bryan and win for this to be over.

"I'm not afraid of you," Nick said, taking another step forward, standing as tall as he could for his six-foot-two-inch frame. He was taller than Bryan but not as muscular.

"You will be when I finish with you."

Nick thought about the best strategy to handle this. Make the first move? "Not if I can help it."

A snort of laughter from Bryan before his fist lashed out and caught Nick under the chin. *So much for making the first move.* Momentarily Nick stopped breathing, and time stalled before he doubled his fists, rammed Bryan in the stomach, and punched him in the face.

Bryan staggered back with a look of surprise and confusion before hitting Nick on the cheek.

Bryan's nose bled down the front of his shirt, and Nick's eye tingled and twitched as it puffed up.

"Hey!" Coach Sullivan yelled.

The boys stepped away from each other.

"Do you knuckleheads want to get kicked off the team for fighting?" Coach Sullivan stood between them, looking first at Bryan, then Nick. He frowned at Nick, as if not believing he was involved.

"I'm going to pretend I didn't see this. You two get out of here, and no more fighting! We need to work as a team. We can't if we're divided. Go home, both of you, and cool off!"

"Thanks, Coach," Nick said, sliding into his car. He started the engine and backed out. Coach was still talking to Bryan, whose face was red, and his nose spewed blood. Nick saw Bryan tilt his head back to stanch the flow of blood.

As Nick drove, his eye puffed up further, and his vision was limited. He looked in the rearview mirror: the left side of his face was normal, but his right eye was closing, and his cheek turned purple.

He parked in the driveway, took his backpack, and went into the house.

"Nick, in here," his mother called.

"It's me," he said and put his backpack on the stairs leading to the second floor. His mother came out of the kitchen.

She gasped. "Did that happen at football practice?" She examined his eye and cheek, her touch gentle, but he winced.

"No, after. Got in a fight with Bryan Cranden."

"Let me get some ice for that eye."

Nick followed her into the kitchen, where his father was chopping vegetables for a salad.

"What's going on?" his father asked when Nick sat down and turned to face him. Whistling, he said, "You'll have a black eye."

"Just a little fight."

The table was set for four people, and he smelled chicken in the oven. He looked dully at the extra plate.

His mother handed him a bag of frozen peas to put on his face.

The peas instantly cooled his pulsing face, and he felt marginally better.

"A little fight?" she asked, giving him a pat on the shoulder.

He moved the bag around, further numbing his eye and cheek.

"Bryan was waiting for me after school, itching for a fight," Nick said. "Bryan's still mad when I teased him about peeing himself."

"That was how many years ago?" his father asked.

"I dunno. Seven or eight."

His mother ducked her head and tried not to smile. "You did that?"

"It was a joke."

"Not a very nice one," she said.

"I wasn't very nice in the third grade." Nick pushed the bag of peas harder into his face.

"And Bryan's still mad after all these years?" His mother leaned against the counter and folded her arms.

"Obviously." His father pointed to Nick's eye.

"Well, that's not all," Nick said, further adjusting the iced peas.

"Oh?" his dad asked.

"What else did you do?" his mom asked, wide-eyed.

He swallowed, remembering when Bryan had asked Emily out in their sophomore year, and she turned him down. "Bryan wanted to date Emily." Even now as he thought of Bryan and Emily, he got a stab of pain in his temple.

"Oh," his parents spoke in unison.

Nick hesitated when he heard the doorbell. His dad left, and Nick heard voices in the living room. His father ushered Cat into the kitchen. Nick took a double take. Cat looked so different tonight, her face free of the black makeup. She was fresh-faced and wholesome—beautiful, even.

Nick's mother came forward. "I'm Nick's mother, Grace Dupont, and you must be Cat."

"Pleased to meet you," Cat said, her eyes resting on Nick holding the bag of frozen peas. Her lip quivered, trying to hold back a smile.

"Nick?" Cat's eyes narrowed. "You in a fight?"

"Yeah, but I didn't start it," Nick said, repositioning the peas on his face.

"Let me guess," Cat said, her voice silky; each word flowed over the other. "Bryan did that to you."

Nick smirked.

"I see the anger in his eyes," Cat said. "He's jealous of you."

"Why?"

"I think things come more easily for you." Cat tilted her head. "Good grades. Football."

His parents stood silently, listening, arms folded, watching their exchange.

"Come on," Cat said, shrugging. "You're popular, a good student, are dating the president of the class, and you have lots of friends."

"Bryan could be that too."

"But he's not," Cat said.

Bryan had been a complainer for as long as Nick had known him. All he did was start fights.

"Who's hungry?" Nick's mom clapped her hands. "I'll get dinner on the table."

"Can I help?" Cat asked.

"No, but thank you."

"That smells delicious, Mrs. Dupont," Cat said, sitting at the table next to Nick.

"Thank you. Good Midwestern cooking," his mother replied and patted her stomach. "But call me Grace, please." Nick's mom placed a platter of chicken and bowl of potatoes on the table, and his father brought the salad and dressing.

"Nick told us something interesting about you," his mother said.

"And what was that?" Cat asked coyly, looking to Nick for answers.

Here it is, Nick thought. The questions, the knotty, tough questions about exorcism, past lives, and the devil's handiwork. He gripped the bag of peas so tightly he tore a small hole in the side, and several rolled out and landed on his lap.

"What did Nick say about me?" Cat repeated.

Nick looked at Cat and saw a flicker in her eye.

"About knowing each other before," his mother said in her offhand manner, throwing out the comment and seeing what sort of response she got. *Fishing.*

Cat gave a short laugh. "I've moved so much, I always think people are familiar."

Nick's mother nodded. "That very thing has happened to me."

"Grace? Grace," his father said with a chuckle, a joke between them. "Who will say the grace, Grace?"

"You give the blessing," his mother said. "Or maybe Nick should?"

"No, no, you go ahead, Dad." Nick put down the peas and listened to his father.

"Our dearly beloved Father, bless this food we are about to receive and nourish our bodies and spirits with your holy ways. Amen."

The conversation stopped as the food was passed around, and everyone started eating. For such a thin girl, Cat had a surprising appetite and ate as much as Nick. And he remembered how she could chug a beer in one swallow. Her stature was deceiving.

"Tell us about your research project. It sounds interesting," his father said as a way to restart the conversation. "I had no idea there were more camps besides the major ones." His father answered his own question. "Of course there had to be. If five million people were killed, the Germans would need more than just the five or six main camps."

"What I find most fascinating," Cat said, "is the

outcome of events seventy years ago still reverberate today."

"How so?" Nick's father asked. Nick could tell his father was gearing up for a discussion on world events. They were alike in that regard; Nick liked history, and so did his father.

"The surviving Gypsies moved to places like Oregon."

"I had no idea," Nick's father said. "What exactly are you researching?"

"Our paper will be on the Gypsies—or Romas—and their persecution throughout time, but particularly at Saumur before the Germans invaded," Cat said.

Nick watched the exchange. *So far so good.*

"And the boys from the school who fought the German Panzers," Nick added.

"I recall Nick saying over a million were killed," his father replied, before taking a bite of his chicken.

"Yes, that's a rough estimate because of their nomadic lifestyle. Historians believe it is much higher, perhaps closer to three million." Cat's speech was articulate, and the words flowed effortlessly, making her sound much older than her sixteen years.

"How did you come by that figure?" Nick's mom asked, listening, her chin on her hands.

"There are Gypsy activists researching that very fact," Cat said, taking a piece of her chicken. "I like the coating on the chicken."

"It's crushed rice cereal." His mom laughed. "A family recipe."

Cat took another bite and chewed thoughtfully. "It gives the chicken a nice texture."

"Thank you," Nick's mother said, giving Cat a

smile of approval. *If you liked Mom's cooking, you were a sensible person.*

Nick watched the exchange between Cat and his parents. So far nothing to indicate rough waters.

"The activists are also working on a memorial for the Gypsies killed in the war. But even now, there isn't much enthusiasm from the French government for such a thing. They want everything to do with the Gypsies swept under the rug."

"Are you French?"

"My adoptive mother is."

"History is always being rewritten," Nick's father said. "And repeating itself."

"And what about the American Indians? Their plight is similar to the Gypsies or any other displaced group. Take the Bible," Cat started.

Danger. Danger. Now she was getting into rocky territory talking Bible history with his father, a man who read and studied the Book daily.

"What about the Bible?" his father asked, leaning forward slightly.

"The Israelites," Cat said.

"True."

"Weren't they driven out of Egypt?"

"Yes, guided by God."

"My point exactly. We've been forcing people to leave their countries for a long time. The Gypsies included."

"You sound very passionate on the topic," Nick's mother said.

"I guess I am," Cat said, running a forefinger on the top of the table. "I suspect I have Gypsy blood."

"Why?" Nick's father asked.

"There is a large population in Oregon where I'm from." She looked up from studying the kitchen table. "I don't know for sure. I just think that." She patted her chest. "In my heart."

Cat's phone pinged from her pocket, and she fished it out. "I'm sorry to eat and run, but my mother needs me at home. An emergency of some sort." She put down her napkin. "Thank you for dinner."

"I'll walk you to the door," Nick said.

"Please feel free to come for Sunday services," Nick's father said.

Nick's mother grasped Cat's hand. "It was lovely meeting you. Please come again."

Did his parents think Cat was the troublemaker as reported by the community rumor mill? It couldn't be confirmed by her performance tonight. His parents seemed to genuinely like her.

At the front door, Cat stood on tiptoe and gave him a kiss on the cheek. "See you tomorrow."

He raised his hand as she got into the Jag and drove away, but lowered it when he saw Emily's car parked across the street. Had she seen Cat kiss him?

Nick dreaded their conversation as he walked toward Emily's car.

She rolled down the window.

"Hi! What are you doing here?"

"I guess a better question would be 'why was she here?' "

"Our presentation?"

"What about all the bullshit about leftovers and not wanting me to come over tonight?" Emily's words were short and heated.

"I'm sorry I lied to you." He reached into the car

and patted her shoulder, but she pulled away. "We had plans to work together tonight. I didn't think you'd understand."

Emily grimaced at him. "I heard about the fight and wanted to make sure you were okay."

"I'm fine."

"You don't look fine. You're getting a black eye."

"I promise we'll have time to discuss homecoming."

She grimaced and made an angry snort. "We'll see."

"What does that mean?" Nick asked as Emily put her car in drive. She glared at him before gunning the engine and zooming away, gravel scattering from her tires.

Nick watched her go. *Shit*. He was in trouble again with Emily.

Chapter 31

"I'm still mad at you, Nick Dupont," Emily said as she confronted him at school the next day. She was breathing heavily, with her hands on her hips, one green-and-white checkered sneaker tapping on the floor.

"I don't know how I can make it up to you," he said with a hopeless shrug.

In some ways he'd be happy when the project was over. He was tired of the drama of working with Cat.

Nick stared at Emily.

"I want you to stop seeing her outside school!"

"Our project will be finished soon," Nick said when the bell sounded, and patted her arm.

Emily hesitated, shifting from one foot to the other, deciding if she had more to say.

"Come on!" Nick took her arm. "I'll walk you to class. We'll talk about homecoming tonight."

****

After football practice, Nick decided to make a quick visit to see his grandmother. He texted his parents. On the way to the rehab hospital, he stopped at the store for a few things he knew she liked, and drove to the rehab hospital.

"Nick!" Grandma greeted him and held out a thin, blue-veined hand toward him. "So happy to see you!"

"Glad to see you too." He pulled up a chair and put

the magazine and box of chocolates on the table within her reach. Her eyes lit up at the sight of the chocolates. Grandma had a bigger sweet tooth than he did. None of the dark chocolate stuff for her—creamy and milky were her favorites.

She turned her attention to him. "You look glum today."

"Oh?" He lifted his head and looked into her eyes.

"Yes, something's different about you. Besides that shiner."

He gingerly touched his cheek before slumping forward in the chair.

"Get that at football?" she asked.

"Sort of."

Grandma snorted. "So what happened?"

"I, er, we got into a fight."

"I can see that."

He didn't really want to talk about the fight with Bryan. "We have a big research project due in World History."

Grandma responded with, "Hmm." And gave him a sideways glance. "Did you find what you needed in Grandpa's journal?"

"No, Cat wants to research the treatment of Romas in France instead."

"Oh?" Grandma peered closely at him. "The girl with black lipstick?"

"Yeah, that Cat."

"What's a Roma?" Grandma demanded.

"Another word for 'Gypsy.' "

"I see. Is Cat a Gypsy?"

Probably. But he responded with, "She's adopted and doesn't know."

"I haven't seen that cute girlfriend of yours in awhile. What is her name?"

"Cat." He realized his slipup immediately. "I mean Emily!"

His grandmother raised a brow. "Honest mistake." There was nothing wrong with Grandma's powers of perception.

He felt his cheeks warm and quickly jumped up. "I better go. I've got homework."

"It was nice of you to stop by," Grandma said.

"I'll come again." He kissed her velvety soft cheek and squeezed her fingers gently before exiting.

On his way home, he called Emily and put her on speaker. "Let's talk about homecoming." He didn't understand what the big deal was. He'd buy her a corsage and wear a nice suit, and they would dance and drink fruit punch unless someone laced it with something stronger.

"Oh," she said softly. "I thought we were going to get together tonight?"

"I just visited my grandmother."

"Hmm."

"What do I need to know?" he asked, pushing down on the gas pedal. He was starving. He figured if he kept it under eighty, he'd be fine.

"I'm wearing a pink dress from Tiff."

"What color corsage?"

"I think white."

"Where to eat?" Nick remembered the drill from the other formal dances they had attended. "The usual?"

"Yes."

"Anything else?" he asked.

"I guess I can't think of anything else," she said,

although she sounded sad their conversation only lasted a couple of minutes.

"I better go and concentrate on my driving."

"Umm. See you at school?"

A question? Why did she need to ask if he was going to be in school? Women!

Chapter 32

That night, Nick joined the cadets in the vast stables, caring for the horses. *I wrinkled my nose at the task at hand in the smelly barn.*

After raking out each stall, I picked up the brush and began currying the nearest horse. Absently, I thought about Chaton and Gretchen, the two girls closest to my heart. The horse pulled away and moved out of reach. I jerked him back and avoided the swinging tail, shifting rump, and stomping hooves.

I was more interested in firing new weapons and driving a tank, not riding around on a horse, making formations—putting on a show. We had read about the Nazis' rout of the countries surrounding France. It was only a matter of time before they'd invade French soil. I wanted to join my father fighting in the underground forces to push them back. Instead, I was stuck here. Oh, don't get me wrong, I worked hard to get here, but that was before the war. I was hungry to fight.

"You there!"

The lieutenant made me stop and lower my guard, and the snapping jaws of the horse swung around and nipped my hand, making it sting and smart.

I heard him laugh as I shook my hand. Taking advantage of my inattention, the horse swung his back quarters, knocking me against the wall.

Prestigious or not, there were bullies here too. I

was popular, but not everyone liked me. I stood stiffly and rubbed my bruised shoulder. It was common knowledge not to sneak up on the horses or riders. Only an imbecile would do such a thing.

The imbecile in question burst out laughing—the lieutenant, a former student, grinned at my discomfort.

"Don't you know not to sneak up on an animal," I replied hotly.

"I hope you're not speaking to me in that tone!"

I turned my back and rearranged my face. And only when my face was neutral did I face him.

The lieutenant picked up a piece of straw and twirled it around. "I've seen Gretchen," he taunted.

Gretchen was my girl. I fought to keep my face neutral, but I wanted to punch him. "I hope she's well."

"More than well. She's a fine girl." He grinned at me.

I remained quiet and waited. If I said more, I'd just provoke him further.

"Are you mistreating this animal?" The lieutenant's nose flared.

"Non. She was spooked when you came in."

"Rubbish! You're not fit to be a stable boy, much less a cadet!" The sullen leader ran his hands down the side of the horse. "Is this the best you can do?"

"Non."

"Then fix it!" he shouted loudly so the other cadets turned to see what was the matter, and several of the horses jerked and stepped away.

"I'm rescinding your visitation privileges for the rest of the month!"

"Why?"

The lieutenant grinned. "I'll be spending all my

free time with Gretchen."

    I grimaced at the retreating back. I'd sneak out anyways and visit Chaton instead.

Chapter 33

The next home football game, Nick was determined not to blow it. He needed to keep his emotions in check and concentrate on the game and not let his thoughts stray. He kept his back to the others as he took a swallow of whiskey from a small flask he thrust into his pack. He felt their eyes on him but didn't care. The whiskey burned down his throat. The warmth settled in his gut, fortified him.

The Laketon Lancers lined up against the formidable Crystal Shores Prep School. The glare of the stadium lights flooded the field. Nick's eyes swept over the Crystal Shores players; they were huge. They could have played the Michigan State Spartans and come out on top. Crystal Shores was one of the best in the state for their school size.

And with the blare of a horn, the game started. The Shores players ran around and over Laketon, and they lost yardage. They were everywhere yet out of reach. Two minutes into the game, Nick was sweating and frustrated. Shores was close to field goal range and...

He didn't see the sideways tackle coming, and momentarily he couldn't breathe. Nick hit the ground, and the Shores player landed heavily on top of him. He lay stunned for a second, trying to get air into his lungs. Grateful when the player stood, Nick lay on his back and looked up at the lights. They danced before his eyes. Gary gave him a hand up.

"You okay?"

"Yeah."

Laketon lined up and watched as the ball sailed through the goalposts for a three-point lead.

Play resumed. *The Germans were swarming over the Loire.* Nick shook his head, but still the tanks rolled forward. He had to do something. *There was a German soldier next to me, and I rushed toward him, headfirst, to knock him flat. I let out a grunt as we tumbled to a heap on the field.*

"What the!" the German yelled.

"Nick!" Coach yelled. "What's going on?"

He shook his head. Nick? That other name. He was Nick, not Jean Claude, and the German soldier was Bryan. How could he have mistaken Bryan for the enemy? A tiny voice laughed in his head.

"What the hell are you doing?" Bryan yelled. "Are you crazy?"

Nick shook his head. "I don't know...I don't feel so good." For a moment he had thought he was someplace else.

Coach Sullivan rushed toward them, waving his arms, and the ref blew the whistle. "You injured?"

"I don't think so," Nick said, moving his head from side to side. The Nazis had seemed so real, he could even smell the metallic artillery and the roar of the Panzer tanks.

"Let's have the trainer check you out." He helped Nick to his feet and led him to the sidelines. "You may have a concussion."

The visions were so real. *The Germans swarmed over the Loire, coming, coming. He was Jean Claude, the student soldier, and Bryan, the Nazi.* His past was overrunning his current life. Oh God, the two were in a struggle for dominance. How could he keep this from happening again?

Coach led Nick to the bench so the trainer could look him over.

"Did you hurt your hand?" the trainer asked.

"Yeah, it hurts." Nick flexed his hands. His hand swelled and throbbed—turning red. "Damn that hurt."

"It might have gotten stepped on." The indentions did look like cleats or even a bite mark. Who would have bitten him?

Nick's parents ran down from the bleachers. "Nick! Nick! You hurt?"

"I don't know what happened," he cried. "I think I'm going to be sick."

The trainer pushed a bucket toward him, and Nick vomited. He wiped his mouth with the back of his hand and took the water bottle the trainer gave him. He took a long swallow, but still the acid residue remained. He took another drink.

"Come on," his father said, holding out his hand. "We're taking you to the hospital to have you checked out. You may have suffered another concussion from that tackle."

The trainer stood. "I think that's a good idea. Have that hand looked at too."

Nick's parents—one on each side of him—led him off the field, where they met Emily.

"Oh my gosh! What's wrong?" Emily panicked.

"Don't know," Nick said. "I feel dizzy." He looked toward the field exit and a hazy figure of a girl by the concession stand.

"Do you need me to come?" Emily asked, rubbing her hands together.

"No, you stay."

"Text me!"

Emily took his uninjured hand and squeezed. He gave her a hug before she ran back to the bleachers.

The hazy figure of Cat called softly to him, "Nick! What's wrong?"

"Cat!" his parents said. "We're taking him to the ER to have him checked out."

She nodded and stepped closer, looking into his eyes. "Your pupils are dilated."

He shook his head. "You're kind of blurry."

"Let me know," Cat said, stepping back into the shadows.

Nick nodded.

"Come on." His father took his arm and helped him exit the field, before driving to the hospital.

In the emergency room, Nick had an MRI of his head, he was given fluids, and his hand was X-rayed.

"Looks like you just bruised your hand." The doctor held up his X-ray. "What happened?"

"I think someone stepped on it."

The doctor chuckled. "Football is brutal. Take it easy for a while."

"Does he need bed rest?" Nick's mother asked.

"No, nothing that serious! Just your normal, nonviolent activities."

Nick was good to go out with Emily then. He looked sideways at his mother, her mouth set in a firm line. She wouldn't want him to leave the house if she had her way.

They left the ER with his hand wrapped, orders to

sit on the bench for a week or so, and follow up with the family doctor.

****

"Are you sure you're up to going out tonight?" his mother asked as Nick got ready for the movies with Emily. Her eyes scanned his, searching. What was she looking for? *Confusion, madness, what?*

"I feel fine." But a small persistent headache throbbed behind his eyes. He didn't want to be babied.

His mother held up her hands. "Okay, fine, call if you need us."

"I will," he mumbled.

Emily rang their bell, and after greeting his parents, they drove to the movie theater.

"How are you feeling tonight?" she asked, pulling at the hem of her T-shirt, tugging it down over her hips.

He had the urge to stop her. He liked seeing a slice of her midriff, winking at him.

"I'm fine. The ER doctor said he couldn't find anything wrong."

"That's good," Emily said.

"So we're going to the new Bond flick?" Nick asked.

"Starts at 7:30. Meeting Gary and Tiffany."

Emily pulled her car into the parking lot for the only movie theater/bowling alley in Laketon, named Laketon Lanes and Movies, not very original, but it beat having to drive to Grand Rapids to watch something, or wait until it came out on Netflix.

Em parked next to a familiar truck, Bryan's, just their luck.

"I wonder who Bryan's with tonight?" Emily asked.

Nick didn't much care. He hoped there wouldn't be any more problems with Bryan tonight. Bryan would be gunning for him after the snafu at the game. Heck—Bryan was always looking for some way to jab at him.

It was too bad he tackled Bryan and not Gary, who might have understood. "I thought you were a Nazi," sounded lame, which it was. Gary would have laughed and shot his hand up in a mock "Heil Hitler" salute and not held a grudge.

Nick purchased the tickets, and Emily bought the popcorn and drinks.

They went into the darkened theater and found a seat by Gary and Tiff.

The previews finished, and the movie started, and Nick took Emily's hand. It felt good to entangle their fingers. He gave her a quick smile.

The movie began in true Bond fashion: beautiful women after James and impossible danger. Nick felt something hit the back of his head.

He turned, but it was hard to see faces in the dark. Then something bounced off his forehead. Popcorn. Nick scowled and whispered, "Hey! Knock it off." He didn't know which direction it had come from, but soon Nick's eyes adjusted to the darkness, and he spotted Bryan four rows back.

"Make me," Bryan whispered-yelled back. He dipped his hand into the popcorn tub and threw three pieces at once. Bryan's date snickered.

Suddenly, someone else stood up. "I'm getting the manager!"

Bryan stopped.

"Was that Bryan?" Emily whispered, looking back.

"The one and only." *Bryan, the bully, the German*

enemy—the lines between the two were blurred and fuzzy.

"Guys! Please!" Tiffany put a finger to her lips to shush them. Gary gave an apologetic smile.

Nick concentrated on the movie, but he was aware of the eyes boring into the back of his head, and the hair on his neck bristled.

He eventually forgot about Bryan.

When the movie ended, Gary asked, "Hey, you want to go for a burger?"

"I'm not really hungry, but I could get a drink." Emily looked into their empty popcorn bucket; just a few forgotten pieces languished in the bottom.

"Sure." There was only one place to get a burger at night, and that was at Del's 50s Diner, formerly a Woolworths back in his parents' day.

They left before Bryan and Rhonda, but they would all probably end up in the same place. Weekends were predictable in small-town Laketon. Anyone over twenty-one went to Grand Rapids for the nightlife, and the under-twenty-one crowd stayed local.

They stepped back into the 1950s, where Del's waitresses wore poodle skirts and saddle shoes. As expected, the diner was packed after the movies and bowling. Nick and Emily squeezed into a booth with Gary and Tiffany. Tiff and Em began their excited gossip banter, when Bryan and his date came down the aisle, Bryan purposefully running into their table, knocking over the salt and pepper shakers and spilling the sugar.

Typical and childish.

"Sorry, bro!" he said, even though he didn't look sorry. "Thought you were a Shores player."

Nick eased out of the booth.

"Nick, please," Emily begged. "Don't fight!"

"I won't." *When had he ever gotten into a fight when they were together?*

"No, the Reverend would never get in a fight," Bryan said, taunting.

Gary got up too and stood between them. "I don't want you guys suspended from school before the homecoming game," he said and pushed them farther apart.

"Who made you the school police?" Bryan asked.

"I did," Gary said. "You guys are acting like babies."

Bryan pushed Gary, but Gary pushed him back. "Don't."

"Outside," Bryan said.

Other football players joined them, some behind Bryan and others behind Gary and Nick.

"Do I need to call the cops?" Del, the diner owner, asked, pushing his way through the crowd blocking the aisle.

"No," Nick said. "We'll settle this later." His eye still had a bluish hue from his last encounter with Bryan.

"Hah!" Bryan said with a short laugh.

Nick sat back down and motioned for Gary to join Tiffany on the other side. Del stood and looked at Bryan. "Will I have trouble with you tonight?"

Sheepishly, Bryan rejoined his date in their booth, and Del went back to the kitchen.

The atmosphere around the table was stilted, with Emily talking about the decorations for the homecoming dance, the number of balloons they ordered, and the DJ from Grand Rapids. Emily and Tiffany were looking at something on Em's phone, their heads close together. Gary and Nick looked at each other with raised brows.

Gary mouthed, "Are you worried?"

Nick grimaced and shook his head. "Nah!"

Gary quirked his brow as if to say, Bryan wouldn't let things go between them.

Nick knew that.

The waitress came over to take their orders. Nick ordered sodas for Emily and himself. Gary ordered a hamburger, and Tiffany asked for a milkshake. Nick fiddled with his straw. He felt Bryan's eyes boring into his head.

He jammed the straw into his drink and sucked it down. "You ready to go?" he asked Emily.

"You drank that fast," she murmured. "Let me finish mine." She did, and he left money on the table.

"I'll take care of it." Gary waved Nick's money away and gave him a low whistle.

"Thanks, man." They left, but Bryan stayed.

Emily looked disappointed. "Why didn't we stay longer?" Emily asked.

"Headache," Nick said.

Emily nodded like she understood.

Bryan was his headache.

"Do you want me to come in for a bit?" Emily asked when she parked in front of his house.

He rubbed at his temples. "No, better not."

She frowned. "I thought you were fine?"

"I am, but I think I need to go to bed."

He kissed both her cheeks and then gave her a chaste kiss on the lips.

She frowned at him.

Something wasn't right. He didn't usually kiss her cheeks, did he?

"I hope you'll feel better by Monday," she said in a hesitant voice.

"Me too."

He hopped out of her car and went to the front door. Nick turned and Emily was still there, looking disappointed and worried.

Chapter 34

I lay awake on my cot, waiting for the perfect time to creep away to see Chaton. The Gypsies had moved their camp several kilometers away, and it would take me longer to reach them. If I was caught, I'd say I was going to visit Gretchen.

The old walls breathed around me, the wheezing sounds of wind squeezing through the cracks, stone against stone, and the groan of the floor settling into place. Some said the place was haunted. I stopped and listened. Hearing nothing alarming, I slid silently out of bed, tiptoed down the hall, and exited the building.

I hurried along the lane until I could see the lights of the Gypsy lanterns and campfires. But as I got closer, I heard shouts and the excited barks of the camp dogs, and saw enormous flames shoot into the air.

I steadied my breath and hid behind a tree and watched the French Home Guard brandishing guns and systematically lighting the wagons on fire.

"You must leave!" Petre, a grocer and head of the Home Guard, shouted and pointed a rifle at the frightened Gypsies.

"Get out! You're not wanted here!" More yelling. More threats.

More screaming as the Home Guard plucked children from the camp. Children who would be given to the good citizens of Montreuil-Bellay or Saumur to be indoctrinated into the Christian life. Their families were forced to flee and leave their children behind.

From where I hid, I could see they had taken Adella, Chaton's little sister. She and two boys huddled together, crying and afraid. One of the Gypsy boys put his arm around Chaton to comfort her. That should have been me comforting her, my arms around her, calming her fears for her sister. But I couldn't let the Home Guard see me. It would be bad, and I didn't want my mother to know I had been sneaking away from school.

One by one the remaining wagons were forced to leave. Chaton's family's wagon, painted red and gold and displaying geometric designs, left the camp and headed down the Rue des Lauriers, forced to leave Adella behind.

In a short time, the camp was deserted. Only the three smoldering carcasses of burned wagons remained.

I trudged behind them, following the dirt side road northward, keeping behind bushes and trees so as not to be spotted. Many of the landmarks and signage naming the roads and lanes were removed to thwart the Nazis, but I'd lived here all my life and knew the roads with or without signs pointing the way. I was gaining on the wagons, but where was Chaton's?

I overtook the wagons, running beside them. "Chaton! Chaton!"

Their wagon halted, and Chaton's head appeared out the back, her long hair flying in the wind, a flag on the currents. "Jean Claude! Oh, Jean Claude, they have Adella!" Chaton twisted a fold of her skirt. "What can we do?"

"I can probably find where they are taking her," I said, straightening to my full height to demonstrate my worthiness of the task. I didn't have a plan exactly, but I'd try to talk to Petre. Would Petre question my interest?

"Then what will you do?"

There wasn't much I could do in this situation.

"I'll think of something."

"How will we find you?" Chaton asked, her words flung away in the wind.

"I'll find you," I said with a resolve I wasn't sure I possessed.

The wagons continued on, their wares tinkling, the wheels crunching, Diesel engines coughing, and the plodding of the horses' hooves echoing in the dark evening air, not a merry sound as when they first arrived, a suppressed, hollow-sounding defeat.

I leaned against a tree to think. What to do? What had my military schooling taught me? Strategy was key. I would need to get friendly with Petre to find out where he had taken the children.

****

"Bonjour, Petre, my good man," I said after a sleepless night. My face was pale from my lack of sleep, but I made an excuse to leave class and go into Montreuil-Bellay. Petre, a grocer, would be looking after his fruits and vegetables spilling from crates outside his shop.

Petre, with weary eyes, heavy bags weeping down his face, smiled briefly.

"Bonjour, Jean Claude! What brings you to town on this gray day?"

I forced a smile. "Boot polish and news for my

fellow students at Cadre Noir."

"Ah, yes, Cadre Noir. You are a lucky boy. I was not so lucky when I was your age. I couldn't meet the standards. I longed for the prestige." Petre's lazy eye gave him the appearance of looking both ways at once.

"You would have been a good cadet," I said.

"Thank you," Petre said.

"We heard rumors of a Gypsy camp," I said, giving Petre a verbal nudge to talk about Adella.

"They are all gone. They were run out of town."

"That is a good thing. And their children?"

It was common knowledge the children were sometimes taken from their Gypsy parents to be raised in proper French homes to save them from the nomadic life.

"We managed to get three," Petre explained.

"Only three?"

"Yes, we have very few places to house them. Would your mother be willing?"

I immediately pictured my mother, her care-worn face, clutching and unclenching her apron in a dither to make such a decision.

"Perhaps. I think she may want a girl. She says boys are too much trouble." I laughed.

"We have a girl for your mother."

"I will ask her." I would bully my mother into keeping Chaton's little sister safe.

****

Later the same day, during the noon hour, I excused myself to go into Montreuil-Bellamy under the guise of checking on my ill mother. With everyone distracted by the coming war and headlines about Hitler's march across Europe, I was waved away and walked the short distance to our small but neat house in the center of Montreuil-Bellay.

"Maman, I have a favor to ask of you," I said, kissing both her cheeks and telling her how beautiful she was. Her joy at seeing me was replaced by fear. Her face fell, and she took a deep breath.

"It is not a bad thing, Maman, but will help our country," I explained, hoping my face didn't belie my duplicity.

She nodded for me to continue.

"You must house a Gypsy child and care for her."

"No!" my mother gasped. "They are so dirty! And suspicious looking!" She clutched at her throat as if she was choking.

My mother was mistaken, as were most of the citizens. I too had once thought that about the Gypsies. Chaton smelled of wildflowers, and I longed to drink in her scent.

"You will clean her and take away her suspicions," I said.

"But what of your father? What will he say if I house a filthy urchin in our home?"

"He is not here. We must all do our part," I said firmly, leading her into the tiny sitting room where a fire blazed in the hearth—her favorite room in their house.

"She can have my old room," I said.

"Your room, but…"

"I will be at the Cadre Noir for another year, and by that time, she may go to a more permanent family."

The time limit seemed to soften my mother's fearfulness.

"It would be nice to have a little girl about the

house…" she said. I could tell she was thinking. Considering. Deciding.

"You always wanted a girl," I said, knowing my parents' troubles at conceiving. "You can make her pretty dresses to wear and teach her to read. She will keep you company by the fire." I waved my arm toward the hearth. "Think how cozy it will be for you to teach her to sew and knit."

"Why yes," my mother said. "That would be very nice."

While my mother still had that faraway look in her eyes, I thought it best to be on my way. "Thank you, Maman. I will let Petre know of your decision."

****

"Maman has agreed to a little girl," I told Petre the next day.

"Thank you," Petre said. "That is one less child to be relocated. The girl is a little thing. My wife and I have two foster children, and we could take no more."

"She will be good for my maman while I am away. Keep her company. Do you have a name for her?"

"Adella."

"Ah good. Maman will expect her."

As I walked back toward the Cadre, Gretchen stepped from a nearby doorway. "Jean Claude?" she said breathlessly.

"Bonjour, Gretchen," I said, kissing both her cheeks. "You look very nice this morning." The surrounding sky was a gray and swirling mass of clouds, foreboding a storm, but Gretchen wore a cheerful red blouse.

She blushed. "What brings you to town?"

"Placing a Gypsy child with my mother."

I heard her sharp intake of breath. "Surely not!"

"Oui. I'm afraid so. We must do our part."

"But they are dirty and smelly and cast wicked spells on people!"

I inclined my head. "This is a wee child. Hardly a threat. She has been well cared for."

Gretchen looked at me sharply.

As if on cue, we heard a canon boom in the background, and Gretchen jumped and rushed into my arms. She was rounder and shorter than Chaton. Her hair smelled of soap and lavender.

"I've missed you, Jean Claude," she whispered.

I cleared my throat. "Me too. But I must get back."

****

Later the same day, during the dark of the night, I waited for the cadets' deep sleep, slipped out of the dormitory, and traveled in the direction of Tours, many meters away. The night was quiet. I took a deep breath as I left the shelter of the school, my footsteps the only sound. My way lighted by the moon. Chaton's family had not gotten far; I spotted their fire and wagons for their family group.

"Bonjour! It is Jean Claude," I whispered loudly to announce my presence.

"Jean Claude!" Chaton ran to me.

"I cannot stay."

She stepped back.

"Your sister is safe with my maman."

"Oh, thank you, Jean Claude! She is a good woman?"

"Oui!"

She kissed me on both cheeks and hands.

"What has happened to your hand?" She stepped

back with a frown.

"A horse bite."

"Maman has something for that." She ducked into their wagon and returned with a small container of foul-smelling salve and massaged the goop into my hand.

"Merci."

Was it my imagination, or did my hand feel better? I held it out, expecting to see the inflamed outline left by the horse's bite, but the ache was dulled by the salve. I tucked my hand into my pocket, returned to the Cadre, and fell asleep.

Chapter 35

On Monday, on his way to school, Nick rehearsed what to say about tackling Bryan during Friday's game. He definitely would blame it on having a concussion, something the ER doctor didn't diagnose, but it was the most plausible explanation.

There was a note on his locker asking him to meet in the cafeteria. It wasn't Emily's writing, but Cat's looping script. Several students gave him a concerned look as he made his way to the cafeteria, but no one said anything about Friday. Nick was glad most everyone had forgotten the incident. Once in the cafeteria, Nick saw Cat the moment he stepped through the double doors.

Her mouth was pert and sexy, colored with dark-red lipstick. She had headphones on, and he could tell she was practicing a new dance in her head by the way her toes tapped.

"What's up?" he asked, putting down his notebook, scanning the room for Emily, and then taking a seat across from Cat.

"How are you feeling?" she asked, concern creasing her forehead. She pulled off her headphones. "I saw you tackle Bryan." She held her hands out wide. "I don't know that much about the game, but I think you don't tackle teammates."

"I thought he was someone else," Nick said slowly.

She leaned forward. "Who?"

"You'll think this is silly." *Should he tell her? She would be the only person to understand.*

"Try me."

"I thought…he was…a Nazi soldier."

"Oh my gosh! You were Jean Claude!" she said loudly.

Several people looked toward them. He motioned for her to keep her voice down.

"I think so," he whispered. "I haven't told anyone else."

"That's good," she agreed. "They'll think you're crazy." She moved her finger in a circular motion by her head.

"I don't know what to do." Nick shuffled his foot under the table. "My parents are convinced I have a concussion."

"Let them keep thinking that."

"But it's a lie."

"Do you want them to have you exorcised again?"

He laughed. "Hardly." Nick broke his whisper, speaking in a normal voice.

"I'll call Dr. Sims and see if she has any suggestions," Cat said.

"Thanks." Nick started to reach for her hand but stopped himself as he saw Veronica walking by.

"What were you talking to her for?" Emily demanded as he exited the cafeteria.

"Come on, Em, we've been through this." He let his arms fall heavily to his sides in exasperation. "She's my research paper partner. I *have* to talk to her."

Emily sniffed. "I hate her for ruining my dress!"

"I know, but she says she didn't do it."

"And you believe her?"

Did he or didn't he? With a sigh, he said, "I do."

"What!"

"So far she's been truthful with me," Nick said apologetically. "I don't think she would lie."

"Bryan saw her."

Bryan was the more likely suspect.

"I don't believe Bryan."

"But he's one of us!"

"One of us?" Nick stared at her dumbly.

"He's lived in Laketon for a long time," Emily said, moving her hands up and down as she talked. "He attends your father's church."

"True, but he's never liked me—he's always causing problems. You were with me when he was throwing popcorn at the movie!"

Emily started to say more but stopped, her mouth hanging open as she thought back to the movie and diner. She started to say something again, gave her head a tiny shake, and remained quiet.

"I should be done with my portion of the paper soon, and then I won't need to talk to her as much," Nick said. "Happy?"

Emily nodded, her mouth set in a grim line, nothing pert or sexy about the way she looked at him.

****

Coach Sullivan began World History by saying, "You should all have some of your paper written by now or at least have a good idea of what you're going to say about your topic." He tapped his clipboard on the desk. "I'll walk around and look at what you've done so far."

Nick turned to Cat. "I don't have anything

written."

She responded with, "I've written a bit so far."

"Can I read it?"

"Of course," she said, taking a folder out of her pack and sliding it toward him. She had written quite a lot. Nick began to read:

WWII in Saumur, France and its Effects on the Citizens and the Nomadic Roma/Gypsies

By Nick Dupont and Cat Thomlinson

The Gypsies, or Romas, are an old population coming from India during the fifteenth century. They became nomads traveling throughout Europe, but primarily Romania. They were feared and persecuted in Europe, especially during the two world wars and Germany's occupation of France in the 1940s.

The Gypsies were rounded up, much like the Jews, and interned. Although not systematically killed, millions died from the conditions in the camps. The recorded history estimates over a million Gypsies died during World War II, but since they had no fixed addresses, the number is believed to be much higher. The largest internment camp was located in France in the Saumur wine-growing region and the nearby town of Montreuil-Bellay. The French citizens in the region thought it was a good thing to have the Gypsies interned. While imprisoned, the Gypsies lost their possessions and, in many cases, their livelihoods.

Nick continued to read. When finished, he said, "That's good."

"What will you write?"

He thought for a moment. "I'll need to talk about what was happening in Saumur when the Germans invaded. The military training school. How they fought off the Germans for two days." As he talked, he moved his fingers, ticking off each point. "We have to tie the two events together. The internment happened because of the truce France had with Germany. They were sort of in cahoots with the Germans until they invaded France."

Nick didn't realize Coach was standing behind him, listening. Coach nodded and picked up what Cat had written. "I like what I heard you say, Nick. This is good too." He shook the paper before placing it back on the desk.

"I'll have something written by tomorrow," he promised.

****

Later, Nick sat before his computer and flexed his hands, arranging his thoughts before writing. His research intermingled with his known facts and those Cat had shared.

He typed: *There was a lot going on in Montreuil-Bellay and Saumur during the spring and summer of 1940 before the Germans actually conquered the area. First the Gypsies were rounded up and imprisoned. Most French citizens were wary and afraid of Gypsies. They feared what they didn't understand. Most Europeans valued landownership and a permanent home; the Gypsies roamed and didn't have traditional houses.*

The Gypsies who wouldn't conform were imprisoned, sometimes in deep holes in the ground, many forgotten at the end of the war to slowly starve to death.

In his head, Nick saw two topaz eyes shine from deep within such a hole as he typed. *It is estimated that over one million Gypsies died in the war.*

Then when the Germans were marching toward the area, the commander of the boy's military horsemanship school—Cadre Noir—organized the boys to fight. Before the fighting, the school's horses were taken to someplace safe. Next the boys and their leaders hatched a plan with the French Home Guard to defend the area from the Germans.

****

Jean Claude nudged him aside. *Sweet Adella. When I visited next, my mother had made Adella a dress and an apron to wear.*

"You must say bonjour to Jean Claude," his mother said.

"Bonjour," Adella said, her eyes downcast and wary.

"You look very nice, Adella," I said, hoping she wouldn't betray me.

"Now you kiss him," his mother instructed.

I bent down to Adella's level so she could kiss my cheeks. She whispered, "Where is my family? Chaton?"

She kissed first one cheek, and I whispered, "They are about five kilometers away, waiting for you." Then she kissed my other cheek.

****

In the morning, Nick printed out what he had written to share with Cat and drove to school to find her. In the cafeteria, he spotted her dark head and also saw Emily waving him over. *What to do?* He stood uncertain for a few seconds before waving back to Emily and walking to where she was sitting with Gary and Tiffany.

"You're late this morning." Emily looked at the

clock on her phone.

"Printing out my paper." Nick yawned. "I wrote most of it last night."

Gary looked stricken. "I haven't even started. Can you help me?"

Tiffany patted his arm. "I'll help."

"I hate writing papers!" Gary grumbled to no one in particular, and Nick laughed.

"Mine's finished," Emily said. "I'm sick of World War II and don't care if I ever know anything else about it."

"It changed the world," Nick said.

"But it was so long ago," Emily said with a pout.

"The war opened doors for women to work, better production methods, and technology," Nick said.

"True, I'm just tired of studying what happened seventy years ago," Emily said with a roll of her eyes.

"I have to agree with Em," Gary said.

"And besides there's still a lot to do before homecoming on Friday," Emily added as if they didn't already know.

Chapter 36

On Friday, the day of the homecoming game and dance, Coach gave his game-night pep talk.

"Now, men, let's go out there and give them our best. Win or lose, we give it our all. Is everyone committed to doing that?" After hearing a resounding yes, Coach's eyes swept over the team, his eyes lingering on Nick the longest. Or so it seemed to him. Maybe it was just Nick's imagination. Maybe Coach had looked at each team member the same way?

"Let's go, team!"

Bryan bumped him. "Don't forget, I'm on your team," he taunted with a grin. "Rev."

"Shut up!" Nick said.

He willed Jean Claude to stay away and not mess with his head in this game. No Nazis tonight. Even with that proclamation, a feeling of dread went through him. The feeling intensified as the game started. Nick was all thumbs, acting as if he had never held or even caught a football. He couldn't keep from fumbling.

"Time-out!" Coach yelled.

Nick huddled with the rest.

"Nick, sit this one out. Let Bryan go in for you. You may still have some residual effects from the concussion you suffered."

"But...Coach..." Nick couldn't think of one reason why he shouldn't sit out. The sound of roaring wind-lashed waves filled his ears, pushing away everything but the mind-splitting sound.

"Yeah, why don't you let me?" Bryan said, giving Nick the biggest shit-eating smirk possible.

Nick gave Bryan the finger.

Bryan filled in for him while Nick paced on the side. Bryan's assistance didn't help their cause. At halftime they were down 14 to 3. Nick followed his teammates toward the locker room, his mind lost in a quagmire of thoughts—like why was this happening to him? A shadow caught his eye. Cat. She was leaning against the wall, her dark clothing blending with the deepening evening gloom. As he walked by, she moved her hand, motioning him to her.

He jogged over, taking off his helmet. "I didn't know you were interested in football."

"I came for halftime," she said, giving him a playful shove.

Nick laughed. "It's got to be better than the actual game."

"I like watching you," she said, giving him a sly smile.

Nick ducked his head, moving the dirt with the toe of his cleats.

"Nick? You're wanted on the field, man," his teammate said. "You didn't hear the announcement to line up?"

"The field?" He blinked into the lights glaring over the grass making it look yellow and not green.

"Yes, they're naming the candidates. Everyone's waiting." Pause. "For you."

Cat gave him a hug and whispered "good luck" in his ear.

Emily would be waiting. Could she see him and Cat from where she was standing? He had a straight line of vision to where Em stood. She'd be mad he was talking to Cat.

"Thanks." Nick, red face and all, turned and loped toward the field. He was greeted with a smattering of polite applause.

He took his place by Emily. She looked beautiful in a pink dress that made her cheeks rosy, but her eyes were wide and watery.

The class floats circled the field.

"What's the matter?" he whispered.

"What were you doing with her?"

The band began playing.

"Talking. She wished us luck."

"Ha!" Emily said. "It looked like you were doing more than talking." She motioned toward the entrance to the locker room. "I bet she wishes we would break up."

"She didn't say that."

"She wouldn't. Do you?" Emily asked. "Do you want to go out with her?" Emily repeated in a low, furious whisper.

Momentarily they were silenced by the roar of the crowd. The senior class won the float contest. *A given.*

"Em!" He tilted back his head in frustration. "No."

"I don't understand why you're always talking to her. And why was she hugging you?"

"We're not always talking." *Why was Em being so unreasonable?* "She was trying to be friendly."

"I bet!"

"You look nice tonight." *Way to change the subject.*

Emily held out the material and let it drop in place. "My blue dress was better, and that bitch ruined it." *Way to stay on topic!*

He rolled his eyes. "Em…Can't we enjoy tonight?"

The way she wrinkled her nose meant she wasn't done with the discussions about Cat or the ruined homecoming dress.

"I told you, you look beautiful." Nick clenched his jaw.

"She better not talk to you at the dance," Emily whispered. "Or I'm going to say something!"

The freshman prince and princess were announced, then the sophomores. Nick caught Gary's eye over the heads of the girls and grimaced, and Gary made his eyes cross. Neither of them cared about being junior prince, but the girls obviously did. Emily bounced a little on her feet in anticipation and shrieked when their names were called.

"It's us!" She turned to Nick excitedly. "We won!"

The glittering crown was placed on Emily's carefully arranged hair and another on Nick's head. She was handed a bouquet of roses. She gave a tentative wave toward the spectators.

"May I present the junior princess and prince, Emily Hendrick and Nick Dupont."

He bent to hug Emily, but she stood woodenly in place. He hugged her, the barb of a rose piercing his uniform. He stepped away and rubbed at his stomach from the sting of the rose.

The senior king and queen were announced last.

"I'm sorry I was talking to her," Nick whispered, giving her a kiss on the cheek.

Emily turned away from him and began walking

off the field. Nick's parents and grandma blocked their way. "Congratulations, you two! Emily, you look beautiful!"

"Thank you, Grace," Emily said. Emily gave Grandma's hand a squeeze. "So glad you were able to come."

"Me too!" Grandma said. "That's a beautiful dress."

Emily's face changed. "I had to borrow this. Someone ruined my original dress."

"Oh dear," Nick's mother said. "Who would do such a thing?"

Nick jumped into the conversation. "Not sure."

"It was Nick's work partner," Emily said.

"Cat?" Nick's father asked.

"Do you know her?" Emily asked.

"Why yes, she came to dinner," his father said.

Emily glared at Nick. "Right!"

They stood looking at each other, neither saying a word until Tiffany called for Emily.

"Nice to see you all, but I've got to go. Gotta check on the dance preparations." Emily turned away from Nick, saying, "We'll talk later."

Not a good omen, "we'll talk later."

"I better get to the locker room," Nick mumbled his excuse to leave.

When Nick entered the locker room, Bryan batted the crown from his head—a playful gesture, but his eyes were hard and cold as sapphires. The crown rolled around the floor before resting on its side.

"Prince Nick," Bryan said with a short laugh.

"Glad it was you and not me," Gary said, giving a low whistle.

****

After the game and their loss, Nick showered and changed and headed to the gymnasium for the dance. The closer he got, the louder the music sounded. Em and her committee had done a nice job with the balloons, the DJ, and streamers.

"Hey! Congrats!" Several people shook his hand and gave him high fives.

"Thanks. Seen Emily?"

Nick found Emily by the punch bowl with several of her friends. She still wore the tiara whereas Nick had left his crown in his locker.

As he approached, Emily didn't look particularly pleased to see him and folded her arms. "Em," he said.

"Don't Em, me!"

Another discussion about Cat.

"Come on, Em, you're my girlfriend. She's new." He moved his shoulders as if trying to get comfortable and then tugged at his collar. "Just being nice."

"Can't someone else befriend her?"

Now she was being unreasonable and childish.

"Will you dance with me?" He grabbed Emily's hand and led her out to the floor.

They danced to a slow song, and Nick held Emily close, smelling her flower-scented hair. They didn't talk, just swayed together until the song finished, and the DJ announced the Homecoming King and Queen.

Nick and Emily clapped with the others. Nick felt the walls beginning to close in. "I need some air."

They left the stifling, noisy cocoon of the dance.

"I'm going to…" Emily stopped abruptly at seeing Cat enter the school. "What's she doing here?" She whispered loud enough for Cat to hear.

Nick thought it best not to answer and shrugged.

"Congratulations!" Cat yelled. "Nice dress!"

Nick smiled, and Emily's eyes narrowed.

"No thanks to you!" Emily said tersely.

"What does that mean?" Cat asked, wandering toward them.

"My. Dress." Emily emphasized each word.

"I didn't touch your dress," Cat said, her voice low and even.

"Ha! Just leave us alone!" Emily took a step toward Cat and stopped.

"Can I at least talk to my work partner?" Cat asked playfully, emphasizing "work partner."

Emily whirled away, her hands making tiny fists as she stalked off to the bathroom.

"She doesn't like me, does she?" Cat asked, with a chuckle.

That was stating the obvious!

"Em's mad about her dress," Nick said, moving over to the wall and leaning against it.

Cat followed him. "How can I convince her I didn't ruin her dress?"

"I don't think she'll listen."

Cat looked surprised. "Why do you defend her?"

He gave her the "*come on,*" incredulous look. "She's my girlfriend."

"She's not right for you," Cat said as she leaned against the wall, one leg crossed over the other.

"How can you say that?" His family loved Emily. *Then an image of another girl, not Chaton, flashed through his mind. A girl on a bicycle pedaling through a picturesque European town, giving Jean Claude a wave.* Nick shook his head, and the image rolled away to the recesses of his head.

"Just the way it is," she said.

"So if that's true, what does it mean?" Nick pushed away from the wall as Emily stood in the doorway and appeared to be searching for him.

"We need to be together," Cat said. "Or we'll continue to chase each other around from one life to the next."

"So we need to be together in order for Jean Claude to go away?"

"Not exactly…"

Emily headed in their direction, her eyes narrow and her nose flared as if she was breathing deeply.

"Should I leave?" Cat asked, taking a step toward the door.

"Probably be for the best."

Cat slipped out.

"Did she leave?" Emily demanded.

"Yes," Nick said.

"Good! I'm so mad at you, Nick Dupont!"

He sighed. He had more immediate worries than Emily being mad at him.

Chapter 37

We cadets stood in neat rows, facing our lieutenant. He had a narrow brow, narrow chin, narrow everything—including his thinking.

He had kept us busy building a fence topped with barbed wire around an old, abandoned barracks on the outskirts of town—a solitary, lonely place. I shuddered at the feeling of despair around the ramshackle building, missing some windows and gaping boards letting in the elements.

I was hoping for news from the front as my father was off fighting to keep the Germans out of France. But the lieutenant was single focused on the barracks, and we could only guess what it would be used for. We had, of course, heard about some of the atrocities in other countries.

Now that the fence was finished, he ordered, "You are to round up all the undesirables in this area! They will be housed here!" He waved his arms expansively. "The Saumur Internment Camp."

My heart sank at his order. But what exactly was an undesirable? My thoughts were scampering around my head, but my body remained completely still. I had the urge to move my feet; my toes were freezing on the bare stone floor. I concentrated on something else and willed my feet to stay stuck to the floor.

As if reading my mind, the lieutenant continued,

"The undesirables are the imbeciles, the Jews, the crippled, the sick, foreigners, and the Gypsies." The word Gypsies shot from his mouth, a pop from a handgun. "They bring sickness and lawlessness to our communities. You are dismissed," the lieutenant said, his words bouncing off the stone walls.

I stood frozen in place, thinking of the wagons and people in Chaton's caravan, until someone elbowed me. I couldn't imagine Chaton's family living in those dismal barracks.

"Pardon," Louis said with a grin. "You going after the Gypsies?" He gave me a smile that hinted at amusement, but something else.

"Of course," I said loudly, perhaps to convince myself as much as those around me, hoping the lieutenant overheard my words. "My duty. But I was thinking about the imbeciles." I watched the lieutenant's retreating figure.

"Ah, yes," Louis said before nodding his head and turning toward the exit.

Foremost in my mind was warning Chaton and her family they were to be rounded up and imprisoned in the newly created Saumur-barracks-turned-internment-camp.

I lost sight of Louis in the jumble of bodies and high-pitched voices and slipped away while the hall was in disarray, and people settled into small groups with plans for their task.

Chaton and her parents and grandmother were about six kilometers away. If someone were to report my black uniform to the commander, I'd say I was rounding up the Gypsies as ordered. After dodging bushes and trees, I reached their small band in the forest. All was quiet in the camp; not even the dogs whimpered.

I called softly, "Chaton. It's me, Jean Claude."

She stepped out from behind a tree, her hair in tangles from the wind and brambles. A boy was with her, and when he saw me, he slipped away. Jealousy stabbed at my gut, wondering what she had been doing with him.

"Jean Claude. You are early." Her cheeks glowed from the wind. The weather was changing, and the scent of dying leaves left an undertone of decay.

I didn't like seeing Chaton with other boys, and pushed my chest against my uniform to show her my medals of accomplishment. "I've come to warn you."

"Warn us of what?" she asked, wrapping her arms around her thin cotton blouse, the outlines of her breasts and nipples visible.

"We are to round up all the Gypsies and others." I looked instead at her head to avoid the unsettling thoughts I was having.

"Round us up?" She frowned and licked at her chapped lips, red as berries.

"I know where you can hide." I stepped closer.

"We don't like hiding," she said stubbornly. "Papa says we must stand our ground."

"You have no ground of your own." I placed my hands on her shoulders, and she stepped closer.

"He believes the land is for everyone…"

I pulled her to me and nuzzled her neck and whispered, "But you must hide, or you will be imprisoned."

Chaton looked back at her family's wagons, shifting feet with indecision.

I continued talking. "The lime caves by the Loire are perfect hiding places." Louis and I had played in them as boys, always careful not to disturb the mushrooms that grew on the walls and floors. The monks, at one time, had stored their barrels of wines and spirits in the caves. They were little used now and rarely considered for hiding places after one had collapsed many years ago.

"We must talk to my papa," Chaton said stubbornly and pulled away from my embrace.

"As you wish, but we must hurry." She took my hand, and together we walked toward her family.

Chaton's father was a small man but with sinewy arms that belied his strength. He was short but powerful and fearless. He was sitting by the fire with one of the boys I had seen buzzing around Chaton.

"Papa, Jean Claude says we must hide."

Her papa looked around their small encampment enclosed by the thick forest of pine, oak, and beech. "More than this?"

"Oui, Papa, to another place that is safer."

"They are coming for you," I said, feeling panic push past the logical part of my brain.

"More like you, you mean," her papa said.

"Yes, like me, but I'm here to help."

"I see." He looked first to his daughter's face and then to me, his eyes sizing me up and down, deciding.

"I have kept Adella safe for you," I said.

"That is true," her papa said with a small nod.

Chaton's eyes darted between them. "We will do as you say."

"The lime caves by the Loire. I know one such cave that is farther away and won't be searched."

"When will we go?"

"Tonight. Meet me around midnight at the river by where you were camped before. We will go from there."

****

I slipped back to the Cadre Noir for my lessons and duties. No one questioned my two-hour absence, but I felt the lieutenant's eyes on me. He always watched me.

"You there, Jean Claude," the lieutenant called. "Come to me."

I stood and approached him where he looked me up and down, eyes stopping on my boots.

My boots were dirty from going into the forest.

"What happened to your boots?" the lieutenant asked. "Were you rounding up the undesirables?"

"Of course," I said.

"You know of the Gypsies' camps." A statement, not a question. "I want you personally to round up all those heathens."

"They have all left the area, sir," I said as respectfully as I could and still differ with the lieutenant.

"They are not all gone!" he hissed, spittle hitting my cheeks as he talked.

I had the urge to wipe it away but stood motionless, urging my eyes to remain neutral and unemotional, but inside, I was anything but calm.

"Oui, I will round them up."

But first I would hide Chaton and her family deep in the lime caves.

"I want to see them tonight!" barked the lieutenant, his words as sharp as the growl of a dog sensing a bone.

Where to locate other Gypsies? I would need to travel toward Lyon and hope to find other small camps. Would Louis help me? I needed to find him.

Chapter 38

A text from Cat interrupted Nick's Sunday afternoon.

—*I need to see you.*—

Nick glanced over at his father, who was also watching the football game on the television.

It was almost five p.m., so he responded with:

—*5:30 P.M.*—

When 5:10 p.m. rolled around, he said, "I'm going to work on my research paper with Cat." Nick picked up his notebook.

"See you for dinner?" his father asked, lowering the volume on the game.

"Maybe."

Cat lived about a twenty-minute drive from his house, in the same gated community as Emily and Veronica. He drove slowly past Emily's house but didn't see any movement or lights. Sheepishly, Nick felt relieved. He drove a bit farther and parked.

A blonde-haired woman wearing a dress and heels opened the door and held out her hand. "You must be Nick. Cat told us about you."

"Nice to meet you," Nick said, wiping his sweaty hands on his jeans. Why was he sweating and suddenly feeling nervous?

"Cat's father will be down shortly." The woman waved him in. "We're going out for the evening, but you two make yourselves at home. Order pizza if you're hungry!"

He never turned down an offer of pizza. "Thank you."

Cat's father, wearing a shirt and tie, loped down the stairs and shook his hand. "Nice to meet you, Nick! We're happy Catherine has friends in Laketon."

Cat, not Catherine, he thought.

Cat came through a door at the end of the hall before he had a chance to take off his jacket.

"Well, we're off!" Cat's parents called from the entryway as Cat led Nick to the living room. The door closed, and the soft thud resonated around the hallway.

"Did you meet David and Joanne?" she asked.

"David and Joanne?"

"My parents." Cat rolled her eyes.

"You call your parents by their first names?"

"They're not my biological parents. I was older when they adopted me, so I knew the difference."

"But still…you should do them the courtesy of calling them Mom and Dad. I bet they would like that."

"I think they prefer it this way," she said.

She motioned toward the massive, leather, L-shaped sofa. They sat down. Nick realized he was clenching his notebook, crumpling the pages. He smoothed it out and placed it on the coffee table in front of the sofa.

He was suddenly aware of her next to him as a tiny shiver ran up his spine. They often sat next to each other in class, so why was this different? They were alone, and he felt an attraction to her closeness.

"What did you need to see me about?" He nodded to his notebook. "Our paper?"

"No, I talked to Dr. Sims again."

"Oh?" Nick sat up straighter.

"About why you tackled Bryan, thinking he was a Nazi." She turned to face him.

"What did she say?"

Cat paused and breathed deeply before saying, "She said the memories may go away if we act on them."

"The war?" How would they act out WWII?

"No, how the war affected our relationship."

"It kept us apart?"

"Exactly."

Was she saying they needed to be boyfriend/girlfriend? He swallowed hard and rubbed the back of his neck.

"I don't think that's such a good idea. Emily won't understand."

"You know, she's not right for you." Cat had a satisfied look on her face until she leaned toward him, kissing him softly on the lips. "Now was that so bad?"

Nick pulled away and licked his lips where they had touched. Cat's kiss was so different from kissing Emily. He shifted. He liked kissing Cat, and his body betrayed him by moving fractionally closer.

Cat ran her tongue over her lower lip. It glistened, and Nick couldn't help being mesmerized by her actions. It was as if an alien had taken over his body, making him want Cat.

He leaned over, his hands on the silk of her blouse, feeling the place where her ribs met her waist, and moved in for another kiss when her teeth bit his bottom lip, kneading gently at first, then harder. His head screamed "no!" but his heart quickened, and he grasped her waist, their lips locked in a battle of biting and kissing.

After a long minute, they jerked away from each other. Nick felt his bruised lips and tasted blood.

"What are you feeling?" she asked, touching her bottom lip with her forefinger.

He remembered lying with Chaton in the blackberry bushes, crushing them with their bodies as they lay entwined with each other. He smelled berries now.

Nick's heart beat rapidly, sending throbs to his temples.

"Do you want to kiss me again?" she asked playfully, quirking a brow at him.

He wanted to.

"No." He swallowed back a lump. "This isn't a good idea. I have a girlfriend." *After all, Emily was his girlfriend, not Cat.*

Chapter 39

It was decided Louis and I would set out for Lyon where we would pass Chaton's camp, and the sounds our horses made would alert anyone to our presence. I prayed they would stay hidden until we passed while searching for other Gypsies to round up. My throat was filled with a lump that threatened to erupt at the thought of what we were about to do. I swallowed repeatedly to keep the growing nausea at bay.

We talked of unimportant things as we rode, the food—all slop—the uncomfortable cots, and the endless schooling on things we would never need to know.

I held my breath when we approached the place where Chaton and her family were camped. The only sounds were the whisper of the leaves against the wind. All was still in the forest. I held my breath as we passed, but nothing gave them away. If Louis knew they were hidden in the forest, he made no gesture, and his position on the horse didn't change.

As soon as we were down the road many meters, I let out my breath. The other Gypsy encampments weren't hard to find. Some wagons had pulled off to the side of the road to rest. We rode up to them, pointed, remained mounted, and commanded the Gypsies follow us.

"Come with us!" I saw some of the men and boys slip away, but I didn't get off my horse to go after them.

I didn't want to run through brambles and bushes in a place my horse couldn't go. We let them escape and contented ourselves with the women, children, and the old Gypsies. If they recognized me, they made no indication. I felt ashamed making the Gypsies walk back to town to be imprisoned in the cold, ramshackle barracks.

When we returned with our prisoners, the commander looked over the Gypsies. The prisoners' eyes were blank, but others showed their distrust and hatred, eyes rimmed with red and noses flaring.

"Well done. Is this all?"

"Oui, the rest have left the area," I said.

The lieutenant didn't look convinced of my declaration as guards dragged the prisoners behind the fence into the barracks as we rode back to the stable to care for our mounts.

"Dreadful business," Louis said. "Just old women and children. Bah! My own grandmother could have done that."

I remained quiet, my mind working on how to get Chaton's family to the limestone cave by the Loire without attracting attention. I would have to guide them one at a time along the narrow path to the cave. I hoped I would have enough time to get them all hidden away.

****

Later during the thick, velvet curtain of night, after the cadets were bedding down for the evening, I lay still and quiet on my cot, feigning sleep, listening for any sound besides the scampering of mouse feet and the creaking of the cots as someone shifted.

At last, I heard the church tower chime the

midnight hour, and eased off my cot and crept toward the latrines. I had hidden clothes in the cupboard in preparation for leaving. I dressed and left.

I saw their huddled forms against the dark backdrop of the city, mainly quiet at this hour. An occasional light showed, filtered through the trees and other buildings. A lonely dog barked at the moon.

"Come," I said softly, looking around for any unusual sounds or activities, but all was calm. "One at a time."

"I'll go first," Chaton's father whispered.

They each carried a bundle of clothing and food.

I guided him along the narrow expanse between the water and the cliffs, toward the farthest cave.

When we arrived, I pushed aside the brush hiding the opening and motioned for Chaton's father to follow me inside. Once inside, Chaton's father produced a candle and lit it so light danced over the walls.

"Bah! Such a smell," Chaton's father said.

I remembered the peculiar vinegar and eggs smells of the caves from my youth. Not a pleasant place to stay, but Chaton's family would be safe here, if they could endure the odor.

I left Chaton's father in the cave and went back to guide the rest.

"What is that horrible smell?" Chaton whispered when she arrived, waving her hand under her nose to dissipate the odor.

"Limestone," I whispered.

Chaton looked around and touched the walls as she circled. Her shadow moved in and out of the candlelight flicker. "We can make do here, Mama?"

Her mother, a silent woman, shook her head and

placed her bundle on the floor.

Good, *I thought,* they would be safe. *"I will come when I can and bring food."*

They had bread, hard cheese, apples, and other assorted bundles of food.

"I must go," I said after hearing the bell toll three o'clock, and eased toward the entrance.

"Thank you, Jean Claude," Chaton said, following me to the entrance. She reached up and gave me a kiss, whispery and delicate, before I slipped through the opening and replaced the brush covering before creeping back to school. The townspeople were wrong about the Gypsies. They weren't the rumored wicked, bad people whispered about in the village. My hand had healed with the balm from Chaton's mother. The Gypsies chose to live their life differently. But was different bad and evil?

Chapter 40

Nick's father had frowned when he returned from Cat's and went upstairs, calling, "Hey! You want to finish watching the game?"

"Can't," he mumbled. "Homework!"

Nick spent the rest of the night sitting at the desk in his bedroom. The lamp glowed on the wood. He traced the circle with his fingertip, his mind a jumble of mixed messages—Cat and Emily. Emily and Cat. He wanted both of them. But that wouldn't work. If he chose Emily, he'd always desire Cat. And if he chose Cat, his life would essentially be over—ostracized at school, his parents disappointed, and his sense of self shattered.

He rubbed his fingers over his lips where Cat's had touched him. The tender part where her teeth bit him made him want her more. This wasn't going to be good.

****

On Monday morning, Nick studied himself in the mirror after his shower. He wiped away the steam and leaned closer, examining his lips. Thinking about kissing her made his hairline sweat, and he had the urge to loosen his collar. Kissing her was so totally different than kissing Emily. His stomach felt a little nauseous. Maybe he should stay home? No, better to act as if nothing happened between him and Cat.

When he arrived, Emily waited by his locker, tapping her foot with a serious, seething look on her face.

What was the problem now?

"You were at *her* house last night!" Emily said, looking at a cluster of her friends standing by their lockers. Veronica nodded to Emily. She turned back to him, folding her arms across her chest. "I think we need a break."

"A break?"

"Breakup," Emily said loudly. "Over."

"Will you let me explain?" Nick stood with his outstretched arms.

"I think your actions speak louder than words." And with that, Emily stomped away, joining her friends who shot Nick dagger eyes and smirks.

"No! You're wrong!" he called after her.

She didn't turn or acknowledge him.

He stood by his locker, shifting feet, not sure what to do until Gary came over.

"Dude!" He gave his customary whistle-tweet. "What's wrong?" Gary followed Nick's gaze to Emily and her friends. "Oh!"

"Yeah," Nick said, looking at the floor. "She broke up with me."

"What?" Gary looked genuinely surprised. "Why?"

"You know why."

Gary shot him a concerned look. "Cat?"

"We haven't done anything." Sure, they kissed. "We're partners; I need to work with her. That doesn't mean I want to date her!" He hoped his loud voice would be overhead by Emily and her posse.

Gary gave Nick a pat on the back. "Women."

He'd have to figure this part of his life out after their research paper and presentation was finished.

****

Coach had written PRESENTATIONS on the board, and people started to panic. Several groaned. Voices were raised as students looked through their notes.

"Hey!" Coach yelled. "I need quiet!" When everything was calmer, he continued, "Can everyone be finished by next week?" Coach asked.

Nick looked at Cat, who hastily wrote something on a slip of paper. *Why don't you come over to my house tonight?*

Why? He wrote back.

To finish.

What?

She smiled at him and mouthed, "Our paper, of course."

He leaned toward her and whispered, "I've got practice after school."

"Anytime you want to come," she said softly.

After football practice and clearing it with his parents, he drove to Cat's house.

He was starving and now wished he would have stopped for a burger.

"Hungry?" Cat asked.

His stomach gurgled in reply, and she laughed.

"I picked up a pizza. Half pepperoni and half supreme. Will that suit you?"

"Sounds great." He set down his notebook and paper while Cat put the pizza and plates on the table.

As they ate, Nick looked over his portion of the paper and, when finished, shrugged. "I think this is as good as it gets."

"I agree," Cat said.

"Then I guess we're finished," Nick said. He wiped his mouth on a napkin. "I'll send you my part, and you can paste it into yours."

She nodded.

"Thanks for the pizza." He started to rise. "I should probably go."

"No, stay. I'd like you to stay for a while."

"I've got homework." Nick hovered between sitting down again and standing. Calculus beckoned, but his heart hammered at the thought of kissing Cat again.

"I've got homework for you too," she said playfully.

What the heck?

He sat down. "What kind of homework?" he asked, not understanding her meaning.

"You'll like what I have in mind. We're going to make Jean Claude go away."

She got out of her chair and sat on his lap and put her arms around his shoulders. "Is this so bad?"

Nick's heart roared in his ears. *He'd be lying if he didn't agree with her. His whole being was aware of her body on his, sending little shocks through his being.*

"How about this?" She bent and kissed him, not the playful, flirty kiss when he arrived. This kiss was long and slow, with him drinking in her breath. Gradually their mouths opened, and they explored with tongues, and Nick found his hands around her waist, holding her close.

"Are…Are we alone?" he asked, pulling back from her.

"Worried my parents will see us?" When he didn't respond, she continued. "No, they're working late. It's just you and me."

Nick swallowed slowly.

"Do you want to sit on the couch and watch television?" Cat got up and patted him on the shoulder.

"Sure." Nick felt relieved. "But I can't stay long. I have a mountain of Calculus to finish."

She took his hand and led him to the L-shaped couch where they sat close together, and she put her head on his shoulder.

This was so totally different than when he was with Emily. He knew he shouldn't compare the two girls—they were so opposite. He turned toward Cat and put his hands in her hair and drew her face to his for another kiss.

"Does she do this to you?" Cat whispered.

"Umm."

"Is that a yes? Or no?" She started kissing his neck, sucking on his skin.

"No, no, she doesn't."

Cat pulled away and laughed. "I told you."

Nick felt like he had been kicked in the stomach. He wanted all of Cat, every ounce, yet he wanted Emily too.

Reluctantly, he pulled away from Cat. "I've got to go," he said softly. "I wish I could stay, but I can't. I'm cheating Emily."

"Oh, I thought you broke up?"

"I guess."

"But you're not cheating on her. We were together before her. If anything, you're cheating on me—on us."

Nick looked at her in the dark, the lights low, making her features shadowy and vague. If he stayed, they would do something he may or may not regret.

Chapter 41

Nick's parents were still up and watching television in the living room when he returned from Cat's. "Did you finish your report?" his father asked, muting the sound.

"We're mostly done, but I've got other homework to finish." He turned toward the stairs.

"You're putting in a lot of extra hours with this report," his father called. "I can't wait to read it when you're done."

He turned back toward them and shrugged. "I hope it gets us an A."

"Grandma would like you to stop by," his mom mentioned.

He felt pulled in so many directions. Pleasing Cat. Getting Emily back. World History. Football. Grades. His head felt as if it would swirl away.

"I'll swing by after practice tomorrow night," he promised, his foot hesitating on the first step.

"She'll like that." His mom smiled.

"Good night, son." His dad waved, taking remote and unmuting the TV.

He took the steps two at a time and went into the bathroom to examine the mark on his neck. He looked closely, and he figured he could pass it off as a scratch. It was faint, and maybe no one would notice. He'd deal with it in the morning and maybe dab on some of his mother's makeup. Reluctantly with a yawn, he opened his calculus book and began his homework.

****

The next morning, he went directly to Emily's locker. "I want to apologize for anything I did that made you think I wanted us to break up."

She studied him for sincerity, looking at him from underneath her bangs. "I don't want you to be friends with her." Emily's demeanor suddenly changed, her eyes angry, asking, "What is that?" She pointed to his neck.

"What?" He reached for his neck. Emily knew. His hand remained frozen in midair. The concealer must have rubbed off. "Nothing, just a scratch."

"Is that from her?"

Emily deserved an answer, but he took the cowardly way out and remained quiet.

Emily shot him a scathing look. "We're over!" She slammed her locker shut. "So over!" she shouted before turning on the balls of her feet and running toward her group of friends huddled down the hallway.

Nick stood rooted. Students flowed around him like water in a rushing stream. Some shot him looks of concern, several smirks, and a burst of laughter from Bryan. Only Gary stopped and clasped him on the shoulders.

Gary whistled. "That was rough!"

"You're telling me!" Nick rubbed at his neck; it seemed to burn under his touch. "I guess I blew it."

"Give her time," Gary said.

Nick wasn't sure time would heal these wounds, but he didn't know if he could ever go back to the status quo. The façade in his perfect life had further split apart.

In World History, Cat frowned when he came in, her eyes following him as he entered the room and sat by her side. They remained quiet. Only their eyes locked together. Nick thought his future was reflected in her eyes—a different outcome than he had imagined, but he was powerless to stop the forces pushing him forward.

****

After football practice and a text from his mother prompting him to visit the rehab hospital, Nick drove the thirty minutes to visit his grandmother. Every time he saw her, she looked better, and her face didn't sag as much, and she was able to get in and out of bed on her own.

"Nick! So glad to see you!" She was always thrilled when he visited.

He leaned over the bed and kissed her cheek. She smelled the same: lilac powder and a hint of peppermint.

"What's that on your neck?" she demanded.

"I scratched myself."

"Is that—" She paused. "—a hickey? Did Emily give you a hickey?"

"It's not a hickey, Grandma. I scratched myself."

"Sure." She continued to look at him and cleared her throat. "Have you read all of your grandfather's journal yet?"

"Not all of it, but what I've read…Believe me, I'm glad he fought that war."

"You speak as if you know?" She tilted her head to study him.

He dreamed of rounding up innocent people to be

imprisoned. "Well…" he said slowly. "We're studying it in class, and it seems real." He let out his breath when Grandma appeared to accept his explanation, although her eyes remained skeptical. What else could she think?

Chapter 42

I needed to find food, or Chaton and her family would starve. My attention was divided by the reports the Nazis were advancing on Paris and where to get food. We were worried and hopeful that we might get a chance to fight. I wanted to join my father in the underground, but I didn't know where he was exactly. All I could do was worry and think of the possibilities.

Chaton and her family had been hidden in the cave for three days. I needed some way to get into the school's kitchens and the storerooms—both secured with formidable padlocks.

I had found a nail in the stables and hoped I could use it to unlock the door to the kitchens. At the stroke of midnight, I eased out of my bed, making only the faintest of creaking sounds as I stood, surveyed the sleeping boys, and exited.

I held my breath as I worked the nail around the lock and then heard the soft, almost imperceptible click. The door creaked in protest but swung open. I stopped, held my breath, and listened for footsteps. Nothing. Only after making sure I hadn't been heard, I stepped into the kitchen and took a loaf of bread from the table, and meat, cheese, and a bowl of grapes from the icebox.

I found a sack and filled it with foodstuffs, closed the door, and carefully relocked the door and slipped into the night.

I heard a footfall and stopped. Was it my footsteps or beating heart? Or was someone following? I remained quiet for what seemed an eternity, but perhaps only five minutes, before easing away from the shadow of the school and down the lane that led past the village to the river.

I heard it again. There was no mistaking it this time. A twig snapped, and a branch rustled. Someone was following me.

I eased the sack down and waited by a tree. My heart thudded in my chest. Someone moved down the lane, slow but deliberate.

"You there!" The voice came from the darkness. "Announce yourself!"

I recognized that voice, swallowed, and considered what to do. I was trapped and couldn't stand here until morning, so in a hoarse voice called out, "Jean Claude!"

"Jean Claude!" came the deep voice. "Where are you going?" My lieutenant.

"Into town."

My fox-faced lieutenant stepped around the foliage to face me. "What is in the sack?"

"Food for my maman.*" The lie came easily and quickly.*

"Your maman?"

"Oui, she is housing a Gypsy child, and my father is off fighting. She needs food."

"We shall see," the lieutenant said. "Pick up the sack and follow me!" He led me back to the school and blew his whistle, signaling all the others to rise from their cots and join us in the great room. The other

cadets came slowly into the room, some hastily dressed in their uniforms, some still in their sleeping clothes, all looking bleary-eyed and yawning. Grumbling and whispers. "Is it the Germans?" "What hour is this?" "I'm still asleep."

"I have called you here on account of Cadet Jean Claude Rousseau who has been caught stealing our food for his mother and a Gypsy child." He let his words sink in to the sleep-confused boys. "Should he be punished?"

"Locked up!"

"Beaten!"

"He should be forced to clean the kitchen!"

"I will leave him to you to do as you please," the lieutenant said before turning and marching away. The cadets surrounded me.

"Please," I begged. "I will put the food back." I scanned the faces, searching for Louis. He must be absent or hidden in the back. "My maman is all alone, and she has an extra mouth to feed!"

Before I could say more, a punch to my gut doubled me over. Then another. And one to my jaw made me see stars before collapsing on the floor. I saw a boot raised to kick my ribs. I closed my eyes. A boom sounded from across the river. The boot grazed me but didn't do any serious damage as I lay on the floor panting.

"What was that?" one of the cadets asked.

"Is it the Nazis?"

"I heard they're coming!"

"My God!"

I was thankful they had forgotten about me as another boom shook the school. The boys stepped away—no longer worried about the stolen food.

The lieutenant ran back. "The Nazis have overtaken Paris and are marching this way!"

I listened as my fellow cadets went back to our sleeping quarters. When all was quiet, I crept back to my cot. I stared unseeing into the dark, worrying about the advancing Germans, Chaton and her family, my mother and Adella. These thoughts and my aching ribs crowded away sleep. I dozed a bit before being shaken awake.

"Up! You lazy lout. You are to wash dishes!"

I was led into the kitchen and faced a towering pile of bowls and pots used for the morning meal. My penitence for stealing the food.

"You will clean everything," the fat cook advised.

My stomach rumbled. Even bruised and sore, I was hungry and hadn't eaten since the night before.

I looked into a huge pot crusted with oatmeal, cooked black on the sides. "This will take forever!" I grumbled.

The cook grinned.

"Shouldn't we be preparing to defend Saumur?" I stammered.

"Non! You are to clean it all!"

At least the kitchen window allowed me a view of the practice arena. I could watch my fellow cadets preparing the horses. "What are they doing?" I asked the cook.

He grunted. "They're taking the horses to a safer place." He put his fists to his hips and roared, "Get busy!"

When I put my hands in the hot soapy water, my fingers felt numb and stretched like sausage casings.

After making a dent in the towering dishes, I looked up from washing to see there was some sort of commotion with cadets milling around. I couldn't tell from this distance what it was about. Then soldiers led a group of people through the arena at gunpoint. I frowned. Was that Chaton's family? Her colorful skirt was the only brightness on this dull, gray day. I leaned forward for a better look and, in the process, dropped a plate. It shattered into a million pieces that skittered across the stone floor.

The cook yelled, "Lout. Imbecile. Stupid boy!"

I hurriedly put the broken china in the refuse container, and when I turned back to the window, her family was gone.

I finished the dishes. The cook pointed to a small room next to the kitchen. I frowned, not understanding, until he closed the door after me and turned the key. I was locked up.

Chapter 43

Presentations for World History research projects started today. Nick thought back to how it all began and the events that unfolded since that first day, when Cat had told him he had lived another life during WWII.

Now as they sat in the cafeteria, Gary grumbled about his paper. "I'll be glad to have this behind me," Gary said, looking into his protein drink, swirling it around in the bottle and taking a swallow. "Maybe I need a cinnamon roll to keep my strength up!"

Tiffany rolled her eyes. Nick snuck a glance past Tiffany to where Emily sat with her friends. He caught her looking his way, but she quickly averted her eyes. He sighed and looked at Gary, who was hurrying toward the cashier to purchase a cinnamon roll. He got up, smoothed down his jeans, and went to Emily's table.

"Can I talk to you?"

She seemed to be debating talking to him, before standing and walking to where he stood. "What do you want?" She folded her arms.

"Presentations start today."

"I know that!" she huffed.

"What I was going to say is that when we're finished, there won't be any reason for Cat to talk to me."

Emily rocked back on her heels and peeked at him

from under her bangs. "Let me think about it."

"Why do you have to think about us?"

"You've changed this year," she said, pushing up her glasses that had slipped down her nose.

"Maybe a bit," he said softly and longed to give her a hug, but he kept his arms pinned to his sides.

****

"Listen up." Coach began class by announcing, "I'll first take volunteers to present your research. Do I have any takers? Extra points for the first two presentations."

Nick's and Bryan's hands shot up at the same time. "Nick and Catherine first and then Bryan and Sam." Nick shot Bryan a smirk, and Bryan gave him a shit-eating grin. They'd see who the better student was.

Coach Sullivan had placed two desks at the front of the room and made a laptop available for PowerPoint presentations and an easel for displays or pictures.

He and Cat had none of those things. They would talk through their presentation. Cat on the historical background of the Gypsies, their internment, and Nick telling about the other significant events happening in Saumur at the same time, namely the cadets at the Cadre Noir fighting the Germans. He smoothed down their paper. He had highlighted the important parts so he wouldn't forget anything.

They took their places at the front of the class. Cat, wearing her customary black leotard, with bright rainbow leg warmers and ballet slip-ons. And Nick wearing his jersey and jeans. He shuffled his sneakers against the floor—anxious to get started and be done and get back to his life before their research presentations.

Cat began, "Our presentation is on the treatment of the Romas—better known as Gypsies—during the Second World War. I've been to France many times and learned of their hardships during the war, so now I'm going to give you a brief overview of their lives before, during, and after the war. Nick will talk about their treatment, particularly in the internment camp in Saumur, France, and how the war affected all the French people."

She paused before continuing. Everyone leaned forward, waiting. "Gypsies are a nomadic tribe of people who originated in India a thousand years ago. They believed the land belonged to everyone for everyone's enjoyment and benefit. But the other Europeans believed landownership was important for stature, so the Gypsies were viewed as strange, backward thinkers. Still are. There is a long history of persecuting the Gypsies in Europe."

Cat stopped for a breath, not once looking at her notes or their paper. "The Gypsies are now protected under the Equality Act in Europe. Many work as artisans and entertainers. But during the war years, they were rounded up with the Jews and others the Germans targeted for their eradication campaign."

Cat's voice, low and calm, had a mesmerizing effect on the classroom. Nick noticed his classmates leaning forward in their seats to listen and look at Cat. She was a beautiful girl—in an exotic way—a dancer when most girls in their class wore jeans and cowboy boots, not leggings and leotards.

She continued talking, stopping only to take a sip of her water. Since she was sitting next to him, he could only see her hands. They stretched and clenched as she

257

talked, accented by her bloodred polish.

"Even though the war wiped out over a million Gypsies, there are many famous Gypsies you may have heard of—Charlie Chaplin and Mother Teresa."

Nick saw a few brows go up in surprise.

She continued, "Ever heard of Elvis Presley and Pablo Picasso? They had Roma blood." Cat finished talking, and now it was time for his part. He mentally gathered what he wanted to say, glanced down at the highlighted parts.

Before he could speak, the fire alarm sounded.

"Everyone to the soccer field," Coach said.

Nick and Cat followed the class and others out the building. In some ways he was relieved to be interrupted, but it would make it so he needed to finish their presentation later.

Coach clasped him on the shoulder as they left the building. "Sorry about that. You may have to finish tomorrow."

Nick rubbed his arms and stamped his feet as they waited for the all-clear signal. Cat slipped on her headphones and began moving her body. The class stopped to watch her, and soon they were joined by others.

Nick spied Emily and Veronica. When Emily saw him looking at her, she turned away. Nick continued watching Cat as she swayed and moved her arms up over her head and then bent at the waist.

The bell sounded, but still the crowd watched her dance. With a final flourish kick of her legs and overhead motion of her arms, she stopped, and several people clapped.

Nick watched her take off her headphones and dip

her head to those still watching.

"You're good," Nick whispered.

"Thank you. I've always loved dancing."

Chapter 44

Louis slipped me a bundle wrapped in newsprint. I frowned at him in the dim light of the storeroom, my prison, but he dipped his chin, indicating I should open it.

Bread and cheese wrapped in an English and French newspaper.

I bent over it expectantly, wanting to know what was happening.

"The Nazis are ensconced in Paris," Louis said.

"What are we going to do?" I asked. "Will we fight?"

And as if on cue, the boom of an artillery shell burst in the distance, rattling the panes in the upper window.

Louis pointed in the direction of the sound. "The Germans."

They were close and advancing.

"What are we to do?" I whispered.

"There is talk of us organizing to help protect the town. But we have no real leadership!" Louis cried.

"So true," I agreed, rubbing my red and water-roughened hands. I perused the papers. The Vichy government had called a truce, but the Nazis marched across the truce and into France.

"So we're to fight?" My stomach tightened from anticipation, fear, and gnawing hunger.

"The commander is in favor of fighting the Germans."

"The students will fight?" My mind went to the antiquated armaments they used in their ceremonial performances. Hardly any resistance to Hitler's advanced methods.

"Oui. We are the only ones left except for some of the old guard."

Louis stood taller as he talked. "We know military tactics."

I thought about the tactics I knew. Use familiar terrain to evade and study the enemy, shoot behind cover, and hide again. Non, I didn't know any tactics, but nodded anyway. I had carried a gun, but it was as ancient as my grandfather who used a similar weapon during the Great War.

"We will need better weapons," I said.

"Très bien. The German Panzers are coming."

Mon Dieu, *we would need the dear Lord and Savior on our side if the Panzers were stalking toward our village. I crossed myself.*

Louis eased toward the door. "I must go now. I will try to come later."

"Oui, merci."

The door closed and locked behind Louis.

I sighed before unfolding and smoothing the newsprint, one in French and another in English. I read the French insert to the Pariser Zeitung, *at least two days old, with news of the gaiety in Paris for the occupying Germans. Was this a way of assuring the French citizens all was right?*

I took a hunk of bread and chewed thoughtfully, avoiding the cut side of my mouth. My stomach was hollow and gurgling for food. I willed myself to chew slowly and carefully.

I turned back to the newsprint. The insert included anti-British cartoons, anti-Semitic and anti-communist views. A propaganda-laced newspaper written by the Germans to be read by the occupied French. All nonsense, and I pushed the paper aside, the newsprint only good for wrapping bread in.

The other newspaper was in English, and I knew English. The Times was many days old but hinted at Churchill's visit to Paris. Had Churchill come to Paris?

I stretched and stamped my feet. I hated being confined this way. There was a war to be fought, and of course, I needed a way to rescue Chaton and her family. Had they been imprisoned?

Perhaps a war would add to the mayhem, and I could slip in and rescue them while others were fighting. Then I could return to the fight. I itched to take aim at the Germans.

While I waited for someone to rescue me, I leaned against the cold stone of the wall with my shoulder and ate more bread and smoky hard cheese, wondering what would happen to me for stealing food. Would my mother hear of my betrayal? Or worse, the news get to my father?

Later I heard high, excited voices beyond the wall. I crept to the door and pressed my ear against the wood. I didn't recognize any one voice, but the excitement was mounting for their service to the French and the Saumur valley. "Vive la France!" "German swine."

How long would they keep me locked up? The

voices faded down the hall; I was alone, and all was silent again.

I went back to eating what was left of the bread and cheese and looked at the grainy picture of Churchill with exiled Charles de Gaulle. De Gaulle was France's true leader and should be leading them. Instead they were governed by Pétain's spineless Vichy government.

A boom shook the building. Chunks of dust rained down from the windowsill. I looked up and watched it settle over the newspaper. To finish reading, I used my forearm to sweep it away.

De Gaulle was separated from the war, locked away from all the activity too. I pounded my fist on the table, further disrupting the particles that rose and swirled in the air, my only companions.

Chapter 45

"As you know, we just finished learning about World War II." Nick wiped his sweaty palms on his jeans. "Much of the information centers on the Jews, but there were many more groups targeted. Their stories haven't been told." He lapsed into French. "*Le camp d'internement eSaumur était situé dans la ville de Montreuil-Bellay. Saumur est une région viticole de France située près de la Loire, le plus long fleuve de France.*"

"Hey!" Bryan said. "No fair. We don't know what you're saying."

Nick stopped, feeling his face warm. Damn, he was speaking French. "Sorry," he mumbled, sneaking a look at Cat who had an amused look on her face.

"Anyway, the Saumur internment camp was in the town of Montreuil-Bellay and was once barracks for troops but put back into service to hold the French Jews, Gypsies, and people who were crippled or mentally challenged. Let me back up a bit. The French weren't really interested in fighting the Germans until after the Battle of France. The interesting thing I learned was that the cadets in the horsemanship school mounted a brief resistance against the German Panzers and held them back for several days. Eventually they overtook the cadets. It was like 14,000 soldiers to 700 cadets." He let that fact sink in.

Nick cleared his throat, rubbed his palms against his jeans again, and continued, "Saumur was a small town, but they made an impact on the war. Even Hitler mentioned the cadets' heroic efforts against his elite troops."

Jean Claude peered over the side, and four haunted faces looked up—three tiny and one big. An old woman with three children. What had they done that was so bad? They were Romas only, just people trying to live.

Nick shook away the image. "At the same time the cadets were fighting off the Germans, the people in the internment camp were struggling to survive. The guards used deep holes in the ground to keep people in a sort of prison within a prison. The holes meant slow death for the inhabitants. Often forgotten for weeks at a time, with no toilets, food, or water. Rats and bugs ran rampant. Over a million Gypsies died, perhaps more, but with no known addresses, it was difficult to keep track."

A shock of cold went through Nick, and his nostrils flared at the smell. He took a sip of water to shake away the feelings. Chaton screamed in his brain from her hole in the earth. "*Help me! Help me! We need food! Water!*"

Nick's hands were clammy again, but he kept them firmly in his lap. "The Gypsies were almost hated more than the Jews. They were creative people who lived a carefree life and lived off the land, traveling from place to place. The people in the towns they visited blamed them for all sorts of problems. Even when France was liberated, some of the Gypsies were still kept in camps like Saumur—forgotten people."

Nick stopped and looked at Coach Sullivan, who nodded his approval. "Nice work. Very interesting. Liked the bit of French you threw in. I didn't know you spoke French?"

Nick gave him a sly grin and shrugged his shoulders.

"Questions?"

Several people open their mouths to speak, then thought better of it and clamped their lips shut.

"Why did you pick that topic, Nick? Catherine?" Coach prompted.

"Cat," she said in a staccato, clipped tone.

"Sorry, Cat," Coach said, flapping his hands at them.

"I have Gypsy blood in my veins and was looking for answers about my family." Her voice held a hint of challenge.

He saw several students raise their brows.

"And did you find them?"

"Some answers, yes. But I'm still searching," she said.

They were both searching.

"Thank you. Job well done," Coach said, picking up their paper and placing it on his desk to grade.

Nick eased from the seat, his back and legs numb from the hard chair. He realized he was holding his breath and keeping his body rigid and upright. His whole body thrummed with electricity. Several people looked sideways at them as they passed down the row to their seats in the back.

Nick sank into his desk and wiped his sweaty palms on his jeans again. He let out a ragged breath, happy to have that over with. Would the dreams stop now?

Chapter 46

The door of the locked room creaked open, jerking me awake.

"Jean Claude, you are needed!" came Louis's urgent whisper.

"What—What did you say?" Momentarily the light from the hallway blinded me.

"Everyone must fight the Germans. Even the janitor."

I got up, using the wall for support. In the hallway, running feet and high-pitched, excited voices echoed off the walls, punctuated by the low booms of artillery at a distance. I would get a chance to fight and redeem myself.

I followed Louis from the room to the hall filled with milling cadets and the clang of doors. I smelled smoke and sweat as I pushed toward my cot and locker in the sleeping quarters for a clean uniform.

I would fight with distinction and honor. Make my parents proud. I would fight and then rescue Chaton and be a hero in her eyes as well.

I dressed quickly, my fingers having trouble with the buttons. "Damn!"

"Hurry. The colonel is to give us his orders." Louis pushed one of the buttons into place for me.

"Merci!" The colonel? We never saw the man, only the lieutenant. I smoothed down the front of my tunic,

followed the other cadets to the great hall, and stood in my assigned place, one row back from the lieutenant and the colonel. The lieutenant's black eyes swept over the boys, resting on me for a moment before going on. His eyes had flickered. He knew I was there and didn't care.

Hurry, *I urged silently.*

The colonel wasn't to be hurried. I hadn't had any dealings with the man with the small mustache, hooded eyes, and a long face, but the colonel had an illustrious career in the French army. He was the colonel over all the commanders and teachers at the cavalry school.

"When will we fight?" came an excited voice in the back.

Colonel Michon frowned. "We will begin when we are ready. Anything done in haste is a waste!" he announced. That silenced the nervous undertones as we waited for his next words.

"Our strategy is to stop them from crossing the bridges." A map of France rested on a tripod next to him. "There are many bridges over the Loire, and we must clear the refugees from them and then blow them up before the Germans can cross." He pointed to each bridge on the map.

I had crossed all the bridges many times in my life and thought back to the Loire, low at this time of year. The summer heat had evaporated the water, so it moved slowly through the valley, a sluggish serpent, its banks exposed but slippery. The Germans would be hindered by their artillery, but they would be able to walk across if the cadets couldn't hold them back.

"Follow your commanders' orders, and we will first help the refugees leave. There is a logjam of

people with all sorts of vehicles trying to cross the bridges, and we must move them away from where we will be fighting. We will fight the Germans. It is our honor!" He raised a fist in the air.

We were dismissed, and Louis and I were assigned to the bridge from Les Rosiers.

The area on and around the bridge was clogged in chaos—cars, trucks, horses, and carts, all struggling to get over the bridge, being pushed by the vehicles from behind. The air hung heavy with petrol fumes, horse manure, smoke, and river debris. The line of cars, wagons, and pushcarts waiting to cross was limitless.

And to add to the problems, a truck was stalled in the middle of the bridge.

"We must push that truck out of the way," I said, nudging Louis.

We took our places behind the truck and heaved with all our might, and the truck inched forward. Soon we were joined by others and pushed the truck off the bridge.

I motioned impatiently for the waiting vehicles to come forward.

"You must hurry. The Germans are coming. Hurry," I urged each one.

Horns honked as if to emphasize the point.

"Hurry. We don't have much time." I nodded to former neighbors and townsfolk. Petre and his family, their car overflowing with suitcases, fruits, and vegetables, drove across the bridge. He handed me an apple.

"Merci."

I kept waving the vehicles forward until my arm and shoulder were stiff from the repetitive motion. The next vehicle was a familiar green sedan. *"Maman!"* I was happy to see my mother leaving. Her head was covered in a somber scarf. She drove grimly, her mouth in a line, clenching the steering wheel, knuckles white.

She turned to me. *"My dear boy! We are leaving, going to the country to room with cousin Helga."*

"Oui. Very good."

Adella sat primly in the front seat, wearing a floral dress with a smock to keep it clean.

I whispered to her. *"I will rescue your family."*

Adella's eyes flickered in acknowledgement.

"I did not hear what you said, Jean Claude," my mother said.

"Safe journeys, and my love to cousin Helga."

"Please be careful!" my mother admonished, before reaching out to touch my sleeve and giving me a fearful look.

I handed my mother the apple and waved them through. The big car rumbled over the bridge and disappeared around the corner, and I was glad they were going someplace safer.

Soon a truck loaded with suitcases, a barking dog, a sewing machine, and bolts of materials came toward me. Gretchen, her tailor and seamstress parents, and little brother were fleeing.

"Bonjour!"

I bent down and peered at the four people crammed in the front of the truck. *"Jean Claude,"* Gretchen said, leaning around her little brother to see me. *"We are leaving for the country! Will you be safe?"*

"I'm doing my part," I said with a shrug. Inside my heart thumped against my ribs.

"Be well. Be safe," Gretchen's mother called.
I nodded as the truck rumbled over the bridge and was gone. I waved the next vehicle through.

Chapter 47

At practice, Coach pulled Nick aside. "The Michigan scout is coming Friday night." He folded his arms. "I'm concerned."

Him too, but Nick stammered, "W-Why?"

"I don't think you're ready." As he talked, he patted Nick's shoulder. "There's something different about you this year."

"It's been pretty stressful." He lowered his gaze to study the ground and his scuffed cleats.

"How so?"

"My grandma in the hospital, and Em and I broke up."

"I'm sorry to hear that." Coach patted his shoulder again. "How about I work with you individually after practice?"

"That would be great." His words sounded enthusiastic, but inside his heart sank. Football had been relegated to the end of the line in his life. It had always been football, football, football, but now his identity was foremost.

"Bryan! Can you stay after to help Nick?" Coach asked.

Bryan grinned. "Sure thing!"

Oh great, not Bryan. Anyone but Bryan. Could he think of an excuse to get out of it? The grandma excuse was getting old.

"Nick's putting in extra time to get ready for the scout," Coach said, motioning for Bryan to throw the ball to Nick. "Throw long!"

Bryan hurled the ball at him, and Nick caught it with an "uumph!"

"Again!" he encouraged. "And I'll run interference."

Coach barred him from the ball and knocked it away when Nick reached for it.

"Visualize, Nick. There will always be someone guarding you from the other team. You need to make sure you're a moving target so you can get to the ball. Let's try it again!"

They practiced over and over until Nick thought he'd collapse from fatigue and sore muscles, and his ribs were tender to the touch.

Coach patted both Bryan and Nick on the back. "Thanks for your help, Bryan."

Nick glared as Bryan answered, "Sure thing, Coach! Always happy to help a fellow athlete."

Nick doubted Bryan wanted to help him; he just wanted to suck up to Coach.

"Football's all about concentration," Coach said when they went back to the locker room to change and go home. "Forget everything else."

****

Nick went home exhausted and starving. He pulled out his phone when it pinged with a text from Cat.

—*I want to see you. Can you come over?*—

—*Can't. Homework*— Nick responded.

—*Don't you want to see me?*—

Of course he wanted to see her, so he responded with:

Cat-astrophic

—Big scout coming to the game on Friday. Tomorrow?—
—K—

Chapter 48

Nick twisted and turned in bed, trying to get comfortable with his ribs. At last sleep came.

I joined the other cadets milling the hallways, excited voices talking about how they will fight the Germans. The lieutenant came toward me. "You will accompany me everywhere! You are not to be trusted. You are a thief!"

I knew it was no use arguing. I swallowed my pride and waited.

"Come!" the lieutenant ordered. "We have new Gypsy prisoners to attend to."

I followed him and a handful of other cadets to the Saumur internment camp. Since the first roundup, the camp had filled steadily. A dark stench hung over the buildings. I felt the bile rising from my stomach and willed the nausea to go away.

"Filth!" the lieutenant said under his breath but loud enough for me to hear.

We stepped through the huge entrance gate and surveyed the inhabitants—all dirty and ragged. Children, old women, a man with one leg, a boy who slobbered and rocked himself in a corner, a rabbi with a long beard and dirty robes, and Chaton's father. I let out a gasp, and the lieutenant looked at me sharply. I added a cough, but the lieutenant saw my reaction. Was Chaton here too?

"You are to punish that man." He held out his hand toward Chaton's father.

"How?" I choked.

"Punish him as you were punished for your thievery."

Punches and blows. I remained where I was, my arms hanging limply at my sides. Then the lieutenant shoved me toward Chaton's father. I had so many questions for him, but first I must slap and punish him. I took a ragged breath, looked around at the cadets and the lieutenant waiting, and swung my fist, hitting her father in the stomach.

He replied with a grunt but nothing else.

"More!" the lieutenant said.

"Say something!" I begged. "Please!"

Chaton's father's eyes were slits of blackness.

With a sob, I hit him in the face next. The angles of the man's cheeks and nose bruised my hand, and I wanted to suck on my smarting knuckles. The man didn't make a sound as blood flowed from his nose, dripping onto his already dirty tunic.

"More!"

"I can't!"

"I said more!" the lieutenant roared.

I swung my left fist in a feeble attempt to hit him under the chin. He reeled back but still made no sound.

"Make him ask for mercy!"

"He'll never ask for mercy!" I shouted. "Don't you see!"

"You are a coward and a thief!" the lieutenant said.

No, I wasn't a coward or a thief.

Chaton, her mother, aunt, and grandmother were

pushed into the camp.

"Non!" Chaton's father finally yelled. "No more!"

Satisfied, the fox-faced lieutenant stepped back.

"You are done, cadet. Now I wish to take a stroll around."

"Can I not wash my bloody knuckles first?"

"You may not!"

I followed wearily behind him. The lieutenant strode around the camp, staying away from the people, but looking in the dim cold barracks before pushing over a pot on the fire, spilling the contents into the dirt—vegetables and a thin broth.

"Clean that up!" he commanded to the old women, waiting and watching.

The women fell on the food, eating and scraping away the vegetables, putting some in pockets for later.

They passed a large metal grate on the ground. The lieutenant stopped and kicked at the side. "You there!"

I peered over the side. Four haunted faces looked up—three tiny and one big.

"Who are they?" I asked with a lump growing in my throat—horrified at what I had seen.

"Does it matter?" He spat on the ground. "Gypsies!"

"They are just people like us!"

The lieutenant turned, his face contorted. "They are not!"

"You're wrong!" I said.

The lieutenant slapped my face. "Shut up!"

We came to another grate that was opened. Before I could stop them, the guards shoved Chaton's mother, aunt, and grandmother into the hole; their cries rose as they hit the bottom with a thud. A guard held Chaton, who struggled toward the hole. I rushed to him and tried to grab Chaton's arm. The lieutenant wrenched me back.

"No!" I screamed.

"In you go, you little hellcat," the guard said as she tried to twist away from him. Her elbow caught him in the ribs, and he doubled over. He straightened and shoved her roughly into the hole.

I doubled over as the gorge burned up my throat.

I coughed and could contain my nausea no longer and threw up on the ground, the splatters streaking the lieutenant's perfectly polished boots.

"Get him out of here!" the lieutenant ordered as a resounding boom filled the air.

"Hurry! No time to waste!" he said to the other cadets. "We must prepare to fight."

The cadets led me to the school and left me there. Louis ran by and beckoned me to follow him.

****

Nick awoke the next morning with a headache and upset stomach. He remembered bits and pieces of his dream. Only the nausea remained. Was he catching something? Maybe he should stay home in bed.

"Mom!"

"Yes?" she called.

"I don't feel very good. I feel like I could puke."

She came into his room while putting on her earrings. "You have been pushing yourself with the extra work on the football field." She came over and placed her hand on his forehead. "You are a bit warm. I'll call the school."

Nick climbed back in bed and closed his eyes.

Would the dream come back?

****

—*Where are you?*— Cat

—*You sick?*— Gary

—*Can you come over?*— Cat

—*No. Sick.*—

He spent the day sleeping, pushing away dreams, and willing his mind to be blank. He was tired of Jean Claude's intrusion. "Go away!" he mumbled. "Leave me alone."

Chapter 49

The buildup to the scout coming to watch the game was taking its toll on Nick's body. His ribs ached, and even with his mouth guard, he had managed to injure the inside of his cheek. Nick crawled out of bed, surveyed his naked, bruised body in the mirror before taking a hot shower and three aspirin.

All this for the Michigan scout who may or may not like what he saw. There was always next year to prove himself.

At football practice, Nick asked the trainer to wrap his ribs.

"What did you do?"

"I think I pulled something."

"I'll wrap you, but you should probably sit out and rest. That's the best thing for bruised anything. Rest. Heat."

"I've been working extra hard to get ready for the scout," Nick said. But that didn't account for all the bruises. He must have run into something and forgotten.

"If you don't take it easy, you'll be in no shape to play." The trainer motioned for Nick to follow him to the office. "Take off your shirt."

The trainer wrapped the adhesive around his ribs.

"Hey!" Bryan burst into the office and stopped when he saw Nick's chest, and then he grinned. "Sorry." He backed out. "I can see you're busy."

"I'll be with you shortly, Bryan," the trainer said.

"That's okay. It can wait," Bryan said, with a quirk of his brow.

During practice, Bryan tackled or pushed Nick every chance he got. Nick gritted his teeth with each impact, only uttering "oomph" once. Even with the tape, his ribs were getting a beating. He leaned over and rubbed them.

"Nick?" Coach Sullivan asked, coming onto the field. "What's wrong?"

"My ribs. I must have done something."

"The trainer said you were black-and-blue." Coach frowned. "How could you forget something like that?"

Nick hung his head. "I dunno."

"Sit out and take a rest." Nick sat on the bench and watched. He wanted to get out on the field and perform, but his ribs ached even with the bandages. He tried concentrating on what the team was doing, but his mind kept going back to Emily and Cat. He knew it wasn't fair, but the differences between them were vast. Cat's kisses aroused him with soda fizzle in his gut. Emily's kisses never caused that tingly feeling, but her kisses were safe and soft, and he liked them too.

Cat was smoke and mirrors, while Emily was real, reliable, and trustworthy. Emily had a solid family and was raised with the all-American girl-makes-good-on-life philosophy. Emily was someone his parents would pick for him. But didn't he get to make that choice?

He knew if he chose Cat, he'd be ostracized, and if he stayed with Emily, he could go on as before. He knew in his head he should pick Emily, but his heart wanted Cat.

When Nick left school, it was already dusk, and

shadows fell over the parking lot. As he got closer to his car, he noticed Cat's Jag. She unfolded her body from her car and stood.

"Hi!" he said. "What's up?"

"Does anything need to be 'up'?" she asked with a quirk of her brow.

"I guess not." Secretly he was happy to see her but swiveled his head to see who else was in the parking lot. Nobody to be worried about.

She gave him a hug, and he winced. "What's the matter?"

"My ribs are killing me."

"Is that something you did at football?"

"I can't remember."

"Do you want to go for a ride? I've got something to tell you."

He was bone-tired and hungry, but the thought of being alone with Cat pushed those ailments aside. "Sure."

"Get in!" She squealed out of the parking lot, and they headed for the main road. "Where to?"

"Get me a burger?"

She laughed and hit the gas. "Coming right up!" Cat slowed as they got to the drive-thru. "Two number ones with cheese," she ordered.

After getting their food, they headed for the beach. There, they ate their burgers and watched the sun slip into Lake Michigan, a puddle of gold before being swallowed into the dark, chilly waters. For the first time today, Nick relaxed into the buttery soft leather of the seats.

He closed his eyes briefly before leaning over and kissing her, then pulled away, studying the shadows and planes of her face, and kissed her again. The fizzing-soda feeling returned, and he wanted more, before shifting in his seat to gather her close and deepen their kiss.

"Do you feel it too?" she whispered.

"I think so." A remembrance on a cellular level of a closeness, holding them together, and a commitment. He didn't know what it meant exactly, only the promise of a union many centuries in the making.

"Me too," she said, kissing him further, running her tongue over his lips, exploring. Another car swung into the lot, momentarily lighting the interior. They pulled apart.

"I guess I should be getting home," Nick said as the other car parked behind them. Their bright lights illuminated the interior of Cat's car.

"I wish they'd turn off those damned lights!" Nick opened the door and got out and shielded his face from the light and walked forward. Nick jumped when Bryan laid on the horn. He shook his head and returned to Cat. "It's Bryan being Bryan."

"What does he want?" she asked.

"Who knows!" He fastened his seat belt. "Trouble."

The lights behind them blinked off. There was no way he was fighting with Bryan tonight. "I should be getting home."

She nodded, put the car in gear, and drove to school so Nick could retrieve his car.

****

Cat wasn't at school the next day but texted:

—*I've got something to tell you.*—

—*Tell me now.*—

—No, in person. Come after school—

When Nick got to Cat's house, he found the hallway filled with boxes. "Are…Are you moving?"

"Yes, for a few months," Cat said, pushing one such box with her foot. "I've been trying to tell you."

"Where will you go?"

"A project my parents need to finish in Oregon."

"Do you have to go?" he asked, clenching and unclenching his fists, suddenly not wanting her to go.

She shrugged. "I have a couple of things I need to do in Oregon."

He nodded. "Can you tell me what they are?"

"No." She studied him. "Are you sleeping?" She touched his cheek.

"Not really."

"You have dark circles under your eyes."

He lifted his shirt and showed her his ribs.

She gasped. "What happened?"

"I dunno. The extra practices with Coach." He shook his head and smoothed his shirt back into place. "I must have done something, but I can't remember." A memory of a kick to the ribs, but that was about it.

Cat's mother came down the hall, carrying a stack of towels. "Why hello, Nick. Pardon our mess."

"You're moving?"

Cat's mother let out her breath. "We regret having to go back to Oregon, but there are some problems we need to fix in our last project."

He nodded and waved an arm over the boxes. "Need any help?"

She smiled and shook her head. "Catherine wouldn't let us leave until after the last football game."

Chapter 50

After all the vehicles had cleared the bridge and an unusual quiet settled over the Loire, we heard the Germans approach. They advanced with thousands of boots marching down the road. In unison—thump, thump, thump—thunder on the ground. They kept coming and coming. I shaded my eyes to see the never-ending line of cars, trucks, tanks, motorcycles, and foot soldiers. The din of so many was deafening. Mon Dieu, *would this end? The frontline Germans stopped at the entrance to the bridge, waiting for the rest of their army to catch up. They didn't hurry and seemed almost nonchalant as they waited, lighting cigarettes and chatting. The bridge would be gone soon.*

Louis and I took up positions at the other entrance to the bridge, blocked from view by the posts supporting the structure. I held an automatic rifle, and Louis had a 3 mm gun. I ran my fingers over the cold black rifle—a relic from the school's museum. Even though ancient, it could and would kill the advancing Panzer soldiers. Could I take aim and kill a man? This was war, but still...I steeled myself. Yes, yes, I could if it meant keeping them out of Saumur.

I stopped admiring the rifle when a person wedged between us.

"Pardon." Another soldier by the smell of smoke, sweat, and blood.

The man, his face covered with bandages, nodded toward the rifle.

"Use mine."

His rifle was newer. I looked over at the intruder's torn and bloody uniform.

The soldier took note of my interest.

"Groupe Franc. I'm making my way back to the front."

"You are hurt?"

"Oui, but I want to fight. To the death if I must. But my sight. My eyes won't focus to fire my weapon."

I studied the man further. His face was covered in bloody bandages, and still he wanted to fight. Would I act the same way if I was in his situation?

"Oui." I turned back to the rows of Germans stretched across the river before taking careful aim at the motorcycle riders, sitting ducks, and firing. At first nothing happened. Had I missed the target? Non, the man slumped over in slow motion as if he were asleep, red spreading across the front of his uniform, a blooming red rose. I had killed a man. I let out a shaky breath.

Next Louis took a chunk from a tank with his hefty gun. Like ants, the Germans scattered for cover, but we cadets kept firing. I aimed again and took out the retreating figures, all the while my stomach protesting and threatening to explode. The Germans returned fire.

"Bien," the stranger said. "Captain de Neucheze would have used your skills." The stranger clasped both our hands in his before disappearing into the trees. He had left his rifle with me.

"I'm running low on ammo," I whispered.

"We must pull back now," Louis said. "They're

going to blow the bridge."

Crouching and scampering away, we took cover behind a large statue of a man on a horse. The base was five meters high. The dynamite exploded, shaking the ground as the bridge burst into flames, spitting debris over the water, the French cadets, and the fleeing Germans. I turned and threw up what little I had into the spindly grass.

I wiped my mouth and wearily sat down as the dust cleared, and all was quiet, all except the beating of my heart. The quiet was more unnerving than the shots and screams.

I sorted through the ammunition. I had about two dozen bullets left.

Next we set up our positions on either side of the statue and began firing over the wrecked bridge into the German soldiers trying to organize back into their lines after the explosion. We were joined by fellow cadets, who rushed toward us and flopped down on the ground, protected by a long-lost general on his iron horse. A few shots pinged off the horse statue, missing the cadets. We all took aim. I pulled the trigger and took out a soldier inching down the muddy bank of the Loire and climbing over the wreckage of the bridge.

"Did you see that?"

Another cadet took aim when German soldiers reached down to haul up their fallen comrade. The three fell upon one another and into the muddy river.

I nodded, my ears still ringing from the blast, before taking aim at a motorcycle's fuel tank. The entire thing blew sky-high, taking out other vehicles and soldiers. Pieces of the bike, trucks, and limp bodies flung through the air.

"Très bien!"

The air hung thick with burning fumes, and my eyes smarted and stung.

I wiped a hand over my eyes and shook my head to stop the ringing. "It's hard to tell the time of day."

"Oui, I think morning still."

My stomach rumbled in protest. It couldn't be helped. We were finally at war, but I needed more ammunition.

"We're going to make a run for it," *one of our cadet companions said.*

"I need more bullets."

"We'll see what we can find." *And with that, a group of cadets left, leaving Louis and me alone again.*

I looked out over what was left of the bridge.

"Do you ever think about dying?" *Louis asked.*

"I can't hear you."

Louis repeated his question.

I couldn't imagine death itself. I wanted to live to be with Chaton again and perhaps run off together to live happily ever after. Her image imprinted on my brain dimmed a bit with each passing hour like the photos of long-lost relatives, the fuzziness overtaking their features and outlines blurred with a brown patina.

"I suppose. You?"

Louis looked at me with a quizzical expression on his face. "Of course! My sainted mother wouldn't have it any other way!" *He gave a short laugh.* "My father finally looked peaceful when he died."

My grandmother had a twisted expression on her face that didn't soften even with her death.

"Do you love your Gypsy girl?" *Louis asked.*

I looked through the rifle's sight as we talked,

waiting for a clear shot, to conserve ammo. I heard his question clearly this time.

"I've seen you sneak away and go to her," Louis said.

"Oui." I looked away from the Germans and over at Louis. The thought of Chaton wrenched my gut further.

Louis took a cigarette from his pocket and lit it, offering it to me. I lowered the rifle and sucked eagerly, the smoke filling my lungs, before handing back the cigarette.

"I think so."

"Why?" Louis asked.

"She is everything I am not."

We sat leaning against the statue, waiting. Neither of us moved until a dozen German soldiers scrambled over the bank, sloshed through the muddy river.

"We should probably go," I said.

The voices from the Germans in their barbed, guttural speech were getting louder and louder as we scrambled away, monkey-style. The Germans had breached the river with or without the bridge. Their armaments crossed downstream where the river flowed weakly, swirling around itself in the shallow muddy currents.

We crawled away from our position past our fellow cadets that had fallen into a heap on the ground. My eyes smarted with tears as I saw their broken and bloody bodies. They had given their lives for freedom. Louis tapped my shoulder for us to continue. He too had tears in his eyes before crossing himself. With weary sighs, we rejoined the others.

Chapter 51

When Nick arrived at his locker on the morning of their last football game, he found Emily there.

"Hi!" He was excited to see her, although he felt a little unsettled about the game tonight.

She gave him a tentative smile. "I wanted to wish you good luck tonight."

Even though they had broken up, Em was supportive.

"Thanks, I appreciate it!" He took a step toward her to give her a hug, but she froze.

She started to say something but clamped her mouth shut as Cat came down the hall. Emily whirled around and hurried away.

"Did I spoil anything?" Cat said with a laugh.

Yes, he thought, but he answered, "No, she was just wishing me luck."

Cat had a pink slip of paper in her hand and fluttered it as she talked. "My checkout instructions."

"You're really leaving?" Nick's breath seemed suspended in his throat.

She shrugged her right shoulder. "I'm used to it. We've lived in four different places in Oregon." She began taking books from her locker.

"Will you keep in touch?" he asked, suddenly worried about her leaving when they had the reincarnation thing hanging over them.

"We don't go for another week, but I need to get packed." She touched his arm. "I'll see you at the game."

He swallowed. "It's been a hell of a year so far."

She laughed. "Sorry for wrecking your life."

Nick grimaced as he considered her words. He certainly wasn't the same person he was at the beginning of the year.

****

Later, Nick looked over the football field where frost had crystallized on the grass, giving it a twinkly, enchanted look. His eyes teared at the brightness.

Coach patted his arm. "You ready to show them what you've got?"

"Ready!" he said with false gusto and rubbed his hands for warmth. His whole body shook with nerves and the chill bite of the wind and Michigan winter. His eyes scanned the bleachers for an unfamiliar face. Would he know who the Michigan scout was? The man with the hat? A woman looking at her telephone? Who could they be? Nick stood as straight as he could and moved his arms, testing the wrapping on his bruised and battered chest.

He certainly needed help to pull this off tonight. He didn't usually pray before a game, but it was worth a shot. "Dear Lord…Help me. I need your guidance tonight…" He inhaled, but it was painful to breathe deeply. The team was running sprints to stay warm on the side of the field. He should be running too, but the cold air and his sore ribs made running hard, and he decided to keep his energy for the game and remained at the sidelines, stomping his feet.

Their opponents were running similar exercises—

the green-and-white Laketon Lancers and the red-and-silver Monroe Nighthawks. Their uniforms made a swirl of Christmas colors as they ran and threw and blocked on the frost-stiffened grass field. Even though it wasn't Thanksgiving yet, the weather made it seem like December.

Gary whistled and poked him and said, "Dude! Glad you're able to play."

"That makes two of us." He rubbed his hands over his chest and felt the reassuring strips of tape binding his ribs.

Gary gave him one final clap on the back, jarring his ribs and making him wince inwardly. How the hell was he to play this way? He needed to grab the ball early and run like hell.

"You ready?" Coach asked.

Nick jumped. "I won't disappoint you!" He pushed all the school drama away and concentrated on football.

"Focus. Anticipate. I know you can do it," were Coach's parting words.

Nick joined the team. The buzzer sounded. The ball was thrown to him, and he took off. It was a miracle he wasn't tackled, he seemed to run with the wind, his lungs burning with the cold air and adrenaline coursing through his veins. He cradled the ball, his legs moving faster and faster. He thought only of the goalposts, coming toward him in a blur.

He was almost there! He could see the line. A ton of bricks fell on him before he crossed the goal line though. He struggled to get away, but the weight was in his chest. On hands and knees, he crawled toward the line until his vision narrowed, and he tumbled into a black hole.

Chapter 52

The medic approached me with a needle, and I shrank away. "*Non! Non!*" What were they giving me? No. I twisted away, but the prick and sting coursed through my veins.

Louis and I rejoined what was left of our cadet class. The sorry-looking group, dirty and discouraged from the German onslaught, huddled together, mumbling our victories but mourning the loss of our brothers. We couldn't hold out much longer without more ammunition and help.

"*Where are the others?*"

I slumped against a tree and listened to the conversations swirling like smoke around me. I needed to get away and rescue Chaton.

"*Shot.*"

"*Killed.*"

"*Captured.*"

"*Any luck?*"

"*I shot seven or eight,*" I whispered, my mind replaying the scenes over and over. The shots, the fallen Germans, the blood, and more blood. My stomach crammed into my throat, and I retched, but I had nothing left to burn its way out of my body.

"*Why did you stop?*"

"*Ran out of ammo.*"

"*I'm low too.*"

"Any biscuits?"

"Non, I haven't eaten in two days."

"Here." A dirty hand thrust a piece of bread into my palm. "Eat this. You need your strength."

I tore into the bread, gagging a bit as the stale crumbs jammed in my throat, but I managed to swallow, the lump filling my stomach.

The cadets were losing the fight against the mighty German army, but it was too late to back out. Would Colonel Michon surrender?

Presently the colonel came to us. "Good job, men. We've kept them out of the town." He passed out what little ammunition he had. "This is it. We will fight until it is gone. You have all done me proud today."

I looked at the meager handful of bullets. I could kill seven Germans, but thousands kept coming. What could I do with seven bullets?

I loaded my rifle and, in a crouch, left the little group to find a position to take aim. The afternoon sun glinted off the metal of the internment camp roofs. Chaton. I needed to free Chaton before we surrendered to the Germans. We were overrun and outgunned. But we had held the Germans at bay for two days.

I slipped into the copse of trees. The trees provided a view of the river, the ant-like Germans lining the bank, and their frenzy of activity.

After a deep breath, I took a shot, aiming for the man who seemed to be giving orders. My shot caught the man in the upper chest. The Germans looked up to where I was hiding and surged forward. I slipped away from the trees, heading through the undergrowth toward the internment camp.

I smelled the camp before it came into view. The

June flowers and budding trees couldn't mask the odor of misery permeating the prison swathed in barbed wire. A figure stepped out from the trees, not a German, but our lieutenant. I would have preferred a German to this man I never liked or respected.

He put up a hand to stop me. "You are a thief and a disgrace to the Ecole de Cavalerie. We should have thrown you out while we had a chance." He spat at me.

We looked at each other for a long time, until the sounds of the Germans coming up the hill, crashing through bushes, tore us apart.

"You are a foolish boy. Look. You have led the Germans to us!"

Yes, but it couldn't be helped. They would be overtaking this whole area in a matter of hours.

"Oui, I was hoping they would kill you, you cruel swine!" I raised my rifle, surprised at how easy it was to do so, and took aim.

The lieutenant's face was frozen with disbelief, his pig eyes tiny and fierce. "Do it! You are a coward!"

Then I pulled the trigger. I was no coward and didn't wait to see where I had shot the lieutenant. I skirted the crumpled body and headed toward the internment camp and to Chaton.

"Are you my relief?" the guard asked me at the barbed fence surrounding the camp. I willed myself to act unconcerned and unhurried, but inside, I felt jittery and anxious.

"Oui, you have earned it."

"How goes the fighting?"

"The Germans are endless," I said.

"I will go and fight." He left, following the sounds of gunfire, shots, and raised voices.

"And may God be with you," I called after him.

The guard slipped away, and I hurried to the back of the camp to the deep holes holding Chaton and her family. The prisoners watched me with fear as I pushed around them. No one touched or tried to stop me. They remained to the side but watched my every move.

"The girl, Chaton. Is she still here?" I asked, breathlessly.

Several people pointed to a grate covering the ground.

A hoarse, breathless cry of "I'm here." They were alive.

"I have come for you."

"Thank heavens! Grandma has gone."

I pushed at the grate with my boot. "Help me," I croaked in frustration, dropping down to dig frantically at the hard ground around the grate.

Several internees leaped forward to help.

I worked in deep concentration, pushing and shoving at the cover, only managing to move it a few meters before I heard the telltale click.

I raised my head to see the lieutenant, his left arm bloody and hanging limply, holding a pistol.

"You should have killed me, Cadet Rousseau, because now I'm going to kill you." He moved his pistol slightly. "And then I'll kill her. She will starve to death in the hole for all I care."

"Non." I leaped toward the lieutenant as the bullet tore into my chest, a hot poker searing my skin. I raised my rifle in a futile attempt and fired.

It was then my world erupted into black and molten lava as I sank down, the sparks fizzling, then one by one extinguished.

My body collapsed and landed with a thud, all the wind knocked from my lungs. As my life blood flowed from my body, I managed to croak, "Chaton, I tried to save you, but…but I…can't…"

Chapter 53

"Nick, Nick, can you hear us?"

"Who's Nick?" he moaned. "My name is Jean Claude."

"You collapsed on the football field," a random voice spoke. "Can you tell us what happened?"

"I've been shot." He tried opening his eyes, but the blinding whiteness made him close them again.

"Shot?"

"Oui, shot."

He felt a prick in his arm.

Although his eyes were glued shut, he heard another faraway voice.

"Nick? It's your mother." A female voice shouted at him. "Your father's following in the car. We're on our way to the hospital."

He tried opening his mouth to speak, but his throat was blocked. Water. He wanted water. He moved his hand. Did it actually move?

"Hold on. We're almost there!" Desperation laced this woman's voice.

Oui, his maman was with him. Chaton too?

"How are you feeling, honey?"

His maman was talking in a foreign language. The voice wasn't his maman. His maman spoke in softly slurred French and this woman in English, the vowels jarring. Something covered his mouth and nose. He couldn't speak. The words—English and French— tangled around each other.

Someone fingered his hand, and he tried to squeeze back, but whatever was sitting on his chest made it difficult to move.

"Can you take my hand?"

He tried, but nothing. He struggled to open his eyes, but they remained glued shut.

His eyes were closed, but he could see everything in a blurry haze. Two women were with him. Both were dark-haired and beckoned him. He searched for their names. One called him Nick and the other, Jean Claude. They stayed with him, fighting for his attention.

He was a disjointed figure swathed and protected in a hospital bed. He came slowly to himself, the feeling of walking through an endless forest, always searching for a way out.

"Nick." A woman pushed back the curtains surrounding his bed and took his hand. "You had us so worried, honey." She squeezed his fingers in a familiar way.

Who was Nick? He knew the name, but not the person. Was she talking to him? She was touching his hand. Yes, she had addressed him as Nick.

"Where…where am I?"

"Spectrum Hospital. You've had emergency surgery."

His eyes flew open.

Jean Claude's chest was covered in bandages, and the radiating heat was tender and intense.

"Was I shot?"

"No, of course not."

"Did we win?"

"Win?"

"Did we win the war?"

"What war?"

She frowned at him. They both stayed silent.

"Why am I here?" he finally demanded.

"A birth defect," the woman said, although he thought she was his mother, only she didn't resemble his mother in the least. His mother covered her hair with a scarf. This woman's head was unadorned.

"A hole in your heart," said the man who came to stand by the woman. His father? The man was his father. Had he come home from the war to be with him?

"You collapsed at the game," his mother prompted.

"Game?" *Surely the conflict with the Germans wasn't a game.* "We are at war; it is no game!"

His mother frowned briefly before responding, "You need your rest."

His parents left, and when he awoke again, Chaton was beside him. "*Mon amour.*" My love.

"*Qui, je suis venu.*" Yes, I have come.

"*Pourquoi suis-je ici?*" Why am I here? "*Ma poitrine est en feu.*" My chest is on fire. "*Suis-je mourir?*" Am I to die?

"*Non.*" No.

When Jean Claude awoke later in the day, the window showed afternoon light. His parents and another man were there, looking down on him.

"How are you feeling, Nick?"

"Pardon?"

"Nick?"

"I am Jean Claude."

He heard his mother inhale sharply, and his father's cheeks sagged.

"Why do you think you are Jean Claude?" the doctor asked.

"What nonsense! Because I am! I was shot!"

"Who shot you?" the doctor asked.

"My lieutenant!" Such idiotic questions. Surely the man knew that.

"I see." The doctor turned to his parents, ignoring him again. "He may just have a form of anesthetic confusion. It is quite common in some patients."

"Did you get the bullet out of my chest?" Jean Claude demanded.

The man ignored his comment and replied, "You should be fine to go home." Home to his narrow cot at the cavalry school or his bed in Montreuil-Bellay? A look passed between his parents and the doctor.

"Will I fight?"

"No, you must rest."

"My *maman* has left town," Jean Claude said.

"I see," the doctor said, but he didn't. Jean Claude could tell he was saying whatever platitudes were necessary to keep him calm.

"And my fellow cadets?"

The man frowned but said, "I'm not sure about them."

"We were overrun by the Germans; surely more are here."

"Perhaps." The doctor pressed a button by Jean Claude's bed, and soon a man in blue scrubs gave him two pills.

"You need your rest."

The voices in his head were tiny, and it was hard to make out all the words. They were speaking about someone named Nick. The ribbons of words flowed around and under each other in an exotic confusing dance, just out of his reach.

"A form of schizophrenia…"

"Treatment?"

"Drugs and therapy."

"What kind of medicine?" asked the woman who was pretending to be his *maman*.

"To keep him from hallucinating."

"I don't think he's hallucinating." His father.

"Has he done this before?"

"When he was a small boy."

"Mental illness can be triggered by a catastrophic event such as surgery."

"It may be a concussion."

Chapter 54

The next day, Nick awoke and looked around. Then he tilted his chin down to look at his chest. An ugly red scar held together by staples sliced his sternum.

The events from the last forty-eight hours came flooding back. Collapsing on the football field, a ton of rocks falling on him, crushing him. A ride in an ambulance. People talking about him. A birth defect in his heart. But still there was a niggling concern of something he was missing. Something important.

A man came in, carrying a chart, looking efficient and professional. "I'm Dr. Garson. How are you feeling today, Nick?"

"Fine."

The man raised his brows and paused as if waiting for more.

"I said I feel better today."

"Good. Can you say your full name for me?"

"Nicholas Dupont."

"Good. Good."

"When can I go home?"

"We'll see how you do when we get you up and moving."

"I want to go home." Nick wasn't sure how long he had been here exactly, but he was already tired of being in bed, taking pills, not having any privacy. "Can you tell me who won the game?"

"The game?" The doctor scratched his head. "Afraid I can't tell you that."

Chapter 55

I surveyed the food tray. No self-respecting Frenchman would eat this slop. Some bread, yes, butter and jam, yes. No anemic eggs for me. At least the coffee was black and strong.

She slipped through the curtains surrounding my bed.

"Chaton!" I said, so happy to see her.

"Hush, I'm not Chaton. It's me, Cat."

"No, no, no, Chaton," he said with a vigorous shake of his head. "Always my Chaton. I tried to save you!"

She folded her arms and studied him.

"I remember! I was shot and killed trying to save you! I didn't leave you to die! I had no choice!"

Cat pursed her mouth as if considering his words. "How…"

"My lieutenant shot me." He grasped her hand. Her fingers felt warm wrapped around his. "I was trying to get you out of the hole when he found me!"

"You were trying to save me?"

"The Germans were coming! I rushed as fast as I could to the camp to free you, but my lieutenant followed me. I tried, believe me, I tried." His eyes filled with tears.

"Hush," she said softly. "I didn't know."

She paused and smoothed the wet hair on his brow.

"I'm worried about you. I hate to go at a time like this. Will you be okay until I get back?"

"You'll be back?"

"Yes, this is temporary."

"You're leaving me this time?"

She smiled, revealing her perfect teeth. "Ha! You're funny."

Nick struggled into a more comfortable position. "Turnabout is fair play, don't you think?"

She tilted her head to the side as if not understanding his meaning.

"Don't you remember? You accused me of leaving you to die!"

"Oh, yes." She gave him a small grimace, remembering their earlier interactions.

"So now you're leaving me?"

"But not to die," she said, nodding toward the IV tube and bag of clear liquid hanging over his hospital bed.

"Feels like it!"

"You're going to be fine and live to fight another day."

He frowned at her. "Fight?"

"On the football field. In the classroom." She moved her arms as if she was conducting the orchestra. "To get better. Regain your strength."

"I guess so. I wish you could stay." He jerked his hand toward his face, but the IV tugged at his hand and he stopped. "I wish I were out of this damn bed!"

"You need to rest." She leaned over the bed and kissed him.

"Cat!" Suddenly three people burst into the room. "So nice to see you!" The woman who called herself his mother said. The man he called Father gripped the wheelchair of the older woman called Grandma.

"I'm just leaving," Cat said, flustered. "I've come to say goodbye. We're moving back to Oregon. But we'll be back, but I don't know when."

"We hope to see you soon," his mother said, opening her arms and giving Cat a hug.

"You will." After a smile and a nod, Cat slipped through the opening and was gone.

His parents pulled up chairs and positioned Grandma's wheelchair by the bed.

"Nick? How are you feeling today?" his father asked.

"Confused," he mumbled. "Sore."

"The doctor said that is quite common after anesthesia and would eventually go away."

He shook his head slightly. "I hope so."

"You need to concentrate on getting well."

Nick sank back into the pillow and closed his eyes. They popped open when there was a knock on the door.

"Hi!"

"Emily!" his father said. "So good to see you!"

Nick's mother gave Emily a hug, and in turn, Emily hugged Grandma.

"I hope it's okay that I came." Emily hesitated before approaching Nick's bed.

Nick managed a weak smile and moved his fingers. "I'm glad you're here." His voice was low and hoarse.

Emily touched the rail at the side of Nick's bed. "I was so worried," she said. "I'm glad you're better."

"Me too!" He stifled a yawn and closed his eyes. Nick slipped into the void of his dreams. Jean Claude seemed to have vanished for now.

A word about the author...

Sue writes 5-star LitPick novels that keep readers of all ages turning pages long into the night. When she's not writing, she's reading, attending author events, or walking her dogs. She has two children and four grandchildren. Snack wise, Sue is a salty-type gal, but wouldn't say no to a chocolate kiss or two! She's not sure she's a reincarnated former novelist, but if she was, she'd want to be Jane Austen, Mary Shelley, or Emily Bronte. www.scduganauthor.wixsite.com/mysite

Thank you for purchasing
this publication of The Wild Rose Press, Inc.

For questions or more information
contact us at
info@thewildrosepress.com.

The Wild Rose Press, Inc.
www.thewildrosepress.com

www.ingramcontent.com/pod-product-compliance
Lightning Source LLC
Chambersburg PA
CBHW051139030726
47504CB00004B/946